BEGGING FOR MERCY

DYING FOR LOVE
BOOK ONE

MISTI WILDS

Begging for Mercy

DEDICATION

Yungblud's "Zombie" carried me through this book. Its haunting beauty is woven into these pages, so I hope they hurt (and heal) your heart as much as they do mine.

Seriously, it's a beautiful song.

Make sure you listen to it for me.

Author's Note

This is a dark romance.

There are mature themes within this book, including red flag main characters who have poor coping mechanisms, bad judgement, and morally gray ideologies. The fictional world this book takes place in is not much better.

Please check content warnings on my website prior to reading.

If you do not enjoy bisexual content and relationships within harems, put down this book and walk away.

(Yes, two of the men are dating.)

CHAPTER 1

—————

REAPER

The steady slap of skin on skin punctuates the air as I rail a needy college student against the wrought iron gate to the city's cemetery. It's long past midnight as sweat drips down my skin and her desperate mewls fill my ears, the rattle of chains keeping the cemetery locked up tight, lost beneath the heavy drum of my heartbeat. It pounds heavy in my skull, keeping me from coming more than the scratch of her fishnet tights over my hips.

Fuck, I just want to come already.

The girl's fake cat tail swishes against my leg with each thrust of my hips, and I quickly wrap it around my fist and tug, making her whine as she's lifted off the ground by the belt cinched around her waist.

"H-hey!"

I hook her to one of the spikes jutting from the mid-bar on the gate and enjoy the freedom that comes from suspension. Grabbing her hips, I slam her down onto my cock and throw my head back as she gushes, her wails reaching a crescendo as she comes first.

It's not my goal to get girls off, but at least it keeps them coming back every year.

"Reaper," she whines, her fingernails digging into the paint covering my shoulders. "S-slow down."

The pain from her claws makes me hiss, my cock jerking as I fill the condom. It's my third fuck of the night but hopefully not the last. Just the last time with *her*.

Breathing hard, I slip from the girl's wet heat. Charlotte? Natalie? I rake my hand through my hair after adding the condom to the pile and zipping up. Only once she starts struggling do I lift her off the gate and set her back down on the ground. Her legs buckle immediately and she stumbles into me, clinging like a grape to the vine as her lips seek mine.

No fucking chance.

I wrench her body away from mine and take three steps back. "Get the fuck out of here, Charlotte."

Her eyes, tinted bright yellow from contacts, narrow into slits. "My name is Natalie, asshole."

Lighting a cigarette that I pull from the carton tucked inside my back pocket, I shrug. "Don't care."

Natalie huffs, clearly annoyed at being dismissed. "I guess the rumors are true. I heard you were a Grade A dick." She adjusts her cat costume, pulling her skirt back into place, and plucks her purse off the fence. "It wasn't even that good."

The moisture gathered around the base of my shaft

says otherwise, but I don't call her out on it. All the girls I fuck find something to complain about, whether it's the body paint ruining their clothes, the bruises from being fucked against a metal gate, or the eeriness of the venue. Not many girls are willing come to a cemetery in broad daylight, let alone in the middle of the night on Halloween, but they'll make an exception if it means getting some action from Reaper himself.

I wish I could say that I came up with the nickname, but sadly, the honor falls to my brother. His tongue is as sharp as his knife skills, I'll give him that. Even though he could charm the pants off of every student on campus, he claims that he's not interested in anyone who's been run-through already, which excludes at least half the population on account of how often I get around.

If it's wet and willing, I've put my dick in there *at least* once.

Once Natalie finally leaves, I pull out my key to the main gate and make quick work of the lock. Fucking the nerd in charge of historic preservation on campus made getting a key easier than getting him off, and *thank Christ*, too, because I'm tired of ripping my goddamn pants from jumping the fence.

Walking into the local cemetery on Halloween night always feels sacred. It's one of the largest cemeteries in the state and nestled directly against Harlin Heights Community College on account of the main building being a sanatorium back in the day, so it's well-traversed, if a little neglected. Ancient tombstones crumble to dust beneath the shadows of thick willow trees, their boughs swaying like sheer curtains in front of an open window. As I walk the moonlit path to our rendezvous point, I keep my eyes peeled for movement in the distance.

I'm not the only one with a hard-on for death on Halloween night.

Although I'm expecting to find couples shacking up in mausoleums, what I'm *not* expecting is to hear the whisper of a woman's voice in my ear. Melodic and melancholy, her hushed song echoes from all sides. I stop in my tracks and peer into the night, half believing that I'm imagining it, and half hoping that I'm not.

I've fucked countless witches and bad little kitties, but never anyone with a voice as haunting as this. My blood pulses in short, jerky bursts as I spin on my heel to locate the siren. Gravel kicks up at my heels and the sound spills into the night. I hold my breath as I listen for her to sing again, but only crickets play their song. Admittedly, if she spotted a shirtless man painted head to toe like a skeleton, she might be too scared to speak. *Fuck.* I dress up like a skeleton every year on Halloween. Girls get off on not knowing my true face as they fall to their knees to worship my girthy cock between their teeth.

But maybe not *this* girl.

"Siren," I call out, slowly spinning in a circle to scan the perimeter. The graveyard stretches for miles in all directions once you reach its center, but we're not anywhere close to there. The outer fence is to my back, and it only extends for a block or two until you hit campus.

Whoever is here has to be a college student.

And all college students within the Harlots' fucked-up fraternities know that I exist.

So which is it? This girl has either escaped the shackles of modern Greek life and is thus unaware of the Reaper's territory, or she's aware but unafraid of roaming tombstones by moonlight.

"Are you alone?" If she's got sense, she won't be alone at night. But if that were the case, there would be no need for her to be silent upon my approach. "I'm alone, too."

Sort of. Zane is hanging out a few miles down, waiting for me to wrap up my sexcapades.

"You have a beautiful singing voice." Compliments don't come easily for me, but this one rolls right off my tongue. "I'd love to match a face with—" A shadow moves inside the nearest mausoleum. A grin pulls at my lips. "—your voice."

The door is slightly ajar, just wide enough for me to know that whoever is inside doesn't want to lock themselves in. Cautious. I'd say *smart*, but since when would hanging out in a cemetery count for brains? I step closer, careful to avoid patches of gravel or crunchy, dried grass from the most recent heat wave. It's fucking hot out for October, and if it weren't for the body paint coating my pores, I'd be drenched in sweat.

I wonder what my siren is wearing. Has she dressed up for the holiday, or is she wearing loose spirit wear emblazoned with the school's hideous double H logo? I lick my lips as I try to picture her as a zombie bride covered in face paint or a makeup-less, freckled slip of a woman with wide, round glasses and her hair tossed into a messy heap at the top of her head. Either is fine. I don't *have* to play dress-up-fuck-up just because it's Halloween. I've had sex with plenty of people who never bothered with a costume.

But no matter how many fantasies flicker through my mind, Siren's face remains as blank as a fresh canvas awaiting the first strike of paint.

I *have* to know.

As I wrap my fingers around the heavy metal door and pull it open, the hinges creak and the sound echoes through the hollow room. Marble floors are covered in a thin layer of dust and cobwebs hang from the ceiling, clinging to the arches of the candelabras.

Recently lit candelabras.

The scent of smoke hangs in the air. I take a steady, slow step into the room. "Won't you sing for me, Siren?" The only thing in front of me is a row of caskets inlaid into the wall, each with a tarnished bronze plaque. Moonlight streams through the wavy glass windows, with a breeze tickling the back of my neck. The farthest window in the corner has been picked clean, the glass panes having long been cracked and removed. Once I recognize that the mystery girl is not in front of me, I turn to check the corners nearest the door.

One lies empty, but the other...

Someone set up a little... I crouch to get a closer look. Picnic? A soft cotton blanket lies across the tile floor. I pinch it between my fingers to find that it's still warm. Two pillows are positioned for someone to sit on, and an open bottle of wine warms by their side. A single taper candle, recently lit and then put out, sits in a holder near a spread of sliced cheeses, meats, and fruits.

A lover's meeting place?

I brush my hand across one of the pillows and hum in the back of my throat. The siren isn't here, but she left her belongings. A quick survey of the room tells me that she scurried to the broken window and hoisted herself through, scratching herself in the process. A deep cut, too. I touch a sliver of glass, its base buried deep within the window pane but its tip jutting out like a thick needle, and spread her cooling blood across my fingertips.

If Zane were here, he'd want to run a blood test to confirm her identity. But it's more fun to go hunting for a girl with a gash in her arm. Or side. Leg? I sit down on her pillows and pop a grape into my mouth as I imagine every place she could be sliced open. It's likely her forearm or her calf. Maybe her thigh? I picture a girl in a pleated mini skirt lifting herself off the floor and slipping through the window in the same way that she's slipping through my fingers. Then I pull a lighter from my boot and light the taper candle, passing my fingers through its flame once it's lit. Her blood fills the grooves of my fingerprints and sizzles in the heat.

Will she return for her belongings and brave meeting a stranger, or will she flee and return in the morning for them?

My phone vibrates in my pocket—an incessant *vrrrrm* that means my brother is getting impatient. We do this every year—it's not like my antics are new or his precious routine is in jeopardy. I'll get my fuck on, as is tradition, and he'll bury our latest victim in a fresh grave so that they won't rot alone.

Sighing, I send him a pin with my location and wait for his arrival. More importantly, I wait for hers.

I wait and wait and wait.

Picturing the bow of her lips.

The tender flush on her cheeks.

The fearful sparkle in her eyes, like a diamond cast in shadow.

Among her forgotten belongings is a worn duffel bag, and inside that bag is a set of matches with a curved *M* on the box, an antique wine opener, a trifold wallet decorated with silver crescent moons, an untouched sketchbook filled with empty pages, and a thick bundle of fabric wrapped carefully around a tiny, polished wooden box.

Just as my brother Zane steps through the doorway with his usual scowl aimed directly at my heart, I attempt to pry open the lock with my bare hands. It's a tiny, golden box missing its key. If the lock were plastic, I could smash it against the stone wall to crack it open. But the little metal locket gleams in the candlelight, taunting me.

"Planning a date?" Zane snags the second pillow from beneath my knees and plops down across from me on the blanket. "That's unlike you."

"I met someone," I muse, flipping the lock up and down with my fingertip. Knowing that it won't open, I set the box down atop the fabric it came wrapped in—a scarf, I think, or some kind of shawl. Soft but not made of wool. Something nicer. I bring the open bottle of wine to my lips and down a few swallows. Did he just insult me? My ego swells. "I can wine and dine with the best of them. All the bitches love me."

"All the bitches *fuck* you," Zane clarifies, snagging the wine and squinting at the label. "They don't love you. Which is why a date is a waste of time."

"Dick," I hiss, kicking his leg. But he's right, I don't date. I fuck. *Hard.* "I didn't plan this. A girl left it. A *siren.*" Licking my lips, I play back her voice in my head, but without enough time to hear her song, it fades rapidly from memory.

Zane flips open her wallet with feigned interest. "Well, this girl—" He tilts her ID towards the light to read her name. "What the fuck kind of name is—her parents must hate her." Sighing, he flicks the wallet shut again. "She clearly isn't interested in having sex with you, so leave her shit where you found it, and let's go." He tosses the wallet into my lap and stands. "Forty-three isn't getting any fresher."

My jaw clenches at the number. It always bugs the shit out of me when Zane turns people into projects. "He has a name," I rumble, slipping the girl's wallet into my pocket as I stand. "*Alejandro.*" One of our youngest kills and undoubtedly one of the most exciting. He really had a thing for Zane—much to my brother's horror. I'm pretty sure Alejandro only slept with me as a consolation prize for not getting into my brother's pants.

But that's the thing about Zane—he doesn't know

how to let loose and have fun. I'm not even sure the last time he let anyone touch his dick—male *or* female. Hell, I don't even know when *he* last choked his chicken.

He is *way* overdue for some stimulation. I bet his spunk is backed up for days. Weeks. *Jesus.* When he finally blows, he'll spew like a goddamn fire hydrant all over the poor, unsuspecting bastard expecting a normal lay.

May God have mercy on their throats if they have to swallow *that* mega-load.

Zane ignores me, which is par for the course when he's irritated. As we walk through rows of headstones towards Alejandro's awaiting corpse, I squeeze the siren's wallet in my palm. It should have more than just her name. Her address. Her *picture.*

A shiver runs down my spine as I slip it into my front pocket for safekeeping. I won't look yet—I want to savor every detail once I'm alone in my bedroom and Zane's prying eyes aren't throwing judgmental daggers at my back. The prick needs to chill the fuck out and loosen the fuck up. Just because I met—or will meet—a mystery girl doesn't mean that I have to fuck her or kill her.

I'll just have a little fun with her. Catch and release.

Easy.

Chapter 2

Mercy

EVERY COLLEGE across the country has its traditions. For some, it means passing under an archway only once you've graduated. For others, it might be petting the "Good Boy" statue of a golden retriever on your way to class each morning. But Harlin Heights Community College, although steeped in surface-level traditions centered around passing classes or earning your diploma, has a layer of tradition hidden underneath the rest that the locals keep alive. One such tradition involves the Harlots' up-and-coming hopefuls, pledges trying to earn their letters through promiscuous acts scattered across campus during the entire twenty-four-hour stretch on Halloween.

Professors cancel their classes.

The library remains closed.

RAs turn a blind eye to the comings-and-goings of their dorm residents so long as no one burns down the building or breaks the toilets.

The boldest individuals have sex in common areas, seeking their pleasure in shadowed lecture halls or on the sofas in the Student Union. But the bravest of all wait until nightfall to seek out the one revered as a sex god among men—a man who paints his entire body in sharp blacks and crisp whites to embody a skeletal appearance and fuck those he deems worthy of his massive *bone*.

It's a tradition I have zero interest in pursuing.

I have my own to fulfill.

Dragging a duffel bag to the cemetery in the middle of the night isn't new for me. In fact, when I'm through with my studies for the week, I often find myself sketching beneath a willow's flowing branches, out of sight from the wandering souls seeking their departed loved ones. It's quieter in the cemetery than elsewhere on campus, and I use the silence to my advantage.

Tonight, however, laughter spills among the tombstones as students try to spook each other or take gothic selfies to share on their dating profiles. Most people stay towards the gate nearest campus, but there are a half dozen of them scattered around the property. They aren't locked half the time, so anyone can wander past the wrought-iron hinges to step onto hallowed ground. I make my way down a familiar stone path and avoid confrontation with couples discreetly fucking on someone's grave. They probably don't even know a single soul buried here—probably don't care—and won't bother to learn their names.

But I know these families. I've seen their names in the records of the town's deceased, dating back centuries to a time when Harlin Heights was an oceanside town whose homes were built from tabby and washed away by summer storms. Although this cemetery is inland, you can still find traces of the ocean etched into the stone or splayed out across the paths as either sand or palm fronds gust by, carried here by the wind. Most prominent families' graves are housed inside mausoleums two or three bodies deep, their structures expanded with each new generation of the deceased.

The Morningstar mausoleum is a smaller building set off from the center of the cemetery. My great-grandmother petitioned to have it moved onto our family land on account of how many dead we house beneath our soil, but the city never granted permission, and the petition was dropped. So while my family keeps the hundred or so graves buried behind the *Morningstar Mortuary* company, I visit the ones resting beside my college campus. On Samhain, the veil between this world and the next is thinnest. I like to think that the dead appreciate drinking wine and eating cakes and crackers as much as they did while alive, so I come here when they have the greatest chance to enjoy having company.

That's the only time I allow myself to sing—when only the dead can hear me.

I don't notice a living soul approaching until it's too late. Preoccupied with slicing cheeses and pouring a glass of wine, I sing a breathy lullaby my mother taught me, unaware that the infamous sex god Reaper is passing by that very moment. It's only when I hear a voice mutter the word *Siren*—a pleading tremor in the shape of a single word—that I peer out the window.

Moonlight illuminates the bones painted on his skin, each one shaded with technical precision. As he spins around, I catch the shifting muscles across his back and gasp at the sheer magnitude of him.

I've heard that Reaper is a god, but I never expected him to actually look like one.

Dressed in black cargo pants and matching combat boots, he hovers on the cobbled path and scans his surroundings in search of something. "Are you alone? I'm alone, too."

Who is he talking to? I look out across the yard to try and find another person, a new victim for his late-night boning, but I don't see anyone. My heart gives an unsteady beat. There's no way that he's talking to—

"You have a beautiful singing voice."

Me.

Shit.

I quickly pinch the wick of my taper candle, extinguishing its flame, and hold my breath. But it's too late—somehow, he's pinpointed my location, because he's looking directly at me. The last thing I want is a confrontation with a sexed-up fiend prowling the night. A security guard telling me not to bring food into the cemetery, sure, I can handle that.

But *this*?

A slow grin curves on his lips as he slinks closer, the sheen of sweat clinging to his neck shining in the moonlight. Handprints and smudges on his neck and shoulders transform him from skeleton back into man, or at least into a hybrid creature that's at once both dead and alive. The spark of fire in his eyes as he moves closer sends shivers down my spine. I crawl across the cool tile floor to make my escape out the broken window in the back corner of the mausoleum. Shards of glass crunch under my feet, making me even more nervous, but if I turn around and run through the front door, Reaper will catch me.

He might think playing hide and seek is a fun type of foreplay, but I'm not interested in playing games. I need to get out of here before he sees me. I hoist myself through the window as carefully as I can, but my caution isn't enough. A shard of glass slices my forearm and drips blood onto my leggings. I land on the ground hard, but I don't have a second to catch my breath. Scurrying behind the next row of graves, I make myself as small as possible as I check my injury.

It's deep, but hopefully it won't need stitches. I should have a hand towel in my bag. I can wrap up—*shit*. My bag. Peering around the tombstone, I catch a glimpse of Reaper staring at the broken windowsill before turning back around. I left my bag behind. He's going to find it any second now.

I stew in silence and consider my options. Depending on the kind of man he is, he'll either be disinterested in my ritual and walk out or he'll be curious enough to poke around. My hands shake as I picture him rummaging through my bag and finding my mother's ashes tucked inside her scarf. I know that I shouldn't take them out of the house, but I hate seeing her stuck on a shelf all day. Dad will dust around her and sing songs with every sunrise, but I know that she wouldn't be happy seeing him mourn like this.

At least when I take her out to the cemetery, she can spend time with the rest of our family.

I'm not sure why Dad decided to cremate her instead of bury her with our ancestors. I haven't asked. Grandma Star says that he's lonely without her near—but if we believe what Mom told us before she got sick, she isn't really locked inside that box. She's in the air. The breeze blowing through the trees. The morning dew wetting every blade of grass or soft flower petal in spring. Each ray of sunlight kissing our faces.

I guess that means I shouldn't bother taking her ashes out of the house, either, but... it makes her feel closer.

Sighing, I clutch my forearm to stop the bleeding and watch for Reaper to leave the mausoleum. Minutes pass. Ten. Twenty. Another man appears, this one's lips pinched in a tight scowl, and enters the same way Reaper had, without an ounce of hesitation. I'd recognize him if he worked here, so he must be another college student. An upperclassman? Graduate student? If the rumors are true, Reaper didn't bother graduating with his class, but he hangs around all the same. Picking up girls with pretty smiles, flirting with jocks on their way back from practice, keeping an eye on the student body like it's his job to keep a head count.

Another rumor puts him as a staff member, but no

one on staff should fuck with students for the hell of it. I don't know what his game is, and frankly, I don't care.

I just need to get my mother's ashes back.

A few more minutes pass before the stranger leaves, then Reaper follows, slipping his hands into his pockets as he quickly scans his surroundings. If he's looking for me, he won't find me. I have zero interest in an introduction.

Once they're far enough away, I quickly rush back into the mausoleum to grab my belongings. My mother's urn is resting on top of the scarf I wrapped her inside, and I breathe a sigh of relief as I run my hands over the box's smooth surface, its lock still in place. Everything looks untouched, more or less. Did he leave my things alone, or will I open my bag to find a dead rat stuffed inside?

My anxiety finally relaxes, and I wrap up the food and return everything to my bag. All I need is my student ID to drop off my things inside my locker—

I rummage through my bag in search of my wallet. When I come up empty, I remove everything and search again. And again. Shaking my bag, I pray that it's found a hidden compartment or slipped out when I wasn't looking. I check the room, but there's nothing other than dust and shards of glass. My wallet is missing.

"Did he...?" Tossing my bag over my shoulder, I step out into the humid air and follow the path Reaper and that man took. I don't hide in the shadows this time, keeping to the stone walkway as I search for them. If he took my wallet, he's an even bigger sack of shit than I thought. Mugging college kids? How low can you get? It's not like I have any money. All that's in there is my student ID, a picture of my parents, an old coin my grandmother gave me, and a handful of business cards for *Morningstar Mortuary*, our family business. Oh, and a debit card. But my bank account balance has been pitiful since I stopped working part-time at the funeral home.

What could he possibly want with any of that?

A scraping sound catches my attention, and a man's sharp voice cuts through the air. "Are you planning to stand there all night?" There's a metallic *clang* that makes me flinch. "Hurry up. I want to go home before the sun's out."

"Or what, you'll shrivel up and die?" Reaper snickers. "You could use some sun. You're pale as shit. It's no wonder you aren't gettin' any. The nerd look is fine, but you have to use it to your advantage. Would it kill you to work out with me? Anyone who lifts your shirt is gonna be—"

"I have abs, asshole!"

"Sure ya do."

The stranger uses his shovel to sling dirt at Reaper. "Shut the fuck up. Nobody asked you."

The sight of grave-digging is so familiar that it's soothing. I've watched my family dig graves ever since I was born, and I've even helped a time or two. We stick to traditional methods and dig with our hands in honor of the dead. Plus, bringing heavy machinery in to dig would damage the land and the graves already set on the property. The Morningstar method is old-fashioned, but it's for a purpose.

I doubt these two are digging by hand for sentimentality, though. But why would they dig at all? It's illegal to rob graves, and it's not like this is a secret spot in the back corner. They could easily be caught by someone... like... me. *Shit.* I need my wallet. Confronting Reaper is a stupid move, but what are my other options? Hoping he drops it? Following him home and digging through his laundry? What if he doesn't even have it?

Sighing, I hide my bag off the walkway and move towards Reaper and his partner. They're working in silence now, the familiar cut of shovels digging into the earth making me feel even more at ease. They've made good progress in a short time, meaning they're either experienced or rushed for time. As I approach them from the side, I get a perfect view of their profiles in the moonlight. Reaper is as imposing as ever. The body paint does little to hide his muscles, and being shirtless means that I'm given a full view of his back. Stripes of naked skin and smeared paint reveal toned shoulders as he throws topsoil into a growing pile. He's focused on his task, hardly looking where he's throwing.

His partner, however, wears a scowl as he digs. The gloves on his hands are skin-tight, but so are the rest of his clothes. A black tank top rides up his abdomen as he cuts the shovel into the earth, and the tears in his skinny jeans threaten to rip wide open. He's more meticulous about digging, prepping the sides of the hole while Reaper sticks to the middle to deepen the space.

I walk up to the tombstone overlooking the plot. Horror quickly washes over me as I realize which section of the cemetery we're in. None of these plots are vacant. These men aren't digging a new grave for some fun Halloween prank. They're disturbing an old one in some kind of sick joke. "Hey, assholes," I call out, unable to stop myself. "You're disturbing the dead."

Both of their heads snap up at the sound of my voice, and Reaper's lips curve into a wicked grin. Ignoring him, I head for the other guy, determined to pry the shovel from his uncaring hands. How could they disturb someone's resting place like this? Do they not care at all? What about the families—

My foot catches on something, and I pitch forward, screeching as I tumble into the dirt. I hit the mound looming outside the grave and slip in the loose dirt, falling unceremoniously fast and hard onto the open earth. The impact knocks the air from my lungs, and my vision blurs. But before I can react, someone grabs me under my arms and lifts me up, setting me back on my feet only to shove me against a dirt wall. The hole didn't look that deep, but apparently my depth-perception needs some work. We're at least three feet under.

While I'm still searching for my next breath, a hand clamps over my mouth. The damp scent of earth and decay fills my nose and tickles my lips. Luckily for me,

I'm used to a little grave dirt. I glare at Reaper as his gaze settles on my face, the sparkle of amusement in his eyes making me even grumpier. He crowds me against the wall, giving me no room to move.

"A lost cat?" His eyes flick up to the top of my head like he's looking for cat ears. "I don't know you, little kitten, but I'm sure I can make you purr—"

The other man scoffs loudly. "Do you *have* to come on to every single fucking person on the planet?"

Reaper tosses a sidelong glance at his partner. "I haven't come on to *you*," he retorts, smirking. "You finally gettin' jealous?"

Ignoring Reaper's remark, his partner drops his shovel and comes to stand beside him. "She's a liability," he says simply, turning his nose up. "You shouldn't have taken her fucking wallet."

Reaper's eyes widen. "Siren?" He brushes hair from my face and smears a line of dirt across my cheek. "So she's not a lost kitty cat."

"She's definitely lost," Skinny Jeans huffs, frowning even deeper than earlier. He reaches into Reaper's pocket and pulls out a familiar trifold wallet with tiny crescent moons patterned along the sides. "This yours?" He taps the corner against my bicep before unfolding it and reading my ID. "Mercy Morningstar. Your parents must hate you to name you after the devil." Flipping through the wallet's contents, he holds up my parents' photograph beside my face and looks between the three of us. "You look like her. Is this your mother?"

I can't answer because Reaper's hand is still over my

mouth, but resentment simmers in my blood as Skinny Jeans casually handles my belongings. That's one of the only photos I have of my parents, and he just—my eyes widen as he slips the photo into his back pocket. I jerk against Reaper's hold while Skinny Jeans reads one of my family's business cards next.

"Morningstar Mortuary," he notates, flicking the edge of the card. "Maybe she's not so lost, after all. Maybe she feels right at home here in the dirt." He puts the card into his pocket alongside the photograph and returns the wallet to Reaper's cargo pants. Sighing, he runs a hand through his unruly dark hair, pulling his bangs back to expose his forehead. "I really didn't want any trouble tonight, but curiosity killed the cat and all that. We'll make room for you, Kitten." He grabs something from Reaper's waist, but before he can make another move, Reaper's hand snaps out and grabs his wrist.

As they glare at each other, I catch a flash of silver in the moonlight. A sharp-tipped knife, serrated on one side, glints in Skinny Jeans' hand.

Adrenaline kicks into overdrive, and so do I. Lifting my leg, I slam my knee into Reaper's crotch and pry myself free from his grasp, dropping to the ground to avoid another grab. I dart for an abandoned shovel and grip it tight, spinning around to *whack* whoever I can. The metal clangs as it hits someone, and Skinny Jeans suddenly shouts expletives.

"*Fuck!*" Gritting his teeth, he lunges for me. "Grab her!"

But instead of grabbing me, Reaper knocks the knife from his partner's hand and slams him into the dirt wall.

"What are you *doing?*" Skinny Jeans snaps, fuming. "Get off of me!"

Reaper's voice, cold and detached, sends shivers down my spine. "No."

"No?" Skinny Jeans sneers. "What, you need to nut one more time? Fine, go ahead, *fuck her*. Then we'll kill her."

Alarm bells ring loud and clear in my head, and I hold my shovel even tighter. These men are crazy. I need to get the hell out of here.

But before I can run, screaming truths freeze me to the spot.

They know my name.

They know where my family works.

They know where to find me.

Even if I run tonight, they could come looking for me tomorrow.

"I won't say anything," I interrupt, trying to keep my voice steady. I swallow the lump in my throat and ignore the heavy beat of my heart. "I don't know who you are or what you're doing. I don't know anything. I'm not a threat." Wincing, I wish I could take that last part back, but it's too late. "Just let me go, and I'll forget this ever happened."

Reaper turns his head and pins me with a cold stare. "No."

Dread coils in my gut. My hands shake as I quickly glance at the knife on the ground. It's too far for me to reach, and there are two men standing between it and me. I would never make it there in time, and if Reaper lets Skinny Jeans go—

"Siren," Reaper calls out, his voice softer. "Pick up the knife."

Skinny Jeans fights against Reaper's hold. "You fucking idiot. She's gonna stab you."

"She might." He takes a deep breath. "But if stabbing me means she'll stick around, then so be it. Fucking stab me."

They're both crazy. Maybe *I'm* crazy. Instead of calling the cops, I carefully maneuver around the two men and pick up the knife. It's lightweight compared to the shovel, and I hold it out between me and the two men. Do I really think that this little knife is enough to take them down? Maybe, if I aim for the jugular. But do I think they could both disarm and overpower me in a split second?

Abso-fucking-lutely.

As I pick up the knife, Skinny Jeans rages against Reaper, but he's no match for the other man's strength. Reaper keeps his eyes locked on me, not bothered in the slightest by his partner's thrashing. Moonlight filters through the clouds and gradually unveils his face. From this distance, I can see the great detail that someone put into the skull painted over his cheekbones, lips, and eyes. The paint contours his features perfectly, making him look like a living, breathing skeleton. But beyond that, I can't tell what he really looks like. If I were shown a prison line-up tomorrow, I'd have no clue which man was him. I stare into his eyes and try to memorize their shape and color—a startlingly beautiful shade of ice blue framed in almond-shaped eyes—then glance at his slicked-back, dirty blonde hair, mussed from the night's events. A lock falls over his eyes, but he pays it no mind, too preoccupied with staring right back at me.

A slow smile curves on his full lips. "You're curious, aren't you?"

My cheeks warm. "Curious about what?"

His gaze flicks to my lips for a split second. "What it feels like." When I don't answer, he hums to himself. "Tell you what. To appease my brother—" Reaper jabs his forearm against Skinny Jean's throat, cutting off his airway. "Let's play a game. Do you like games, Siren?" Skinny Jean's eyes bulge as he turns his attention on me, like I'm the one to blame for his current situation. After a few seconds, his eyes roll back in his head and he collapses into Reaper's arms, allowing the latter to lift him out of the hole and lay him down beside the mound of dirt. Turning back to me, he lifts an eyebrow expectantly.

"I, um…" Shit, do I like games? The cogs in my brain stutter as I try to form an answer. "I don't know?" Flustered, I take a step back, making sure to keep the knife between us. If Reaper can knock out a friend—*his own brother*—there's no telling what he'll do to me.

It's hard to tell what Reaper is thinking with all of that face paint obscuring his features, but I'm pretty sure he looks… sad. After a moment, he sighs. "Look, if Zane has his way, you won't make it out of this grave alive. The only chance you have is—"

"To play a game," I interrupt, finishing his sentence.

His expression brightens. "Exactly. I knew you'd catch on."

All games have rules. There's always a winner and a loser. But there's also a win condition. If I'm smart, I can beat Reaper and his brother Zane at their own game. And if not, I can always call the cops.

"Okay," I say slowly, not entirely convinced. But my priority is getting the fuck out of here so that I'm not assaulted, murdered, or buried alive. Talk about a shitty Halloween. "What game?"

"Let's call it... hide and seek. With a twist." Reaper's teeth glow in the moonlight. "You have one year to convince us not to kill you. If you fail, by this time next year, you're joining Alejandro here." He reaches outside of the grave to pat a human-sized lump wrapped inside a bedsheet.

Oh God, is that what I tripped on? A body?

I can't help but voice my thoughts. "Are you *crazy?*"

Reaper shrugs, like the question doesn't faze him. "Hard to know, Siren. I don't feel crazy."

Fucking hell. I feel like the biggest idiot for leaving the house tonight. Who knew that the most notorious fuck-boy on campus was also a psycho? Taking a quick breath, I rack my brain for other rules for this game. "I need a win condition," I blurt out, trying to think of easier ways to win. There's no way I'll convince crazy people to let me live if I know their secrets.

Like the fact that they're *murderers*.

"You know, like, something I can accomplish that means I automatically win." I'm pulling this out of my ass, but Reaper seems focused. He tilts his head to the side and observes me silently, like he's contemplating what I'm saying.

"Yeah, you convince us not to kill you."

"Something else," I insist. "Like, uhh, like—" What do I know about Reaper? He sleeps with students in unconventional places, like the city cemetery, and never takes them out on dates. He's a really good lay, but no matter how much people beg, he barely learns their names and never calls them after. Having sex with him would be just another conquest for him. So what if— "You fall in love with me."

He stares, unflinching, for a long moment. "You want me to fall in love with you?"

I wish I could take everything back, but there it is. Out in the open. "I don't *want* that," I insist, grasping at straws. "But I know your reputation. You don't love anyone. So if I can get you to fall in love with me, I win. You can't kill me. Him, too." I nod towards Skinny Jeans. "If either of you falls in love with me, neither of you can kill me."

Reaper takes one step closer, then another. The pit is small enough to fit a body, so it only takes a moment for him to close the distance between us. Grasping my hand, he lifts the knife towards his face and pushes the sharp edge over the ridge of his brow. As it breaks the skin, a trickle of blood trails down his cheek. "Deal." He brushes his lips over my cheek, and the warmth of his breath makes me shiver. "But if you fall in love with *me*," he whispers, his voice like a scratch in my skull, "I get to kill you the moment I find out."

Something wet and warm drips onto my cheek, sliding down the side of my face until it touches the corner of my lips. A metallic scent fills my nose, and I swallow a gag, but Reaper's eyes dilate the moment he realizes what's happening. With one hand crushing my wrist and his body suddenly pinning me to the dirt wall, he lifts his fingers to my face and smears his blood into my skin. The knife digs deeper into his eyebrow, slicing him open and bringing more blood to the surface. He groans as it spills down his face and drips onto his chest, *onto mine*, and I gasp as I feel a distinct *lead pipe* digging into my hip.

"Get off of me!" Shoving him as hard as I can, I manage to push him back and keep the knife. Blood drips down my palm, slicking my grip on the handle, and I take gasping breaths as Reaper stumbles back. His gaze is unfocused, eyes wide, as he stares in my direction without really seeing me.

All I can stare at is his dick.

If I thought his brother's pants were tight, Reaper's are suddenly tighter. There is no room for imagination. The thick outline of his cock, including the imprint of the swollen tip, sends alarm bells ringing in the back of my mind.

There's no way that monster would ever fit inside of me.

Not that it ever needs to—I can make Reaper fall in love with me *without* him ever fucking me. Besides, that's not the goal. I can convince him not to kill me, and that's fine. He doesn't have to fall in love with me.

...but it would be satisfying as hell to put a man like Reaper in his place.

"One year," I say firmly, wiping my bloodied palm on my thigh. The blood is sticky now that it's drying. "I convince you not to kill me or I make one of you fall in love with me. Then I walk away unharmed. You can't touch my family or my friends. That's cheating. No blackmail. No bribery. No—"

Reaper shakes his head with a small laugh. "Okay, Siren, calm down. This is between you and me. And Zane," he adds, glancing at his brother before turning back to me. "I'll make sure that no harm comes to your family or friends. You have my word."

I doubt I can trust the word of a murderer, but it's a start.

Sliding down the dirt wall opposite me, Reaper slumps, tossing his legs out in front of him the moment his butt hits the ground. "One year," he murmurs, staring at me as he wipes the blood from his face with his wrist. "You better get out of here before Zane wakes up. He won't be happy when he learns about our agreement."

Swallowing hard, I nod. "Okay. How—how do I find you?" I can't very well win the game if I can't interact with the other players.

Reaper's smile is full of charm once again, nearly

knocking me off my feet. "Don't you worry about that, beautiful. We'll come to you." He doesn't help me climb out of the pit, but he doesn't ask for the knife back either.

I'm halfway home before I realize that Skinny Jeans still has my parents' photograph in his pocket.

CHAPTER 3

ZANE

My brother is a goddamn fool.

If burying Forty-three wasn't bad enough on its own, Kane started humming a melody he *swears* came from his "Siren"—the girl who assaulted me with a shovel—while we walk back to the car. Like he's *happy* that he left a loose end for me to burn.

"The game is stupid," I say for the third time, unable to wrap my brain around the logistics. Because there aren't any. "She's going to call the cops. They'll sketch our faces and put out an APB for anyone matching our description. It'll be all over the news." Anxiety claws at my ribs like a rat climbing a ladder, the tiny beast desperate to avoid dark sewers filled with nothing but the rot and stench of death. That's what awaits Kane if this shit gets out—*the death penalty.*

Forty-three isn't an arbitrary number I pulled out of my ass. It's the number of kills we've made since we started this venture as undisciplined teenagers. Not that our first was intentional—it was self-defense. *But still.* That's forty-three murders under our belts and forty-three missing persons cases within a few hundred mile radius of the city. Not to mention all the bodies we regularly disappear for the local bratva families.

Even the Baranovas' influence can only go so far if this shit hits the national news.

We're usually smarter than dumping bodies into fresh graves. Forty-three—Alejandro—was an exception on account of Kane's soft spot for the man. He insisted that we bury Alejandro with his family since *they mean everything to him.*

I never should have allowed it.

Dragging a hand down my face, I make a sharp turn onto the next road on the right, the one headed for the outskirts of the city—what's known as *Old Town.* The historic district, home to the city's oldest houses, is set against the mountain range to the north. The richest settlers chose to live opposite the beach, so their houses stood longer against the test of time. Only families whose names date back centuries still reside there. The Baranovas, I've been told, even have land hidden among the towering evergreens.

My brother and I have no such claims to property or fortune, but a certain curious little kitten does.

Kane idly peels layers of paint off his hands and wrists while I drive down a long stretch of road. The sun will be rising soon, its colors already peeking over the horizon. The scent of salt on the ocean breeze gives way to earth and pine the further from the cemetery we drive. It takes a few false turns for my memory to kick in, but once thick, wrought-iron gates come into view right where the slope of the mountain begins, I know we've found the right address.

Morningstar Mortuary.

Slapping his hand on the roof of the car, Kane *whoops* loudly. "Hell yeah, I knew you didn't get enough of a taste. Let's go." He sits up in his seat, leaving paint strips to flutter to the floorboards.

Crinkling my nose, I smack his shoulder as we approach the gate. "Stay in the car. You're peeling. It's evidence."

His brows lift beneath his bangs, finally flattened after a few hours spent digging in the dirt. "No way, you'll hurt her." He hops out of the car before I've cut the engine. "I gave my word. She has one year to live." Squinting against the headlights, he covers his eyes. "Are you coming?"

It's with the greatest patience that I watch Kane climb over the gate. We're not even thirty seconds into this operation, and he's grinning like a kid breaking into their best friend's bedroom window on a school night. He always does this—getting too close to our targets, too invested, only to bleed when they do. It's what makes his artwork potent enough to sell for hundreds of thousands of dollars each.

He feels things deeper than most people.

It gives me room to feel even less.

I scratch the prickle on the back of my neck and exhale through the nerves skittering across my skin.

There's no room for anxiety tonight, only action. I grab onto the iron bar and hoist myself over the fence—not as quickly as Kane, but fast enough. I jog to catch up with him on the gravel path. The sky lightens through the canopy of trees. Songbirds greet the morning with eager chirps, and Kane takes it all in with breathless wonder.

I'd thought he would be too enamored with our scared little kitty cat to appreciate the scenery, but apparently, he can make time to smell the damp earth and listen to the sounds of the forest preparing for daybreak. Although the weather's been warmer on account of the blast of heat coming up from the south, the sweat on my skin chills me to the bone. I'm not as thick as Kane. He may burn a thousand calories fighting and fucking his way through the day, but not me. I don't have the metabolism or the muscle mass.

Definitely not the libido.

I steal a glance at Kane while he's preoccupied with kicking a large rock into the ditch beside the path. We're not related, barely even brothers on account of us never staying under the same foster family's roof. I try not to think about it. The past doesn't matter as much as the present.

As the sun crests over the unseen horizon and flecks of the palest blues turn to vibrant pinks and brightest oranges, they paint Kane's body in an iridescent shimmer, highlighting the artwork painted all along his body. The whites and grays turn to color, and it's then that I can see the flaws along his back. Not the scratch marks from his nightly conquests—but the flimsy lines and incorrect proportions pretending to be arched ribs and blocky vertebrae.

He can't reach his back to complete his masterpiece, so he enlists me to complete the picture every year, and every year, I fuck it up. In the dark, though, and with their thoughts on little more than his cock, Reaper's victims don't care that I miscounted the rungs of his ribcage or fucked up the shading on his spine. It's not like they're paying attention.

Not like I do.

Drawing a breath, I tear my gaze away and focus on the changing landscape. Trees give way to swaths of open earth, and ancient, unmarked headstones begin to appear. This land is some of the oldest in the city—and the most hallowed. The only people who come here are the Morningstars themselves or their clients, the winding stretch of road keeping curious eyes away.

Unless they're on a mission to skin a cat.

The funeral home sits at the front of the cemetery, recently remodeled to appear approachable and comforting. Landscapers have installed a small pond, complete with croaking frogs and a pair of ducks idling in the water. Kane hovers at the waterside for only a moment before continuing down the path towards the back house —the real centerpiece of the property—Morningstar Mansion.

It's not actually a mansion, hardly more than two thousand square feet and sagging into the dirt on the back end, but it overlooks the oldest graves from before Harlin Heights was a city. An old church is nestled up the slope of the hill leading up the mountainside, its white-washed walls having long since faded to a grievous off yellow. Kane would have a better name for it—something stupid like *butter yellow*—but to me, it's just fucking ugly.

Kane bounces in his step as we approach the house from the back porch. Its front faces the main lot of graves, but its back faces the road. We skip the steps in favor of climbing over the dilapidated railing, its chipped paint sticking to my palms. Kane leaves flecks of body paint in his wake, just as I predicted. The skeleton covering his body has cracked, and pieces slough off carelessly, leaving a trail of salt and pepper everywhere he goes.

Grabbing his arm, I keep him from trying the back door. I point up to the second floor window, the candle flickering in its eave no match for the sunlight breaking across the yard. We only have a few minutes until it covers the entire area, and we're sitting ducks if Mercy's father has a gun on site... and every man worth his salt has a goddamn gun in this town.

But as Kane boosts me up to the window overhead, it isn't Mercy's father we see in through the screen door. An ancient woman with hair white as the purest winter snow peers unflinchingly at us, an antique lantern in her hand. I kick off Kane's shoulder and scramble through the open window, leaving him to deal with the old woman, because my target is in sight.

Mercy's asleep.

My heart pounds as I knock over the candle on the

windowsill and tumble onto a desk. Papers and pens scatter to the floor as I catch myself, banging my elbow in the process. With a hiss, I clutch my ringing funny bone and glare at her limp form beneath a mound of blankets. It's not *that* cold, but she's bundled like she's fighting a fever. I roll my eyes and move to her bedside, ready to right the rules of this stupid game.

If I'm playing, I have a say in how this shit show ends.

She looks peaceful in her sleep. Waves of midnight hair spill across her white pillowcase, accentuating just how pale she actually is. Skin smooth as porcelain covers her cheeks, down the hollow of her throat, across the length of her collarbone. Icy blue veins streak across her chest and over the curve of her breasts, dipping beneath the blanket before I can glimpse any further. In the dark of the cemetery, I wasn't quite sure what I was looking at other than a fucking problem.

But here, with the morning glow of dawn illuminating her beauty, she's a goddamn angel.

Too bad I have to clip her wings.

In the two seconds it takes to pin her body to the bed and cover her mouth, she wakes. Her eyelashes flutter like a firefly's wings, and the moment her eyes open, I lose my breath. We stare at each other as the songbirds outside mock me. This isn't some fairytale—it's not love at first sight.

I don't know what it is.

A problem, I remind myself, clenching my jaw. "You," I hiss, pressing her deeper into the mattress. She's limp beneath me, not even trying to fight. What's *wrong* with her? It would be easy to snap her neck. Smother her with a pillow. Shove a bottle of pills down her throat and force her to swallow. Her fight-or-flight response must be broken—it's why she didn't run last night when she had the chance. Why she didn't stab Kane or slit my throat. Why she didn't call the cops.

I draw a deep breath and say what I came here to say. "You're a stupid fucking girl." Anger rises in me like a tide, boiling and unstoppable. Sweat breaks out across my skin despite the chill in the room. I can hardly breathe, and she just sits there. Watching. Waiting. Is she even awake?

She blinks, and only then does she take a deep breath through her nose. A myriad of emotions cross her face before they settle on *tired*. She looks so small and fragile beneath me. Like I could break her without trying.

"You should have let me kill you." My voice scratches in my throat, and I swallow dryly. "Now you have an entire year to wonder. Will it hurt?" I dig my fingernails into the soft flesh of her cheek. "Will you suffer?" Shaking my head, I can't help but laugh bitterly. Our victims don't normally see their deaths coming. We wine and dine them up until their final moments, because it makes the sudden switch around that much more painful for them.

And delicious to watch.

"How will it happen, I wonder?" I sit up and straddle her waist, removing my hand from her mouth to pin her wrists over her head. Even her bed frame is an old, rickety metal thing, creaking at the slightest shift of weight.

"Slow and cold as your life seeps from your body like water from a tap..." I tap her inner wrist with my fingertip, admiring the flutter of her heartbeat. A flush creeps across her cheeks, but who's to say what from? "Or a quick flash of pain before it all goes dark? I wonder." I hum to myself, trying to picture Mercy's final moments. But all I get is a blank void of static in my brain.

Her voice is a tender caress on my senses. "I don't think I'll convince you not to kill me."

I lift an eyebrow. "So you're not as dumb as you look."

"I could kill you," she murmurs, whisper sweet and gentle despite her declaration. "Is that what you want?"

My blood runs cold. "The hell did you just say?"

She repeats herself. "I could kill you." Her eyes, a warm auburn, suddenly brighten. "Is that what you need? A way out?" She clenches her fists over her head. "I may not know much, but I know grief when I see it. Your eyes—"

I tear my gaze away from her face to stare at the wall over her head. Its paint is peeling like the rest of this fucking place.

"—You're hurting."

"Shut *up*," I snarl, baring my teeth. "You're insufferable. I can't wait to fucking kill you." Closing my eyes, I take as deep of a breath as I can and refocus on the purpose of my visit. "The rules of the fucking game. You can try to make my brother fall in love with you, but I want something else."

If she thinks she can kill me, *ha*, fat fucking chance.

But reverse-murder-schemes bore me. And "convincing me not to kill her," as she allegedly declared her win condition, is equally as stupid.

I lower my lips to her ear and breathe in the scent of lavender on her pillow.

Someone has trouble sleeping at night.

"For me not to kill you, I want..." A shiver rolls down my spine, and I dig my knees into the mattress. My feet hang over the edge of the bed, the furniture just as inadequate as the woman beneath me. Hatred boils in my gut like lava. This is why I don't get involved. Kane's the one who handles our targets—I can't handle interacting with them. I grow impatient and irritable, and they end up running away before we've closed the deal.

But Mercy *can't* run away. Not if she wants to live.

Licking my lips, I hum against the shell of her ear. "You can't have sex with Reaper."

It's perfect. Kane will tie himself in knots over this girl and try to fuck her two ways from Sunday. It's how he attaches to people—his love language is physical touch. I can't count how many times I've woken up to Kane smothering me in bed. It started when we were in the system as kids. Now that he's a grown ass man, he's rarely home at night, and we keep separate sleep schedules. But if the weather's bad and either of us can't sleep, we revert to old patterns and seek each other out for comfort.

All it takes is a crack of thunder to turn two men into babies.

I'd roll my eyes every goddamn day if I didn't need him just as much as he needs me.

Mercy suddenly turns her face so that our eyes are locked. Her warm breath fans across my cheeks. "That's like having a death wish. I know his reputation." She finally struggles against me and tries to pull her wrists free. "He sleeps with anything with a pulse." Her hips press into mine as she bends her knees, and I struggle to keep her pinned. "Why don't you want me to have sex with him?"

The retort *why does it matter?* is on the tip of my tongue, but I hold it in. "This is how I win the game," I say simply, huffing as she continues to writhe beneath me. "Stop fucking moving."

It's her turn to huff. "Get the fuck off of me, then."

I jump off of her the moment I feel heat stirring deep in my gut. There's no fucking way I'm entertaining *that* reaction. "If Reaper fucks you in any way—anal, oral, vaginal, titty fuck—"

"*Jesus,*" Mercy shouts, quickly sitting up and throwing a pillow at me. "Get the hell out of my room! I won't sleep with him!"

"—or if you fuck him, I'll be the one collecting your life, Kitten. Before the year ends."

Her mouth pops open. "*Kitten?*"

The nickname slipped out on its own. I frown. "Mercy. Whatever." Turning back towards the window, I push her desk to the side and throw one leg over the sill. "That's my rule. Break it, and you die." I jump down to the porch, and the wood splinters beneath my weight. I quickly hop onto the ground and peer back up at the window just in time to find Mercy glaring at me.

"If I get *you* to fuck me," she shouts, disturbing a pair of birds hanging out on the rooftop, "then *I* get to kill *you*!" Her skin is flushed bright pink, the sun's rays painting her in warm brushstrokes that give her a new spark of life she didn't have a moment ago.

I chuckle under my breath, but it's short-lived. Kane appears from the back door of the house, a half-eaten cookie trapped between his fingers. "If you *what?*" He wipes a crumb from his upper lip and jumps off the porch in one huge leap. Turning on his heel, he nearly stumbles to look up at Mercy's window. "Tell me it's not true, Siren. You'd rather fuck him than me?" A flash of hurt in his baby blue eyes almost makes me feel bad.

Of course he's more concerned about the sex than he is about the homicide.

I clap him on the shoulder. "It's her win condition. Don't worry about it. Never gonna happen." I raise my hand high and flick Mercy off. "Deal, bitch."

Let the game fucking begin.

CHAPTER 4

MERCY

THERE ISN'T enough coffee in the world to scrub my mind of the last twelve hours. *Not even.* I don't know how long I lay in bed after making it home from the cemetery, but it wasn't enough. Washing Reaper's blood off my face went about as well as it could have, and I left my clothes in the mud sink to soak out the blood and dirt.

My thoughts inevitably drift back to the man who climbed through my bedroom window. *Skinny Jeans.* What did Reaper call him?

Zane?

I chew on his name as I hover in front of the coffee pot and sip my third cup. Reaper's infamous on campus, but I've never heard of him having a sidekick. Or a brother. I guess no one cares about Reaper's backstory so long as he fucks like a god. But if I'm going to make him fall in love with me, I'll need to learn more about who he is and what he likes. Sighing, I set down my mug and stare out the kitchen window at the gravestones criss-crossing through the property. Not only do they know where I live, but they trespassed to deliver a message.

They could kill me in my sleep if they really wanted to.

A headache brews in the back of my skull, and I quickly swallow the last of my coffee. Standing here isn't going to solve anything. I need to think. Come up with a plan. Research. If the rumors are true, Reaper has been a part-time student at the college for the past five years. There has to be a record of him somewhere. A name. A picture. *Something.*

Maybe I can dig up some dirt on Zane, too.

My best bet is to get someone in Greek life to talk. I don't know any of the sorority girls, so that's an automatic bust. But the thing about Reaper is that he's not just into chicks—he's made rounds in the frat houses, too. If he's lettered, he comes from money or pedigree. If he's not, they let him in on account of something he can offer them. Drugs. Booze. Sex. Connections. I wrack my brain for any defining features from last night, but other than how muscled he is, I come up empty.

I pull out my phone and send a quick text to Sam—the only frat boy I know—and invite him out for coffee. My treat.

While I wait for his reply, I retreat to my bathroom to put on my makeup for the day. Heavy eyeliner. Dark lip stain. A white lace bow in my hair. I draw a wing on my left eye and stare at the curved line. Without thinking, I draw a straight line down the side of my cheek and stare at the black streak, the gears slowly turning in my head.

Someone had to paint Reaper's body last night.

Someone talented.

Like an art student.

I close my eyes and take a deep breath, conjuring the faces of every student in my studio classes. As senior-level classes, there aren't too many students enrolled. I pick through the faces and weed them out one by one, starting with people who I know are in relationships. After that, I go through what little I've gleaned from their artwork and narrow the focus even further. By the end of this ten-minute exercise, I'm ready to tear my hair out.

I don't have a clue who would help him.

Thankfully, my phone chimes just as I'm about to wipe my entire face clean and restart my makeup.

SAM

Sure. Meet me after practice? 8:00?

I quickly send confirmation and erase the random line of eyeliner running down the side of my face. I should tell Sam that I don't want to see him to *see him*, but I'd rather catch up first and then delve into the dirty details about Reaper and Zane.

If anything, Sam will be a welcome distraction for my impending demise.

By the time I walk the few blocks from campus to Sam's frat house later that evening, he's already waiting outside for me. Freshly showered after football practice, he grins at me and bounds down the front steps to meet me on the sidewalk. Once he's within range, he throws his arm over my shoulders and pulls me in for a half-hug.

"Where have you been hiding?" he teases, giving me a once-over. His gaze lingers on my fishnet tights before he shakes his head. "Enjoy your favorite night of the year?"

I roll my eyes, but my heart isn't into it. "It was a scream."

"Well, tell me all about it. You hungry? We could go to Papa Joe's." He looks at me expectantly.

"I thought we were going for coffee."

"Coffee doesn't count as food, Mercy." He pokes my stomach. "Have you eaten today?"

My stomach growls at the prospect of food. He's right, I haven't eaten all day. I've been too nervous about the prospect of running into Reaper and Zane again. "Fine," I concede, the two of us changing course for the local pizza joint. "But you're paying."

Sam keeps smiling as he shoves his hands in his front pockets. "I'd never dream of anything else." The evening air is cooler than yesterday, making jeans the staple of the season. His letterman jacket sports a proud double H patch for *Harlin Heights College*, but the fact that we even *have* letterman jackets is the biggest joke of the century. We barely qualify for competitive sports as a Division Three school, and that's only because the local alumni funnel money into the college's coffers like their lives depend on it. It's not like many of us are earning our Bachelor's degrees here. Most local kids move away to bigger schools with more promising graduation rates, but those who stick around don't graduate.

It's as if the student body disappears once senior year arrives.

Sam and I fall into comfortable small talk, our ease of companionship a testament to how long we've known each other. After Sam's mom died when he was a teenager, our dads ended up joining the same grief counseling group and dragged us both to the teen meetings for sons and daughters suffering similar losses. Out of everyone in the group, Sam was the most magnanimous, leading discussions and encouraging others to participate. He even got an outcast like me talking. No one's a stranger when it comes to Sam.

He has a way of bringing out the brightest versions of people.

As soon as we've settled into a booth in the back of Papa Joe's Pizzeria, he doesn't waste any time getting to the point. "Tell me what's on your mind. You don't randomly ask me out on dates without a reason." He throws an arm over the back of his seat and stretches his legs, bumping my knee with his.

"This isn't a date." I fiddle with the paper strip from my silverware.

"Oh, so it's business? What could Mercy Morningstar possibly need me for?" After a moment, he snaps his fingers. "You need a male model again, don't you? You don't even have to ask. I happily accept."

I kick his foot under the table. "I don't need a model." Our server brings us complimentary water and garlic knots. I take large gulps of ice water to keep from blushing at Sam's playful grin. The last time he modeled for my sketches, things got heated between us. We didn't take it further than kissing—despite his flirting, Sam is a gentleman—and we agreed to keep our relationship platonic by the end of the series. *But still.* I don't need to open that door again unless I'm ready for whatever waits on the other side. Right now, I need to focus on staying alive rather than hooking up with my closest friend.

"I need to tell you something." I fold the napkin band into uneven triangles before flattening it out and redoing it more evenly. "I met someone last night."

Sam's eyebrows hitch. "Yeah? How'd that go?"

Umm.

"He wants to kill me."

Sam's smile tightens. "Seriously, Mercy, no offense, but we need to work on your punch lines."

"*Seriously*, Sam, I'm not joking." I flick the triangle at him, hitting him square in the chest. Lowering my voice, I lean across the table so that no one but Sam can hear me. "I caught Reaper and his brother burying a body in the cemetery." The memory resurfaces like a bad dream, the taste and grit of grave dirt on my tongue churning my stomach.

"Reaper? Like, *the* Reaper?"

Our server interrupts to take our order, and we both say the same thing: a large vegetarian with extra parmesan packs. Once they're gone, Sam sets his forearms on the table and leans across to whisper back. "I don't believe you."

I considered this outcome while Sam was at practice. I don't need him to believe me so long as he tells me everything he knows or gets me in touch with someone within Reaper's inner circle. Still, Sam's disbelief hurts more than I anticipated. "Why not?" I cross my arms over my chest. "Am I not pretty enough to be his type?"

"You're not stupid enough to be his type." Narrowing his eyes, Sam scoffs. "Besides, isn't it a little too 'on the nose' for a guy named Reaper to be a killer?"

"I know what I saw." I clench my jaw and quickly decide to give Sam the full details. "He and his brother tried to kill me after I caught them burying a body. Well, Zane tried, but Reaper stopped him. I'm not sure why. Trust me, I've spent all day thinking about it." I take a sip of my water. "But it gets even weirder. They want to play some kind of fucked-up game. The loser dies by the winner's hand." A shiver rolls down my spine. "They gave me until Halloween next year to win the game."

Sam sits completely still, his eyes searching mine. "You're serious."

"As the grave," I say dryly.

"Not funny."

"Kind of funny."

"How do you win the game?"

This is where I lie. "I have to figure out who they are and why they kill people. Like a detective." The ice in my glass rattles as it melts. "What do you know about Reaper's brother Zane?"

"Hold on," Sam interjects, holding his hands up. "Why don't you just go to the police? You can't play their game. The odds are stacked against you." Counting off on his fingers, he lists all the reasons why the game is rigged. "They could lie about who they are. They could try to kill you before the deadline. Reaper's like a ghost, Mercy; he's in and out of the frat houses whenever he pleases, there one second and gone the next. I can't tell you how many times I've walked in on him dicking someone down, then as soon as they're finished, he disappears." Sam crinkles his nose in disgust. "But anytime I've asked around—because he's broken more than one virgin's heart—I don't get any answers." He sighs and rubs his forehead. "The game is rigged. They want you to lose."

I seal my lips tightly together. "I'm aware."

"Then why play at all?" A muscle in his jaw tics. "We should go to the police. Let them handle it, Mercy."

Instead of following that line of thinking, I backtrack. "What do you know about Zane?"

Sam chokes on his water. "*Please* let this go."

Interesting.

"Why are you avoiding the question?"

Our pizza arrives, but neither of us looks away from

the other. Our server refills our drinks and retreats quickly, sensing the tension in the air.

"There are some things within Greek life that you should stay out of," Sam says, choosing his words carefully. His gaze flicks over my shoulder for a moment before returning to me. We aren't exactly in a private venue, so people are going to see us together. If he spills sacred fraternity secrets, there could be consequences.

I nudge his knee beneath the table, and he reaches under to keep me still. Grabbing my thigh over my knee, he squeezes, his fingertips slipping through the holes of my fishnets. His Adam's apple bobs on a swallow. "You're playing with fire."

"I wouldn't ask if it weren't important." A sharp pain tears through my heart, and I have to look away from Sam's piercing stare. "Isn't my life worth something?" My voice trembles, and I take a sip of water to cover.

Sam sees right through me, like he always does. "Hey," he breathes, gently brushing his hand across my knee. "Of course it is. You know I didn't mean it like that." Part of grief counseling is coming to terms with your inner demons, and Sam had a front row seat when I first met mine. Depression is one fucked-up bitch. "Let's eat, okay? We can talk about this later." His gaze shifts behind me again, and he pulls his hand back.

"What's wrong?" I glance at the plexiglass panel behind his head, but it's not reflective enough for me to see what's behind me.

"It's nothing." He splits the pizza in half and slides

three huge slices onto his plate. "Don't let the pizza get cold." He turns the conversation to our families, classes, and plans after graduation. We've had these conversations before, so the familiarity is comforting, if not a little boring. It's been a while since I've had a conversation that didn't involve reading the latest obituaries in the newspaper and divining which family will contact us for funerary support. I'm a bit out of practice.

After paying and boxing up leftovers, Sam dabs up a few guys at another table on our way out the door. Only once we're safely down the block does he relax.

"Tough crowd, huh?" I nudge his shoulder with my elbow. "Remind me why you pledged?"

"Legacy," he murmurs, nudging me back. "You know how family shit goes." We walk another half a block before he glances at me from the corner of his eye. "Has your dad asked yet?"

I exhale slowly. "Not since the last time." It's no secret that my father is trying to convince my older sister Lilith and me to take over the family business, but I have no interest in soothing the bereaved. "I think he's waiting until Christmas to bring it up again."

"Naturally." Sam chuckles softly. "Gotta have you and Lilith in the same room for that talk."

"Grandma Star is in on it this time."

"Oh, yeah?"

I nod. "She says someone needs to keep the dead company after she's gone. I think she's still waiting for me to inherit *the gift*." I say the last part with air quotes.

"After two decades, I think that ship's sailed. Her best bet is to wait for a grandkid to arrive."

Not that I'm having kids anytime soon. Even Lilith, at nearly thirty years old, hasn't shown any signs of settling down. "I think Grandma's upset that times have changed."

No one visits the cemetery to pay respects to their ancestors, and most of Grandma Star's clients have passed away. Spiritualism isn't as popular as it once was. Newer generations would rather consult an EMF reader than seek out a medium.

I take a deep breath and frown at the cracked sidewalk. None of this solves my problem. If I had *the gift*, I'd march right back to that grave site, dig up the body of that poor soul Reaper and Zane killed, and get him to spill their secrets.

Reaper's voice suddenly rasps in my ear like a bad dream, and I spin around to find empty air behind me. Grabbing Sam's arm, I stare wide-eyed at the empty space. "Did you say something?"

Sam's forehead crinkles as he looks between me and the empty concrete behind us. "Um, no?"

"I heard a voice just now." I clutch Sam's arm so tightly that he bends at the waist to accommodate our height difference. "Is there anyone missing from your frat? From any of them?" My brain fires rapidly, jumping from one idea to the next. Reaper used a name last night when he talked about the dead body. We were standing in a grave. A *marked* grave—with a family name engraved on its headstone.

"I need to go back to the cemetery," I blurt out, dragging Sam across the street. The grounds aren't too far from here. Maybe a few blocks. Thirty minutes tops if we speed walk.

"Whoa, there. We can't walk. It's getting dark out." Sam pulls me to a stop and plants both hands on my shoulders. "My car's parked off of Jefferson. Let me drive you." He steers me a few streets down to the public lot where his truck is parked. Gravel crunches under our tires as he pulls out onto Jefferson Street. Taking a right, he swings around to the cemetery within a few minutes. Much faster than walking.

Once we're parked again, he clicks the *lock* button on his door and flips a switch to engage the child lock on mine. "What are we doing here, Mercy?"

I rapidly jerk the door handle. "This isn't funny, Sam. Let me out."

Headlights from a car passing on the street illuminate his face in blinding detail, accentuating the frizzed tumble of brunette hair sticking to his forehead. Freckles dot his cheeks, one for every day he's spent out in the sun over the past three years of football practice. But his eyes—a vibrant green that belongs to glass, not flesh— seem to glow. "Not until you tell me the truth." He grips the steering wheel so tightly that the leather creaks. "Please, Mercy. I can't help if you're not honest with me."

Turning my face away to look out the window, I don't answer at first. What can I say? I heard a voice in my ear that sounded like Reaper, but clearly wasn't, repeat the name he used to identify the corpse he was in the middle of burying?

Grandma Star would believe me, but I'm not sure that Sam will.

"His name was Alejandro," I say slowly, catching Sam's reflection in the side-view mirror. "The man that Reaper killed. That's his name. If we go to the grave, we'll find his family plot. Section F, fourth row back." I try to flip through the surnames I've read a hundred times in the cemetery's catalogue, but they blur together in my mind. I need to walk to the section to jog my memory.

I need to find out who Alejandro was to determine why Reaper killed him.

Sam runs a hand down his face before cursing under his breath. Undoing the child lock, he sighs. "This whole situation is *F'd.*" He slams his car door once he slips out, then comes around to help me down. As soon as my feet touch the ground, he grabs my hand and holds on tight. "Don't walk ahead of me, and don't wander off on your own. We're doing this together."

A small smile curves on my lips. "Scared of the dark?"

He scoffs. "Scared that you'll get kidnapped, actually. C'mon, I don't want to be here any longer than we have to." As we walk beneath a streetlamp, he catches me smiling. "What?"

Shaking my head, I try not to laugh at his expense. "I think you're scared, Samson Wright. I didn't know a linebacker could spook so easily."

It takes a moment for him to respond. I've nearly

forgotten what we were talking about, but even then, what he says doesn't make sense.

"I wish you'd stayed home last night." Sam's jaw clenches as the graveyard comes into view. "Reaper's bad news, Mercy. I hope you know what you're getting into."

The side gate creaks as I push it open. The damn thing is hardly ever locked. Whoever watches the grounds does a shit job at securing it. I squeeze Sam's hand as we step across the threshold onto hallowed ground. "I don't," I admit honestly, "but I'm ready to find out."

CHAPTER 5

REAPER

THE CIGARETTE in my hand goes out, the orange sparks at its tip fading to gray. I keep relighting it, thinking that I'll be able to focus better with a few more puffs. Instead, I've burned through half a pack and have hardly taken any hits. I toss the butt onto the mausoleum rooftop and sigh, dragging my fingers through my hair. I didn't get any sleep today, and neither did Zane. Halloween always fucks with his sleep schedule, making him irritable as fuck and terrible to be around.

I left the house as soon as the sun went down. After a successful hunting season, I'd normally find a busty brunette to wile away the hours with, but I've got a one-track mind that's playing on a loop.

Mercy wants to have sex with Zane.

At least, that's her *win condition*, he says. As if she would come up with that on her own. No matter how much I've pestered him about the rest of their conversation, he stays mute, refusing to fess up.

He did something. Said something. I know it.

But forcing myself into Mercy's life so soon after seeing her—nearly twelve hours ago—breaks other boundaries we've set for the hunt. We're supposed to lead them in slowly at first, only ramping up in the final stages. With Mercy, I want to start on full speed and burn right through her.

Hence the cigarettes. My mind keeps spiraling on everything I *shouldn't* do, which consequently, is everything I *want* to do.

Voices carry across the cemetery. It's not uncommon for people to be here in early November with Día de los Muertos around the corner, but I recognize these voices. *Both* of them. I perk up immediately, craning my neck to check all of the nearby entrances. One. Two. Three..

There.

Siren is walking hand-in-hand with a frat boy I've never had the pleasure of seducing, but I've seen him around. He's a junior, I think, but he's been in the frat since his first year enrolled. I don't pay much attention to the politics of Greek life, but I've seen enough to know when someone is there on daddy's dime instead of their own volition. This guy—football star, pretty smile, business major—never seems like he wants to be here.

I'm not sure if he wants to be *anywhere.*

But he looks pretty goddamn content holding Mercy's hand.

A tear of tension rips through my shoulders, and I roll them back to ease the strain. I haven't laid public claim on her, but I will. Soon, but not yet. Let him hold her hand for now, but within a month or two, I'll make sure she—and the entire student body—knows who owns her.

Because when Zane and I choose a target, we claim *everything*. Mind, body, soul. *Life.* I take a deep breath and try not to let impatience get the best of me. Zane says that it's one of my many faults—as if there are that many —that I get too attached too quickly. He could serve to get more attached than he does.

I pull my phone from my pocket and take a picture of the two of them holding hands, capturing a coy smile from our girl. I frown at the screen as soon as I see it, disliking how she's smiling for another man. At least it isn't reciprocal; he looks like he's got a stick up his ass. Wound up tight. Looking over his shoulder, about to jump out of his skin—

A slow smirk curves on my lips. Did my little siren tell a friend about our deal? Is she trying to protect herself from me?

I wonder what Zane would make of that.

My phone vibrates moments later, just as Mercy and Pretty Boy cut across a row of graves towards the section we visited last night. "Yo," I answer, still smiling. Zane isn't nearly as amused as I am.

"She has a boyfriend?" His voice clips at the end of each word. I can picture him glaring at his phone.

"I don't think so," I answer honestly, staring at them from a distance. "It looks like they're dragging each other around. Almost like they're fighting."

"Lovers fight."

"Hm." What would Zane know about that? "Still, he doesn't look happy to be here, but she's all too eager to visit Alejandro again."

Paying her respects to the dead? She should have brought flowers.

"What are they doing there?"

Like I know. Rolling my eyes, I switch the phone to my other ear. "Want me to walk over and ask them?"

Zane falls silent. "You shouldn't."

...but he wants me to.

Grinning, I jump off the mausoleum rooftop and stumble a few steps into the grass. "Say less," I tease, chuckling. "Want me to put you on speaker?"

"God, no. Put me in your pocket."

"What a snoop. She won't know you're listening." I'm sure that's the idea. "Taking an interest in her already? That's unlike you." Visiting her this morning was unlike him, too. He doesn't normally pay this much attention to our targets, preferring that I handle in-person interactions. Texting, sure, he'll text up a storm if the mood strikes. But seeing them in person?

Not his thing.

I'm tempted to put him on video and flip him around so that he's eye to eye with Mercy. I'd love to see the utter shock and horror on his face.

"I'm not interested," Zane snaps, clearly in denial. "Just find out what they're doing."

"Roger."

I slip the phone into my front pocket and make my way to Alejandro's family plot. He has three generations buried here, including his younger sister. I'm not sure what she died from, but according to Alejandro, his parents never recovered. I'm not sure that he did either, truthfully. In his final moments, he wished to see her again. It was touching—and the reason why we buried him with her.

Mercy is crouching in front of Maria's tombstone when I approach. She doesn't hear or see me, but Pretty Boy does. He's on high alert, clenching his fists and preparing to defend Mercy's life on sight. I can see it in his eyes. You can't fake that kind of determination.

"Easy, boy," I murmur, unable to keep the smile off my face. In another life—or maybe just another year—I'd go after him, too. "What's your name?"

"I'm not a dog," he growls, looking very much like a guard dog as he plants himself between me and Mercy. "What the fuck are you doing here, Reaper?"

Mercy quickly turns at the waist, her eyes beautifully wide as she spots me. "He's here?"

Yes, Siren, I'll find you anywhere.

"I should be asking you that." I nod towards the grave. Zane and I did a good job recovering it to make it look untouched, but it's not perfect. The more they walk on the topsoil, the more our facade comes undone. "I'd appreciate if you didn't step on Alejandro and Maria. It's disrespectful to the dead."

"Why'd you kill him?" Mercy stands up and wipes her hands off on her skirt, a deliciously pleated black skirt that hangs just above her knees. I lick my lips and admire the view of her porcelain skin beneath her fishnet tights.

Goth girls always know how to put on a show, no matter the season.

She blushes bright pink at my stare. I might have hit a nerve.

I'll have to keep hitting them.

I pretend to think about answering her question, taking my sweet time to shift my gaze back up to her face. "Why do you want to know?" It's unusual for our targets to ask about our previous kills, but then again, none of them ever had a heads-up about our pastimes. Mercy's a rare exception. The only one.

That's what makes this year's game so thrilling. I can feel the excitement pumping through my veins with every single beat of my heart. "That's privileged information," I continue, cracking my neck with a jerk of my head. Exhaling, I groan. Damn, I needed that. "I don't think you've earned it yet, beautiful."

Pretty Boy Guard Dog bares his teeth, doing a very good impression of a German Shepherd. Even his hair's scraggy. "That's the game, right? Figure you out, and she gets to live." He glares at me. "What kind of a man threatens innocent women for fun?"

"I'm not threatening." I slide my gaze back to Mercy, enjoying the corset she's wrapped around her body. I bet tearing it off of her would be a fun little challenge. She might even try to bite me. "It's a promise, one that I fully intend to keep. But—" I click my tongue against my teeth. "Siren, when were you going to tell me you had a boyfriend? I could make this a two-for-one deal."

I don't *want* to include Pretty Boy, and Zane will rip

my head off if I agree to it, but seeing her spine snap into place is *so* worth the bluff. She pushes herself to her feet and tries to pull him behind her, but he refuses to move, so they glare at each other and stand arm-in-arm.

Cute.

They answer at the same time, only in opposites.

"No fucking way."

"Do it."

Then they glare at each other some more.

I cross my arms over my chest and enjoy the aggressive posturing between them. I hope that Zane can hear every heated word.

"You are *not* dying for me."

"Who's talking about dying? I'm talking about living!"

"You're crazy if you think I'm letting you in on this."

"What, you don't think I can handle it?" Pretty Boy tosses his hand out towards me. "Mercy, I can handle him, trust me. I've taken on bigger bastards than him."

Chuckling, I resist the urge to grab my crotch and show him what he can *really* handle. "As touching as this is, I'll have to decline. This is a solo operation."

Pretty Boy's eyes snap to me. "You have a partner. She deserves one too."

So she *did* tattle. I can't be too upset about it—I'm loving this new side to her. "As long as you know what's at stake..." I trail off, wondering just how much he knows. "But she did promise to fall in love with me."

She gasps, having the audacity to look scorned. "I did not!"

A shadow crosses Pretty Boy's face. "Tell me the rules of the game."

"No, you're not joining—"

"*Mercy.*" He turns away from me to grab her chin and force her to meet his eyes. "Let me help you."

I watch their interaction with keen interest. What's their relationship? Friends? Exes? Lovers? Whatever it is, his tactic works. She nods at him and wraps her arms around his neck to pull him closer. Then, she whispers in his ear.

My cell phone burns my thigh, overheating from the length of the call or, more likely, from Zane's fury. He may act calm and collected on the outside, but he's a ticking time bomb waiting to explode. I haven't been able to light the fuse after all these years, but if he's as interested in Mercy as I think he is, this could be what pushes him over the edge. We've never done a double-homicide, and that could be enough to force his hand. He'll have to join in on the fun.

I'm just not sure how Pretty Boy will change the terms of the game.

At any rate, he's clearly displeased by the time Mercy's done sharing secrets. He's boring a hole in her head with the intensity of his stare. To her credit, she's unflinching despite the pressure.

"You can still back out," I offer. "I'm more than happy with Mercy as my only prize."

"Shut up." He finally breaks Mercy's gaze to glare at me. "And let me in on the deal." Stepping in front of

Mercy, he pushes her behind him. "If I get Mercy to fall in love with me—"

Zane curses loudly from my pocket.

"Then neither of you can touch her." He lifts his chin. "That's my win condition."

I stare at Mercy's wide-eyed shock, enjoying the way she freezes on the spot. "So it's a race?" I shake my head, knowing that Zane is going to *hate* this. "And what about you?" I nod towards Pretty Boy. "Shouldn't we have a little fun with you, too?"

"Not interested." He clenches his jaw. "I'm only here for Mercy."

"Fine," I concede, sighing. "Whoever gets her to fall in love with them first has the honor of deciding her fate. But when you fail—because you will, or you'd already have won her heart—"

Pretty Boy flinches.

"You both die."

CHAPTER 6

SAM

THE ENTIRE DRIVE back to Mercy's house is silent. Neither of us speaks. I can't say what's on her mind, but I know what's on mine.

Mercy lied to my face.

She told the truth, sure—*eventually*. But if we hadn't run into Reaper in the cemetery, I doubt she would have come clean. She would have let me go on believing that all she had to do to win this twisted game was figure out some psychopath's real identity, when in reality, she's supposed to make him fall in love with her.

I don't know who's more fucked in the head: Reaper for toying with her, or me for thinking I have a chance at beating him.

There's no way that Mercy will ever fall in love with me. But damnit—I have to try, don't I?

We agreed last year that we were going to remain friends. Not friends with benefits, not emotional rebounds, but *friends*. People who look out for each other. Who stick around to let them know when we're being assholes or when we need to stand up for ourselves. To tell the truth, no matter how much it hurts.

And Mercy *lied* to me.

I cut the engine once we park in her front driveway. Crickets sing like the lead instrument in an orchestra, filling the silence with the sounds of nature. An owl hoots somewhere nearby, and a possum crosses the front yard on its way to the tree line. Life remains vibrant even in the darkness. I've always said that Mercy puts on black makeup and nail polish to keep people away, but underneath the black leather and combat boots, she's just as down to earth as the rest of us.

She has hopes and fears, too, like me.

I happen to know every single one.

Or so I thought.

Sighing, I close my eyes and take a deep breath. "You should have told me the truth from the beginning." If I had known that love was involved, I would have—I don't know—told the cops? I run the idea through my head a few times, and in every scenario where I file an official report, I get laughed out of the station. No one would believe that a serial killer wants a college girl to fall in love with him *or else*. But I would have believed her.

That's what friends do. We confide in each other. We trust each other. We pull each other out of the fire before we get burned.

"We could run away," I suggest halfheartedly. "Start a new life." It sounds as stupid as I feel.

Thankfully, Mercy doesn't laugh. She reaches over

the middle console and pries my hand off the steering wheel. Setting it in her lap, she plays with my fingers, tapping my knuckles with her fingertips. "I can't leave my family, Sam."

Some truths hover in moments of silence like these. They float in the air like a vapor that we pretend we're not breathing in, when all the while, it's slowly suffocating us. She can't leave her family because they can't handle another loss.

I could leave mine, though. I'll *gladly* leave everything behind if it keeps Mercy safe... and away from Reaper. I drag my free hand through my hair and try not to think about him, but my thoughts spiral. Memories of running into him at frat events or football after parties blur together, but one thing remains constant.

He's always fucking around.

Mercy shouldn't get involved with someone like that.

Bracing myself for another lie, I clear my throat. "Are you a virgin?" I keep my eyes on the tombstones ahead of us, trying to keep myself from picturing Mercy at one of those parties, spread out on a pool table while Reaper dicks her down. He does that to virgins—makes their first time a spectacle. Something *memorable.* My face twists into something heinous, but that's how I feel when it comes to Reaper.

Downright disgusted.

"Is that so bad?" Mercy throws my hand back at me like I've burned her.

Fuck. She thinks I made that face because of her. "No, Mercy, that's not—"

She pops open her door and climbs down from the cab, slamming the door in my face. I quickly hop out behind her. "Mercy, wait—that wasn't—I don't care if you're a virgin!"

Spinning around, she bends over and picks up a rock. "Then why did you ask?" Throwing it at me, she screams in frustration. "*God*, if I could lose it, I would, okay? No one wants to have sex with The Dead Girl!"

I barely have time to catch the rock before she's turning back around and storming across the yard. I'm aware of her reputation on campus. She says that it followed her from high school—that not enough of the local kids moved away after they graduated, so she's been labeled *weird* since day one, Freshman year. But I didn't think that would fuck up her chances of dating.

I mean, *look* at her.

She's fucking gorgeous.

As I follow her inside, I say a quick "*hi, Grandma Star*" and wave at Mercy's grandmother. The old woman barely sees me, too focused on whatever spirits are dancing in the moonlight, or so she says. Without a word, she pops open the cookie jar beside her and hands me a homemade sugar cookie. "Play nice, dear," she mumbles, waving me on. "Mercy's troubled lately."

Yeah, no kidding.

When I head upstairs and push open Mercy's bedroom door, a chair she used to block her door clatters to the floor. "You really need to get that fixed," I say without thinking. Then I have to dodge a shoe thrown at my head. "Nevermind, I'll do it." Replacing the broken lock and adding a few deadbolts should help keep Reaper at bay. But I'd feel better if she let me stay over—or better yet, if she came back to my place.

"You can stay with me until we figure this out." I pick up the shoe she threw and roll it over in my hands. It's one of her many combat boots, all identical, with laces instead of buckles because she likes them tight. "We can move back to my Dad's if you want. He's never there. It'd be like our own place." I doubt she wants to spend all semester surrounded by testosterone and beer at the frat house.

She plops down on her bed and kicks off her other boot. "I won't make you do that. Samuel sucks."

I shrug and lean against her doorframe. Can't argue with that. My dad's a dick. "He doesn't have to know."

"He won't notice his son shacking up with The Dead Girl?" Mercy shakes her head. "Don't you have to marry for pedigree or some shit?"

"Please don't call yourself that."

Fluffing her pillow before getting comfortable, she takes a moment to respond. "Everyone else does." She closes her eyes, and her mouth curves down. "Maybe that's why Reaper likes me. I'm already dead, so it's less work."

I don't like hearing her say his name. When she first brought him up, I thought she was joking. I *hoped* she was. But seeing him tonight brought everything into focus: Mercy has a target on her back, either because she's a virgin he wants to ruin or because she interrupted their body dump. Either way, he's interested, and it makes my skin crawl. I've never liked that fucking guy.

Mercy pats the bed beside her. "Don't just stand there. Sit."

Like a dog, I obey, closing the door before coming to sit beside her. She stares at the ceiling, and I stare at her. I mean really, *really* look. The dark circles under her eyes worry me, but they aren't new. She's always had trouble sleeping. I grab the lavender spray from her nightstand and spritz the air before lying down with her. The bed creaks beneath our combined weight. "Is there more that you're not telling me?"

She crinkles her nose. "Well, you already know that I'm a virgin. What more is there to say?"

I roll onto my side and prop my head up on my elbow. "I'm serious, Mercy."

"So am I." She glances at me before staring at the ceiling again. "His brother Zane says that Reaper can't fuck me, or he'll kill me. That's his win condition. I can't have sex with Reaper."

Thank *God.* That's the best news I've heard since this nightmare began. I hide a smile beneath an unconvincing cough. "Why does he care?"

"How should I know?" She rubs the back of her eyelids. "I think it's because of how easy Reaper is. He'll fuck anything. So if he gets in my pants, like he probably wants to, it's an easy win for them."

"Nothing about you is easy, Mercy Morningstar," I murmur, brushing the back of my hand over her upper arm. "If he'd known that, he wouldn't have picked that as his condition." I've never known Mercy to have a crush on anyone, let alone hookup with someone. Now it makes sense. "Why didn't you tell me that you were a virgin?"

"I didn't think it mattered."

"It doesn't," I say gently, "*yet*. But it will if Reaper finds out. That's why I asked."

Reaper's a fucking bloodhound when it comes to virgin pussy. He'll find out sooner or later... so it's better if she weren't one.

I try to keep my voice even as I say what's on my mind. "I could help you." My heartbeat spikes at the thought of Mercy giving herself to me. I've never been with a virgin, but knowing that it's Mercy's first time would make it special. She deserves more than a good time. It needs to be special. After everything she's been through, I'd like to give her something no one else could. More than my friendship. More than sex. Something... deeper.

A flush colors her cheeks. "Are you saying that you want to sleep with me, Samson Wright?"

I swallow, suddenly at a loss for words. *Yes* feels like the understatement of the century. "I—"

Mercy suddenly rolls onto her side and covers my mouth with her palm. "Don't," she whispers, biting her bottom lip. "I don't... want to ruin anything. You mean a lot to me, Sam, and sex will just complicate things." Her blush deepens to scarlet, trailing down the curve of her neck. "Besides, it's not like you're in love with me or anything, and I only want to have sex with someone I love. That's why I'm still a virgin. I know that I said I'd throw it away if I could, but I just…" She trails off, lowering her hand and looking away. "I'm just frustrated. It's hard to find love when no one even looks at you."

Brushing my thumb across her cheek, I tuck a loose strand of hair behind her ear. If only she could see what I see. She's more than some family legacy or a lost artist.

No matter how dark it gets inside my head, she's the girl who always brings me back to the light.

"I see you, Mercy Morningstar. I've always seen you." Pressing a kiss to her forehead, I breathe in her scent and tuck it deep inside my chest for safekeeping. "The offer still stands. When you're ready, I'm here." I pull her into my arms and hold her close. Neither of us sleeps, but there's a comfort here unlike any other I've felt.

I won't let *anyone* take that away from us.

CHAPTER 7

ZANE

BY THE TIME Kane makes it home, I'm ready to tear him a new asshole. I couldn't sleep after learning that he invited another player into the game, but not only is there one other person to worry about, it's Samson fucking Wright. His father is one of those corporate guys who make shady deals in the background. Killing his son will turn heads our way, no matter how cleanly we go about it. And if we kill Mercy and leave Sam alive?

That man will strike back if we take his pretty little friend away.

It's a lose-fucking-lose situation now, when it was so simple before. No one would mourn Mercy Morningstar's disappearance, but Sam is another story. The heir to the Wright fortune is a face we can't erase so easily.

Kane steps through the front door, and I'm on him in two seconds flat. Shoving his chest, I snarl at him. "What the *fuck* were you thinking?" His back slams into the wall. "Sam Wright isn't a target."

He looks at me without a spark of recognition in his eyes. "Should that name mean something to me?"

Frustrated, I wrap my fists in the front of his t-shirt and haul him into the living room. "*Yes*, it fucking should. You didn't recognize him? You've tried to sleep with him twice." I keep a detailed record of every frat brother and sorority sister that Kane has sex with, and Sam's name has never made it onto the list. I don't think he's into men. Tossing Kane onto the couch, I pick up my laptop from the kitchen island and hand it to him. "Here. Read his file."

While Kane browses Sam's school records, I pace from one end of the apartment to the other, burning my usual path across the carpet. I'm wearing it thin from how often we do this. "You know that I look into all of our targets."

"I know."

"So you can't be surprised that I'm vetoing this."

"You can't veto it. We won't get Mercy if we don't include him. You're the one who insisted on killing her," he reminds me, frowning at me over the top of the moni- tor. "We could have fucked her last night. Had a little fun. I could have made her forget all about Alejandro."

I'm going to have an aneurysm. My head pounds in time with my heartbeat, and I have to close my eyes. Why does his solution to everything always involve his dick? I take a deep breath in through my nose. "What are we going to do?" I open my eyes to find Kane staring out the balcony's glass doors.

"We'll make it look like an accident. Put them

together. The police could find them this time, and then it's not our problem. His dad won't search the city for their killer if it's ruled an accident or suicide." Kane leans back and sinks into the pleather couch, carelessly tossing my laptop to the side. "They looked close. We could make them seem like they're dating." He's frowning as he says it, but it's not a bad idea.

"That could work," I say slowly, moving to the window to close the blinds. "They could be dating for real now. He says he wants her to fall in love with him." Sure, he might say it's to save her life, but he wouldn't have chosen that condition for winning the game if he didn't already want her to fall for him. "He could win. He has a headstart."

"Bull*shit*," Kane snaps, punching the cushion beside him. "She doesn't like him that way." But I can tell he's not convinced; his forehead crinkles as he glares at his fists. "She *doesn't*." Switching gears, he jabs a finger at me. "Just sleep with her, man, and it'll all be over. Then you won't have to worry about the other guy. But we'll wait to kill her until next year; I want to watch her spiral."

Displeasure sours inside my gut. It's not that she isn't pretty—she's got this haunting quality about her—but I just don't *feel* that way about her. Kane can drop his pants for anyone, but I don't want her anywhere near me. Not like that. "No," I answer simply, "I don't think I will."

I can't wait to watch her fail over and over again, tripping over herself as she gets more desperate with each passing month. I wonder if she'll grow bolder the closer we get to the deadline. But, realistically, I doubt we'll make it to the spring with this game. It'll probably be over by the new year, and Kane and I can move on with our lives.

Speaking of—"Are you graduating this year?"

The sudden swing in conversation turns Kane off. He pushes himself off the couch and tries to hide in his bedroom. I block him from closing the door. "You're a fifth-year senior. You need to graduate." We can't keep killing in the same place or we'll get caught. We've already had a few close calls with the feds. At this rate, we'll have to go underground and join the Baranovas in their illegal deals just to stay under the radar.

I *really* don't want to have to learn to speak Russian.

Kane grabs his sketchbook from the desk and flips to a random page. "I don't need to graduate. I already have a portfolio and enough clients to keep us running for years."

I prepare myself for our usual argument. He doesn't want to leave the city, and he doesn't want to stop pretending that he's a student. But he's an artist—he can live and work anywhere. "Then drop out."

He scratches a line onto the page. "I'm good, thanks."

"You don't even go to class."

"I finished them all."

Sighing, I retreat to the living room and grab my laptop. Pulling open a new browser tab, I log in to his student portal and open his graduation profile to check his transcript. He's taking one studio class this semester, and then he has one more before he's officially done with his Bachelor's of Fine Arts. "It says here that you have a studio class."

"I turn in my assignments after hours."

"So you don't actually go?"

He ignores my question, but it gives me space to think. I click back to Sam's student profile and confirm his major before searching for Mercy's.

Fine Arts.

Senior.

She's in the same grade and discipline as Kane.

If we're going to win this game, we need to work smarter, not harder. Sam has the upper hand on account of his relationship with Mercy. We're at a disadvantage.

It's time we changed that.

"You're going to class," I inform Kane, snapping my laptop closed, "because Mercy will be there."

That catches Kane's attention. He drops the sketchbook and pencil onto his bed and jumps up like he's ready to leave immediately. "She will? You're sure?"

"If you're both enrolled in Painting Level III with Mrs. Lebottowitz, then yeah. Next semester she has to take an Exhibition class, and then she's graduating." I nod my head. "Same as you."

Kane claps me on the shoulder and grins. "Guess I'm graduating with our siren. You should be thrilled."

My smile pinches, but I play it off well enough. I'll be glad to get out of this city, so graduation should convince Kane that it's worthwhile. Mercy, however, is still as much of a problem as she was the moment she stumbled into our sights.

I can't kill her outside of the game, or Kane will leave me.

So all I can do is push them into as many situations as possible to make her fall in love with him *without* sleeping with him. Because if Kane gives her that piece of himself, it's only a matter of time before he carves out his heart and puts it in her hands. I've seen this time and time again with each new target, and every year, it gets harder and harder for him to pull back right at the cliff's edge, just before the fall.

And if Kane falls in love with Mercy, a woman who doesn't deserve an ounce of his attention, it might be the one thing that finally breaks me.

CHAPTER 8

MERCY

FOR THE FIRST time in years, I wake up to the sound of an alarm. I struggle to move my body, and panic quickly sets in until I realize that I'm not trapped in a waking nightmare—Sam is in bed with me. The warm breath on the back of my neck and the arms wrapped tightly around my waist tell me that he stayed the night after I dozed off.

We weren't cuddling when I fell asleep, but we sure as hell are now.

"Sam," I murmur, grabbing his arms. "Wake up. Your phone—"

He sighs into my hair. "Five more minutes."

I squint at the ancient clock on my wall and struggle to read the numbers. "What time is it?"

"Seven."

Seven? I slept all night?

"You had a good night," Sam mumbles, easily reading my mind. "I kept your demons away."

"Ha ha," I reply dryly. But truthfully, I'm in shock. "I haven't slept through the night in—"

"Years," he finishes for me, humming deep in the back of his throat. He finally reaches over the side of the bed and blindly turns off his alarm. "I guess that means I'm your good luck charm. Who knew I could be so effective."

I roll my eyes and crawl over him to get off the bed. If he's going to stay the night more often, I'll need to move my bed away from the wall so this doesn't become a problem. My knee digs into his thigh, and he inhales sharply, grabbing my hips. Our eyes meet across the scant distance between us, and he makes a choked sound. "Let me help you."

The words echo his sentiment from last night, and my face burns.

Sam offered to have pity sex with me so that I could lose my virginity.

"I've got it," I insist, but he's already rolling us over. The bed is too small for two grown adults, so what starts as *help* rapidly turns into disaster. We slide over the edge of the mattress together and tumble onto the floor, bashing skulls and jamming elbows. I hiss through my teeth as a jolt of pain shoots up my arm, but it's Sam who brunts the worst of it. I brace myself with an accidental jab to his crotch.

He wheezes in my ear and croaks like a frog, rasping something that sounds like *probably deserved that* before flopping onto his back and throwing his forearm over his eyes.

"I'm so sorry!" I quickly sit up and hover over him, unsure how to help. "That was an accident!"

"It's fine," he swallows, setting his hand on my thigh. "I'm fine." His phone blares again, this time with a powerful bass line. He sighs, grabs his phone from off the floor, and swipes to answer. "Yeah? I'm not home. Of course I'm coming to practice. Meet you there." It's one of the shortest conversations I've ever witnessed, but Sam scrubs a hand down his face and rolls up into a sitting position. "Water," he murmurs, staring at the sunlight streaming through my window. Then he looks at me. "I've gotta go. Practice." His smile is apologetic. "Can I drive you to campus?"

I run a hand through the tangles in my hair. "Um, yeah. That'd be great. Let me change..."

Sam helps me stand. "Great. I'll see if your dad is up." Before he leaves, he hovers in the doorway. "Hey, uh... about what I said last night—"

"It's okay," I interrupt, not wanting to go down that path before I've had coffee. "We don't have to talk about it." At the sight of Sam visibly deflating, I quickly add, "I'll let you know if I change my mind. Deal?"

A delicate blush blossoms across his cheeks, and he clears his throat. "Yeah. Sounds good."

Sam's late to practice, and consequently, I'm late to my morning studio class. I try to be quiet as I walk in, but the door creaks and alerts the class that I've finally arrived. Thankfully, everyone's too busy painting the model posing in the center of the room to do more than throw me a quick glare before returning to their work. Our instructor, Mrs. Lebottowitz, raises an eyebrow but doesn't comment. I've never been late in my entire college career, so this is new for both of us.

What's worse is that someone is in my seat.

I walk around the classroom to take my spot by the arched bay windows and find a burly man making broad strokes on his canvas, the blocks of color pale enough that I almost miss them. Rather than follow instructions and color batch with a specific palette, he's chosen to pair the lightest pastels with a deep indigo, creating a striking contrast that pulls the figure off the page. I stare in awe as he switches brushes and paints a beautifully tapered line to delineate the model's thigh.

Who the hell is this guy? I glance at Mrs. Lebottowitz to find that she's staring too, but not at the painting—at the man. I force my gaze away and take the stool next to him, quickly shuffling around the room to grab my paints and supplies. It takes a few minutes to get in the zone, but once I'm there, the rest of the world falls away. I mix a deep magenta and pair it with a light peach, taking a page from my neighbor's book and switching up the assignment. By the end of the first hour, my shoulders are screaming. I stretch my arms over my head and peek at the canvas beside me.

The first painting's finished and set aside to dry, turned to face me as it rests against the foot of the easel. I stare at the bold color choices—a pale blue set against deeper tones, lush violets, and a slash of red across the figure's face. Any blending he achieved was done messily and fast, but it gets the job done.

He takes his time on his current painting, tracing the arc of the model's brow with such delicacy that I'm drawn in, the paintbrush tucked between my fingers slipping. The brush tips down my canvas and creates a cracked line directly in the middle.

"Shit," I breathe, dropping the brush onto my tray. The scraggly line is ugly as hell, cracking through the model's torso like a trench. I grab a paper towel to dab the paint, and a hand snatches my wrist to stop me. I look up and meet a familiar set of icy blues, the sunlight catching flecks of silver in their depths.

"Don't," Reaper murmurs, tipping his head towards mine. His voice wraps around me like a caress, sending heated shivers down my spine. I barely recognize him in a normal setting, yet here he is, statuesque like a Greek god in a plain white t-shirt that stretches across his chest and bleached jeans slung low over his hips. Now I know what Mrs. Lebottowitz has been staring at all morning.

At night, his presence is like a voice in the back of your mind, intimidating and powerful even while hidden. But during the day, you'd never know he was capable of murder until he's swinging the axe over your head. Charm radiates off of him in waves, and now that I'm paying attention, it isn't just Mrs. Lebottowitz who's swayed by him.

So is our model.

The smile on her lips looks like it was made for him,

the arch of her body sensual and inviting. Our nude models rotate their positions around the room so that everyone has a chance to paint or sketch from different angles, and today, my side of the room is supposed to be turned towards their back. But she's chosen to forego the schedule and aim her breasts towards the frosted windows—or, rather, in Reaper's direct line of sight.

He pays her no mind, however, keeping his eyes on mine. "Use it." Glancing at my tray, he picks up a clean paintbrush and dips it into the paint. "It's more interesting."

I stare at him for a full thirty seconds, the silence between us palpable. His smile grows, turning into a smirk as he flexes his arms. "Go on, Siren. Paint. Or am I too distracting for you? Should I leave?"

With a glare, I whip my head back around and re-wet my brush, careful to remove the excess paint before returning to my canvas. I draw a short line on the hollow of her throat, ignoring the dark line a few inches below. Keeping my voice down, I ask, "What are you doing here?" Frustration makes my brushstrokes sloppy, and I have to set down my brush and stretch my fingers. This is a longer studio class with sessions that range from three to five-hour stints. I didn't check the schedule to know which day we're on, but only one hour has passed. There are at least two more left before class is dismissed, and I *really* need to pass this class. Leaving in the middle of a session docks points from your project grade. This month, we're experimenting with color and light when a model shifts their position in the middle of a painting.

Will you recover, or will you embrace the movement as part of your work?

Reluctantly, the model turns her body around at Mrs. Lebottowitz's suggestion, finally turning her back towards us. Having one fewer set of eyes on us makes me bolder, and I drag my easel and chair closer to Reaper's. "What are you even working on?"

The moment my eyes land on his canvas, I'm at a loss for words. The woman in the painting isn't tall and lithe like our model—she's hunched over her canvas like a gremlin, but her legs stretch on like knives, dipping through the floor to touch the scratch of earth painted beneath. A canopy of wilting leaves, looking eerily similar to those on the oak tree behind us, hangs over her head. He isn't following the prompt at all, choosing instead to mix fantasy and reality.

But his work is really fucking good. The technical precision required to paint the swell of her cheek in one stroke, the colors shifting from an off-white olive tone to a rough lavender, is hard to miss. Then there's her lips —the tiniest swipe of red reminiscent of an older Japanese style—is simple yet elegant. I'm both devastated and impressed, and it makes me want to pack up and leave.

I've *never* left a studio class early before.

Reaper rakes his fingers through his hair, exposing his forehead and mussing up the top. "It's not my best work," he says gently, "but it's good enough for this class."

I stare at his painting to avoid meeting his eyes.

"You're not enrolled in this class. You snuck in here to torment me. You stole my *seat.*"

He chuckles under his breath. "Someone has an inflated ego."

"I do not!"

Mrs. Lebottowitz hushes us as she walks by.

Picking up his paintbrush, he reaches over me to dab the far edge of my canvas with the same deep blues on his own. Our shoulders brush, and I resist the urge to topple him over for the sake of everyone else in the room. I can't ruin class for *everyone.* I pick up my paintbrush dipped in pure white and press my hand against his, fighting every one of his strokes with my own. The paint mixes on the canvas, creating a wave-like translucence.

"I'm a student," he says finally, tapping my knuckles with his fingertip. "I haven't been in class because I complete all of my assignments at my home studio. You'll have to visit sometime."

Home studio? *Visit?*

"What are we, friends now?" I scoff. Lowering my voice, I continue. "Last I checked, you wanted to kill me."

His hand hovers over the canvas. "I *do* want to kill you." Turning his face towards mine, he ghosts his lips over my temple. "But I want so much more than that, Mercy. Won't you give it to me?"

Tingles spread down my arms. "Give you what?"

Carelessly dropping his brush on the floor, he turns my hand over and explores my inner wrist, tracing the blue veins trailing up my forearm. "Everything I want."

Distracted by his touch, I idly swish my paintbrush back and forth without truly seeing what I'm doing. "And what is it that you want, Reaper?"

"Call me Kane," he murmurs, suddenly pressing his nose into my hair, "when we're like this." The gesture is intimate enough to make me blush, and I have to force myself not to react.

"Kane," I amend easily, tucking this new piece of information away. Sam agreed to help me look into Alejandro's family this week. It'll be easy to add brothers Kane and Zane to our search. "What do you want, then, Kane?"

"You." Gripping my chin, he turns my face towards his, stealing my breath in one fluid motion. "Will you sing for me, Siren?"

My heartbeat increases its tempo, and I find myself at a loss for words. No one has ever asked me to sing for them before... and no one has ever *looked at me* like this before. Kane's touch is gentle, but his gaze is piercing, slipping into my heart like a dagger.

"Okay."

The corner of Kane's lips curves upwards. "Yeah?" He caresses my jawline. "That makes me so happy, Mercy. *So* happy." Still smiling, he lets me go and returns his focus to his painting, suddenly invested in completing the piece.

I stare dumbly at him for a few minutes before I slowly turn my body back towards my easel. I pick up my dropped paintbrush and clean the entire set before continuing my work, unable to focus with the jagged black scar tearing through the figure. But I don't paint over the mistake; I leave it where it sits, knowing that I can work around it and salvage what's left.

With Kane, I have a feeling that I'll be doing a lot of improvising to save what pieces of myself I can. Because if it's that easy for me to give something up the moment he asks, I'm in deep, deep trouble.

CHAPTER 9

REAPER

MERCY SAID YES.

If seeing her in class today wasn't enough of a rush, witnessing the way she melts in my hands is enough to make me downright *giddy*. Once class is finally over, she meanders around the room at a leisurely pace, going so far as to clean the sink so that she doesn't have to confront the fact that she agreed to something I want.

Without a single word of protest.

My cheeks hurt from the smile I've been wearing for the past two hours. My god, I never come to these classes, and now I know why. True art can't be dictated by some old fuddy-duddy telling us to *feel the weight of the brush* and *see the curve of her waist like the waves of the ocean*. Art has to be felt in the marrow of your bones— it's bringing raw experience to life for others to see. It's like if telepathy were real and we could read each other's minds. That level of intimacy is exactly what I try to embody in my paintings. I want whoever looks at my work to know the agony I felt as I plunged a knife into Alejandro's heart—to feel the rush of chasing him through a moonlit meadow—to taste the love pouring from his veins.

I haven't sold his paintings yet, so I hope to show them to Mercy before our time is up. To let her know that even in death, I'll capture her beauty with the utmost reverence. There's a method to my madness; it's why Zane has stuck around as long as he has. I don't kill out of boredom. I help people feel the full range of emotions that the human soul has to offer.

Someday soon, I'll ensure that Mercy not only understands it, but that she experiences that euphoria with me.

When there's nothing else she can distract herself with, Mercy slings her crossbody bag over her shoulder and finally glances at me. I'm practically bouncing on the balls of my feet, eager to get out of here. "Have you eaten?"

The tiniest twitch on her lips makes me wonder if I asked the wrong thing.

"No," she answers honestly, "but I'm not hungry."

"I'll have something delivered." Taking her hand, I eagerly pull her out of the studio. It's only a few blocks from the Fine Arts building to the cemetery, and I want to relive the moment I first heard her voice. It won't be accurate on account of the blazing sun outside, but it'll be close enough... I think. And if not, we'll just have to come back after dark. Once we're outside, I slow my step and walk hand in hand with her down the sidewalk. Heads turn our direction, the students within the frats no doubt recognizing me from my late-night rendezvous, and a few even take pictures.

Mercy tries to pull her hand free, but I don't let her.

"Reaper," she hisses, forgetting to use my real name as she digs her nails into the back of my hand. "Let me go. People are staring!" She must not be used to the attention, because she blushes like a virgin, her pale skin turning the brightest shade of red.

I stop to stare at the flush trailing down her neck and disappearing beneath the collar of her dress, some kind of ruffled, layered ensemble with a thick belt strapped around her waist. It leaves her thighs bare from her knees up, but she chose high boots with a zillion criss-crossed laces. There's no way I'm ever getting those off without a knife.

Pinpricks of pain from her death grip help me refocus on the whole woman rather than her parts.

"Stop looking at me," she snaps, clutching onto my hand even harder. "Or I'm not going anywhere with you."

Taking a breath, I lift our joined hands so that she can see the damage. Her nails have broken through the skin, creating crimson crescents where she's drawn blood. "I'm not the one with my claws out. Relax, Mercy. I'm not going to do anything to you today. At least let me look." I give her an appreciative once-over. "I like what I see. Is that a crime?"

She relaxes her death grip and has the decency to appear concerned. But when it comes to the apology, I'm not sure if she means it. "Shit, I'm sorry?"

"It's okay." I squeeze her hand to reassure her. "I can handle a little blood. But you should get used to this." I brush her hair off of her shoulder, enjoying the warmth of her neck. "Because I'm not going to stop touching you, Siren." I keep us moving, tugging Mercy along while completely aware of the whispers in the courtyard and not caring in the slightest. People usually talk about my dick game, so I've been told, and this will give them something even juicier to gossip about.

Reaper has a girlfriend.

Mercy might not see it that way, but over the next few months, she'll come around. They always do. Go on a few dates, make them feel special, learn what makes them tick. I usually let them show me pieces of their world, but this time, I want to show Mercy parts of mine... and learn where the two intersect.

It doesn't take long for Mercy to recognize the path we're on. Color me impressed; not many students take this detour. The pathway is covered in moss on account of the shade from the canopy of trees overhead, so it blends into nature particularly well. The grounds staff doesn't keep up with this spot since students aren't supposed to come here—but the fact that Mercy simultaneously perks up *and* wilts makes me smile. "Don't worry," I tell her, "I promise that I'll be on my best behavior today."

She purses her lips like she doesn't believe me, and that's fair.

I wouldn't believe me, either, but it's not my fault.

Sometimes even the smallest moments are worth living to the fullest.

When we get to the side gate, I grab the key from my pocket and unlock it. Pushing it open, I gesture for her to enter first. "After you, beautiful."

As she crosses the threshold, she eyes my key ring with interest. "Where did you get that?" she asks, watching as I shove it back in my pocket. "Are you the reason the gates are never locked?"

I can't help but chuckle. "Guilty as charged." I walk up the stone path ahead of her, eager to reach the mausoleum. My heartbeat thrums the closer we get, and it's hard to keep waiting on Mercy to catch up. I glance over my shoulder to find her swishing her skirt back and forth across her thighs, a pleasing hum falling past her lips as she hops along a line of concrete pavers.

It's actually *adorable*.

She leaps off of the final stone in the sequence, and I jump forward to catch her mid-flight, scooping her into my arms easily. She gasps as I spin her around by the waist. "Let me down!"

"I told you, you have to get used to this. Besides—" I lower her to the ground but don't let her go, interlocking our hands and bringing her knuckles to my lips. "Aren't you supposed to be the one making me fall in love with you?"

The way her eyes widen—that little catch of her breath—means that I'm winning.

Until she *shoves*.

I tumble backwards and trip over an overturned

brick on the path. In that first moment, she's grinning in triumph, but in the next, I'm grabbing her hand and pulling her down with me. Her bubble of victory bursts before my eyes, and I inhale the sweet taste of surprise as we collapse onto the grass. Not willing to let her get away, I drag her body on top of mine and grab her hips to keep her in place. "Easy there, Siren. I bruise easily."

She smacks her hands against my chest as she sits up, a cry of frustration tearing past her lips. Torn blades of grass stick to her dress, and her chest heaves with each labored breath she takes. "You're insufferable!" Smacking me again, she huffs. "I wouldn't fall in love with you if you were the last man on earth! Get a *grip!*"

"That's too bad," I muse, enjoying her squirming. "I'd be good for you. Not only am I an excellent lover—"

She snorts in disbelief.

"—but I'm a good listener." I tilt my head to the side and admire the view, the smooth canvas of her thighs wrapped snugly around my hips. Planting my feet, I roll my hips in the cradle of her thighs, sighing at the friction. I'm not above dry humping, especially when my partner keeps blushing like that. My cock stirs as I imagine her grinding on my thigh, her plush tits bouncing as she takes her pleasure. "Sing for me, Siren." I grab her thigh and greedily widen her stance, moving her body to where I need her. "That's it," I groan, rocking my hips. Heat builds exactly where I want it, and within seconds, I'm rock hard for her.

A tremor courses through her body, but she doesn't fight against me this time. Slowly, *very slowly*, she grabs my hands and starts to move her body over mine. Her lips part on the tiniest intake of air, but she doesn't sing like I want her to. By now, other women would be grinding all over my cock, desperate for it. But Mercy takes her time, like she's hesitant to give in to the pleasure.

It makes every little touch and tease ten times hotter.

I'm the one losing my cool. Rapidly.

"Mercy," I rasp, swallowing hard. "Touch me." The word *please* hangs on the tip of my tongue, but I refuse to let her have that kind of power. I can give her my body —but I won't give her anything else. Taking her hand, I guide her under my shirt and over my stomach, placing her palm flat against my chest. My heart races as she brings her other hand up and presses down on my sternum, mashing her tits together so that the tops spill out of her dress. I stare at her chest while she *finally* lifts her hips and—*stops*.

"Kane," she purrs, arching her back. Her cleavage dips towards me, giving a perfect view of the freckle hiding just out of sight beneath the top of her dress. I sit up and grab her waist, eagerly shoving my face in her tits and licking that tiny speck of skin. She fists my hair and gasps, but I don't stop there. I kiss every inch of her chest until I reach her neck. "Siren," I breathe, nipping her throat. "Sing for me, beautiful. I need to hear you." My fingers slip beneath her dress, gliding up the back of her thigh as I suck a bruise onto her skin.

Pain rips through my scalp as she pulls my hair and tears my mouth off of her body. It blends beautifully with the muted pleasure of her rocking hips, and I moan. "*Fuck*, baby," I rasp, staring up into her doe eyes. Those pouty lips deserve a kiss, but she's not letting me get close enough…

"Why don't *you* sing for me?" Cupping my jaw with her free hand, she presses the pad of her thumb to the plush center of my bottom lip. "Don't you want to please me, Kane?"

Fuck, she's good.

I swipe my tongue against her thumb, and she pushes it inside my mouth.

"Suck," she commands, not giving me a choice. She pushes in past the knuckle and trembles as I do as she asks, hollowing my cheeks and making a show of it. If there's one thing I'm good at, it's sucking dick, and a finger can't compare. But the way Mercy's eyes flutter, you'd think I *was* sucking her dick. Her cheeks flush bright red, and I'm suddenly enraptured, unable to look away. Imagine if I was sucking her *clit*. Fuck, she'd come undone.

"G-good boy," she praises meekly, popping her thumb out and cupping my cheek. Saliva smears across my lips, but I don't give two shits. I'd much rather have her cum all over my goddamn face.

"Let me eat you out." I lift my hands up her skirt and grab the elastic of her panties. I bet she's soaked. Licking my lips, I abandon her underwear and grab her ass, pulling her up my body. She fights against me—stubborn fucking woman—scraping her knees on the dirt and landing woefully far from my face. With a growl, I try again, and she falls forward, smashing my face with her pillowy tits.

It's not what I was hoping for, but it's still nice.

She scrambles off of me fast as lightning, though, and I don't have a chance to enjoy it. Standing up, she straightens her skirt and plants her hands on her hips. "No thank you."

Most girls like—no, *love*—being eaten out. Face sitting, however, can be out of their comfort zones if they're not confident in their partner's ability to breathe orrrrr... they're inexperienced.

I stare at Mercy with fresh eyes, taking in the flush of her skin in a whole new light. I'd imagined her as a blushing virgin earlier, but I hadn't hoped for it to be true. That would be too perfect. *She* would be too perfect. Rather than straight up ask her about it, I arch my arms over my head and flex my hips, giving her a good, hard look at my erection. I'm tenting like crazy, and it's impossible to miss. When she does me the favor of staring at my dick, I make a show of it, running my hand down my chest until I reach the button of my jeans. I pluck my waistband, eager to strip down.

"Want to see?"

If spontaneous combustion were possible, Mercy would burst into flames. A layer of sweat suddenly clings to her skin, and she shifts her weight from foot to foot, biting her sumptuous bottom lip.

What I wouldn't give to slide my cock between her lips.

Popping the button and unzipping my fly, I slowly

inch my pants below my hips, giving her plenty of time to change her mind. Turn around. *Give herself away.* My balls tighten as I imagine driving my dick into her slick center and pulling back to find my shaft smeared with blood. *Fuck.* There's nothing like virgin pussy. Creamy, delicious, eager—

I grab my cock through my boxers and thrust, groaning. "C'mere," I rasp, squeezing my shaft. "I want you to touch me."

It's like Mercy wakes from a dream. I half expect her to wipe drool from the corner of her mouth, but no, she stands her ground, having the audacity to feign boredom. "If you need to come, then come already." She crosses her arms over her chest. "It's not *that* impressive."

Blood rushes to the head on top of my shoulders.

What did she just say?

Oooooh—

With a smirk, I pull my boxers down and free my dick, feeling it slap against my stomach. Mercy's eyes widen and she stops breathing, but I *don't* stop, quickly hooking the elastic band beneath my balls. With one hand cupping my jewels and the other wrapped tightly around my shaft, I stroke eagerly. Vigorously. Tossing my head back and moaning. *Shit.* This wasn't meant to feel this good. I only wanted to get a rise out of Mercy, but instead it looks like I might actually—

It takes a pitifully short amount of time for me to come, my dick pulsing in my palm as thick ropes cover my stomach. The last few spurts drip onto my hand, and I drag in a lungful of air, feeling my thigh muscles twitch.

I hate that she had to see that. Her first impression of me is going to be the wrong one. She's going to think that I can't last—that my dick game is *weak*. I quickly sit up and wipe my hand on my jeans. "Mercy—"

Her hand covers her face, and it looks like she's trying not to laugh.

My ego bruises immediately, flaring white hot. I jump to my feet, making her flinch. Grabbing my waistband to hold up my pants, I close the distance between us in three short strides and grab her hand before she can run away. "*Mercy*," I repeat, unable to hide the venom from my voice. "Clean up your mess."

"My—" Her eyes flash and she tries to pull away. "*Your—*"

I slap her hand against my abs, stickying her fingers in my cum. Together, I smear our hands in the mess, knowing that she'll find it gross. That she'll run. *That I can chase her.*

My release is still warm from the heat of my skin, and my muscles twitch beneath her touch. "*Your* mess," I repeat, "because this is your fault."

Her eyes narrow into slits. "*What?*"

"If you had let me eat you out like a good girl…" I lace our fingers together with my hand covering hers. "… then this cum would have been inside you where it belongs. Instead, it's been wasted." I click my tongue. Oral sex would have been the appetizer, but after she'd come all over my face, I would have loved to bury my load deep inside her virgin pussy. The anticipation is going to kill me. A trill of electricity shoots down my spine, tingling my balls and making it that much harder to focus on anything other than the way Mercy's mouth forms a scandalized, yet goddamn sexy, perfect *O*.

"Y-you're the one who started jerking off!"

"You didn't stop me," I point out, lifting an eyebrow. "I think you enjoyed the show."

She chokes on her saliva, coughing but not denying it. "How could I stop a nymphomaniac?"

Whooooa, hold on—

"I'm not a nympho." I grip her fingers tighter. "Repeat it. Say, 'I know you're not a nympho, Kane.'"

She digs her fingernails into my stomach, attempting to rile me up. But I'm already burning for this girl, and the pain only makes me want her more. I lick my lips and ignore the warmth pooling in my belly. "Say it," I growl, grabbing the belt cinched around her waist. "Tell me that I'm not a nymphomaniac!"

That's the biggest fucking insult I've ever heard. I don't fuck people just to get my rocks off—I fuck people so that I can feel every goddamn beat of this rock inside my chest. So that I can feel every breath that fills my lungs. Every scratch of nails on my skin and scream blasting my ears. It's the purest form of life, feeling every cell in your body set on fire. I burn from the inside out over and over again, because it's the best goddamn feeling in the world.

A virgin won't understand that.

I can't help but laugh at the irony. God, the one woman I can't wait to sink my dick into thinks I'm a sex addict. What a fucking joke. I release Mercy's hand and her belt and use my shirt to wipe the cum from between my fingers, but I leave the mess on my torso. It's going to be a bitch to clean without a shower. Clenching my jaw as tight as I can, I resist the urge to scream. "Get out of my sight."

Mercy's doe eyes pain me this time. "I didn't mean to upset you."

Too fucking late. "Go home, Mercy. I don't want to see you right now." Fixing my jeans, I try not to glare at her, but it's *really* hard.

I've never wanted to prove someone wrong so badly in my entire life, but I have no clue how to do that. If I have sex with her now, she's just going to think that I'm adding another notch to my bedpost. But explaining the nuances of my sexual appetite isn't something I want to share with anyone, let alone the woman who just insulted me to my face.

I'll have to calm down if I'm going to win the game, but with twelve whole months ahead of us, that doesn't have to be right now. Besides, maybe some distance will make her think about her mistake and how to make it up to me. I avoid looking at her as I turn around, knowing that if I see a tear in her eye, I'll *really* want to make her cry.

Pretty girls don't fall in love with the men who put them there.

CHAPTER 10

SAM

WHEN I'M on the practice field, it's usually easy to let all the shit brewing in my head fade away until the only sensations left are the hard knocks on my body and the smell of freshly cut grass. I always look forward to challenging drills and tackle runs because every bruise on my body is a testament to the life I've chosen—far away from my father and the never-ending pressure of the Wright family legacy. But the one good thing he did for me was take me to those counseling sessions after my mom died.

That's where I met Mercy Morningstar, the girl patiently waiting for me on the sideline. We agreed to meet up today, but I figured she'd want space after our impromptu sleepover. Instead, I find her standing at the sideline near the other girls watching their boyfriends practice. I glance in her direction every chance I get, often enough that Coach calls me out on it and my teammates rag on me. But it's all good-natured fun. I get my tackles in, and she gets to watch me tear through the opposing team's defensive line.

I work a little harder for her, unable to help myself when a pretty girl watches me play.

As soon as the whistle blows and we wrap up for the morning, I jog over to Mercy, unable to keep the grin off my face. "Hey, cutie. Haven't seen you here before." She looks just as pretty as she did this morning, wearing a ruffled skirt with a belt. Or is it a dress? My eyes travel from her face to her body, and that's when I see it.

A goddamn *hickey.*

My mood sours instantly. I try to keep my voice level as I clutch my helmet to my side. "What have you been up to?" Swallowing, I tear my gaze back up to her face, but she's already covering the spot with her hand, a pretty pink blush on her cheeks.

Oh, that's a hickey, alright, and for some reason, I absolutely hate it. In all the years I've known Mercy, not once has she ever had a mark or bruise on her skin. I always thought that she had good veins, but I guess that was wishful thinking, because here's all the proof I need. She bleeds like the rest of us.

"I had class," she replies, pulling her hair over her shoulder to try to cover the mark. It's too close to the front for that to work, so all she does is frizz the ends of her hair. "I, um, ran into Reaper. Or he ran into me. He was in my seat." She frowns, the little divot between her eyebrows driving me crazy.

But not as much as the thought of Reaper's teeth on her throat.

I tap the same spot on my neck. "You've got a—" I can't bear to say the word *hickey*, so I pivot. "Bruise. Did he touch you?"

She avoids my eyes, and I want to scream. Tossing my helmet to the ground, I close the distance between us and grab her chin. Tilting her head back, I examine the mark on her neck. It's not nearly as bad as I imagined, but he had to have enjoyed himself. I know *I* would have.

"Yes," Mercy answers honestly, "but we didn't... really... do anything?" The divot between her eyebrows deepens. "Sort of?"

My blood simmers at her uncertainty. "What does that mean, Mercy?" Mental images of him pushing her against a wall and shoving his hand down her panties make me even hotter in all the wrong ways. "Did he hurt you?"

She tries to shake her head, but I'm still holding her chin. "No, he—" Her flush deepens. *Fuck*, I've never seen her this flustered. Is he winning? Does she *like* him?

Do I need to change for Mercy to fall for me?

"—he, um, masturbated in front of me."

Jesus Fucking Christ.

What a goddamn degenerate.

"In the middle of class?" It has to be almost noon by now. Her class starts at eight-thirty and my practice started at nine, so there's at least a thirty-minute window unaccounted for. "Or after?" I hate asking for details, but I need to know what I'm up against.

If he's bribed his way into her classes, I might be in trouble.

"After." Mercy grabs my wrist and removes my hand from her face. "But I'm not here to talk about—"

"Did you enjoy it?" I grind my teeth as I think about her standing there—sitting? Fuck, where were they?—getting wet for another man. I'm not usually the jealous type, nor have I crossed the friend line with Mercy since we decided to remain platonic, but that wasn't *my* wish, it was hers.

Now the lines are all crossed and tangled, and I can't figure out what I'm supposed to do. Listen to her talk about Reaper jerking off and torture myself with the details, or force myself into the situation and remind her that I'm just as much of a man as he is. I'm better. Healthier for her. I'll make sure she drinks enough water and takes walks in between painting sessions. I'll hold her at night to keep her nightmares at bay, and I won't tease her about all the makeup she wears to bed. I'll be here for her, like I always have been, but more than before.

Better than before.

I run my hand through my sweaty hair and try to get the image of Reaper stroking his cock out of my mind, but all I can think about is Mercy turning the exact shade of red she is now while she watches him. "Well?"

She meets my ire with her own, straightening her spine and crossing her arms over her chest. "I pissed him off, actually. It was great. I had soooo much fun laughing at his dick. It's really tiny, you know. I don't know how anyone thinks it's this massive monster cock."

That's because when it's buried in your ass, it could split you in half. Looks can be deceiving. I've seen

Reaper's cock first-hand—not by choice—and I know how hard he pounds. The bastard fucks hard and likes it when his partners scream.

"Did you tell him it was small?"

"No, but I laughed."

"You *laughed*?"

Talk about a man's worst nightmare. Mercy's giving him a run for his money.

"That's probably the worst thing you can do to a man's ego," I inform her, unable to keep from grinning. Fuck, I can't believe she laughed at his dick! "Bravo."

"I didn't mean to!"

"That doesn't matter." I unsnap my shoulder pads and start removing my gear. Shit's heavy. "He's going to remember this for the rest of his life."

Until he can prove her wrong, at least. If I play my cards right, though, he won't get the chance.

"I know I won't forget it," Mercy mutters, more to herself than to me. She gets this faraway look in her eyes, and I know she's reminiscing or fantasizing or, fuck, I don't know what's worse.

"Stop that," I grunt, tapping her forehead. "No picturing another man's cock in front of me. It's not allowed."

Ignoring my new rule, she starts describing Reaper's cock. "I never realized they were so veiny. Are all dicks like that?" Her eyes flick down to my crotch, and my dick gets ideas, thickening to half-mast.

I clear my throat, feeling the tips of my ears burn. She can't possibly want to compare my dick to Reaper's, right? I'm imagining things. That little sparkle in her eye is a figment of my imagination. Pure fantasy. There's no way she would ever suggest—

"Can I see it?"

My heart stops beating, and I stare at her lips to make sure I heard her right. "Come again?"

She blushes furiously, pinking from the tip of her nose to her hairline. "I, um, asked if I could see it."

There's no way this is *actually* happening to me right now. I'm being pranked. There's a hidden camera. People are hiding in the bushes to jump out and laugh at me the moment I pull my dick out for her.

"See... what?" I ask, still not believing that I'm hearing her right. I have to be having an acute case of heat stroke.

"Oh God," she squeals, smacking her cheeks. "I'm so sorry, I'm being so insensitive right now. I can't just go around asking guys to see their dicks—"

If only she knew how many would volunteer.

"—and you've been so generous already with trying to save my life—"

There's no trying, I *will* save her from this idiotic game before she gets herself killed.

"—I'm so sorry!"

"Don't be." Gently taking her hand, I give her a reassuring squeeze. "I'll show you."

She bites her bottom lip. "Are you sure?"

"Yes." *Dear God, yes.* "But not here." I chuckle under my breath, and thankfully, it helps her relax. "Let me shower first. We can grab some lunch, head to the Registrar's office, and knock out two birds with one stone. No one's ever there, so while I'm researching Reaper and his brother, you can research..." I gesture towards my crotch. "My dick."

Shoving my arm, Mercy laughs. "That's super cheesy. And perverted."

I shrug, but being cheesy and perverted doesn't bother me if it gets me the girl.

The Registrar's office is in its own building across the street from the financial aid office. It's busiest during the first few weeks of the semester, so seeing as we're in November, things are dead quiet. Mercy and I waltz through the front doors and breeze up to the counter where one of the cheerleaders—her name is Abby— beams at me.

"Sam!" she gushes, coming around the counter to give me a hug. "What a surprise!"

I offer a polite smile but quickly grab Mercy's hand and lace our fingers together. I'm not here to see Abby like she thinks. This is a business meeting.

Well, business with a dash of selfish curiosity on my part.

"This is Mercy, my girlfriend." I squeeze Mercy's hand, but thankfully she plays along, swaying her body into mine. "Mercy, this is one of the cheer captains, Abby. She said she'll help us with our research project."

Abby pouts. "I said I would help *you*, Sam. I didn't

realize you were bringing someone with you." Sighing, she takes a key from the lanyard around her neck and gestures for us to follow her. "I could get into serious trouble for this." We walk down a short hallway until we reach a back office. The walls, bookshelves, and desk are completely bare save for a desktop computer. "We're still waiting on the new hire, so you can use this desk. I already logged in for you." Lingering close, she brushes her hand over my chest and bats her eyelashes. "You owe me."

I remove her hand and take a step back, bumping into Mercy. "I'll hook you up for your next exam. Poly-Sci, right? Still can't pass?"

Abby's face flushes crimson. "It's a hard class, okay?" She turns an ugly glare on Mercy. "I bet *she* couldn't pass."

"Actually," Mercy interjects, stepping up beside me. "I have a 4.0 GPA. What's yours?"

I damn near laugh out loud. I know for a fact that Abby's GPA is in the lower 3s. It's fine for undergrad, but she'll have a tough time getting into a graduate program without boosting her GPA, which I can also help her with. "Text me your class list," I offer, "and I'll ask around the frat for help. I think John is a PolySci major. You know John?" I give a brief description, embellishing a few details for Abby's benefit.

She perks up, albeit reluctantly. "Thanks, Sam," she murmurs, quieting down. "I'll leave you two alone."

"Thanks." I close the door behind her and spin around to find Mercy already typing away on the keyboard. Placing my hand on the back of her rolling chair, I peer over her shoulder. "You don't waste any time, do you?" She types in the name *Kane*, pulling up a list of every senior-level student enrolled with that name. There are at least three hundred. "You'll want to cross-reference with Reaper, but uh, there's a typo. His name is Zane."

Mercy grunts. "Reaper's name *is* Kane."

Kane and Zane? "What kind of names are those? Are they twins?"

"Not that I'm aware of." She clicks the filter icon and tries different settings. "But you know how we are about names around here. You lucked out with Sam."

Being named after my father—Samuel Wright—hardly feels like good luck. "Samson sucks just as much as Zane and Kane, thank you very much." I spin her chair around so that she's facing me instead of the screen. Her warm, auburn eyes travel down my body until they stop at my crotch, eye-level to her from this height, reminding me of the *other* reason why we're here. I place my hand on my belt and tug the strap. "But a name like Mercy..." The leather unbuckles, and I unsnap my fly. "She's the lucky one. She can get whatever she wants." I pause with my hand on my zipper. I shouldn't get ahead of myself, but my cock sure does want to. It twitches with anticipation. "Do you still want to see it?"

She bites her bottom lip and flicks her gaze up to mine, making it impossible not to imagine what it would feel like to have her hands on my body instead of mine. "Are you sure it's okay?"

"Positive." I unzip my jeans and lower them a few inches. "Ready, baby?" The endearment slips out, but she doesn't bat an eye, blushing as she nods.

"Yes."

I pull my dick out slowly, stroking it a few times to get it hard. It grows within seconds, turning rock hard in the blink of an eye, and suddenly, I don't know what to do. Did she want me to jerk off or just show it to her? My throat clicks on a swallow. "So, um, not all dicks are alike." I lift my cock to show her the underside, drawing her attention to the line that stems from shaft to tip. "But they all have this part, and the underside of the head —" I stroke my thumb as I describe the spot. "Is usually very sensitive." Pleasure coils in my gut, and I draw a deep breath. "Sizes and shapes can vary. Some are thicker than others, or longer, or curved. There's really no 'one size fits all' situation. They feel different too, when they're inside. So I'm told." The tips of my ears heat as I rub the head next. "I'm circumcised, so you don't have to do anything to reveal the head, but some guys have fore-skin that covers it at first."

Shit, does she know this already? Did she pay atten-tion in sex ed?

"I'm rambling," I groan, staring at my dick in my hand and suddenly feeling *very* stupid. This isn't sexy at all—it's ridiculous that I thought it would be. Giving Mercy an anatomy lesson—real sharp, Sam. "You can just, uh, look. All you want." I take a step back and hop up onto the edge of the desk beside the computer monitor.

Mercy looks between my cock and my face like she's undecided which she should speak to. "Thanks." Her smile helps me relax. "I will." She goes between glancing at my cock and staring at the monitor in small doses, clicking through the menu options and looking back at me while the information loads. Once she's done researching Kane and Zane—which I have absolutely no clue if it was successful or not—she rolls her chair closer to me. Grabbing my knees, she pries them further apart and gets a better look, turning her head to view my dick at different angles.

"You can touch me," I murmur, taking her hand and gently sliding it up my thigh. The barest touch is torture, the warmth of her palm burning my skin through my jeans. "But you don't have to if you don't want to." I emphasize this by giving my shaft one long, steady stroke. "I'm content just like this."

Sucking her bottom lip into her mouth, she looks up at me beneath those gorgeous, curved lashes. "Show me what to do."

Oh, dear lord, heavens above. I'm going to the fiery pits of hell after this. Straight down to the very bottom with the dregs of society, every single one of us perverted, greedy, twisted souls.

Because I do exactly as Mercy asks. I show her how I like it. Wrapping her hand around my length, I cover her hand with mine and stroke slowly, building pressure as we glide over the head. I hold in a groan and lean back on the desk to give her a better vantage point. "See how—" my voice catches—"there's liquid at the tip?" I rub her thumb over my slit, gathering my precum on her fingers. "Now spread it down—*yes*, like that—" She flicks her thumb over the tip and rubs my precum beneath the head, exactly where I showed her was sensitive, and I have to hold my breath.

My heart feels like it's going to explode.

Mercy lowers her head and inhales. "It smells different."

Fuck. Me.

"Yeah," I rasp, swallowing hard. "It'll get thicker, too, when I'm close. You should be able to feel it."

Her eyes dilate the tiniest degree, and I can practically taste her curiosity. "Are you close now?"

I take a shallow breath to keep from panting. Sweat drips down my neck, and I have a really hard time staying still for her. "Keep stroking and I will be." I haven't come from a hand job in years. My own doesn't count. But every time I hook up with a girl, a handie is a precursor to a blow job or sex. It never lasts long and is only part of the pregame event.

But I might be rethinking my strategy with Mercy kneeling between my thighs.

She strokes faster, the puff of moist air breezing past her lips making me hotter. This isn't a blow job, and I'm not asking for one, but *shit*. She would look so good taking me into the back of her throat. Her free hand clutches my thigh as it twitches. "You're trembling."

I can't reply other than to moan, carelessly throwing my head back as it slips free. Her fingers glide over my shaft, caressing beneath the head, grazing my balls—the sound of Mercy spitting accompanies the wet, warm drip of her saliva down my shaft, and I lift my hips off the desk to guide her hand. *Shit. Fuck. Fuuuuck.*

Thrusting in time with her strokes, I groan as she brings me to the edge and dangles me over, her spit quickly speeding up the process. "I'm gonna—you might wanna—*fuck*," I hiss, jerking my hips as my balls draw up, emptying in steady pulses that send tremors wracking my entire body. Cum shoots out in rapid fire succession, shocking Mercy enough that she gasps.

"Oh!"

A streak grazes her cheek and clings to the edge of her lips, painting her in pearlescent white. I drag in a lungful of air and greedily watch as my cum stripes her chest, too, dirtying her innocence.

I'm glad it was me and not him.

I can't say that I'm sorry, so I pull my t-shirt over my head and wipe the cum off her cheek. I hesitate to wipe her lips, reluctant to remove my scent from her skin, and she swipes her tongue up to lick herself clean.

"Fuck, Mercy," I whine, unable to help myself. "Careful with that tongue, or I'll come again."

She smiles and gives me the cutest little giggle, the warm flush on her cheeks filling me up inside. I smile back at her. "Clean yourself up, dirty girl, so we can finish up in here." The room smells like cum, and as soon as Abby finds out, she'll start trash-talking me behind my back, I know it.

After she's wiped herself off, she swivels idly in her

chair while I reach over her to search for Alejandro instead of the brothers. "Do you want your shirt back?"

I grab the t-shirt and drop it to the floor. "We'll take it with us." Sneaking a peek at her, I smile at how focused she is on my arms. Once she realizes that I've caught her, she quickly turns her attention back to the monitor.

"What have you found? Was he a student?"

"Nope," I answer easily. His name doesn't appear in any student records, past or present. The ones who were similar didn't match the picture we found on social media of a local missing man. He's been missing for two weeks, so the search is still ongoing.

I ask the question that's been on my mind all morning. "Why don't we go to the police?"

Mercy's expression flattens. "In this city? You know how everything's handled behind closed doors. Your father has enough money to hide anything he deems scandalous. I think his precious son inserting himself into a murder investigation would count."

The mere mention of my father is enough to ruin my post-nut bliss. I click the mouse harder than necessary. "He doesn't have to know. We could put in an anonymous tip."

She sighs. "About a body in a cemetery? They'll think we're stupid."

I relinquish the computer to her and drum my fingertips across the top of the desk. "You really want to play their game?" It's the stupidest thing I've ever heard, toying with someone's life like you're playing a hand of poker. I know that my father trades in important things, too—weapons, contracts, information—but not *lives*.

Not that I know of.

"They're going to cheat. They won't give you an entire year. *Us*," I amend, frowning. "They won't give us that kind of luxury of time, no matter what they say."

Mercy peers up at me, a frown on her face. "You don't know that."

Scoffing, I kick her boot with the toe of my shoe. "You can't possibly believe that they'll play fair. They're murderers."

"They're still people."

"If you tell me that 'they're just like us'—"

"That's not what I'm saying."

I wave my hand to give her the floor. "Okay, then explain."

She leans back in her chair and scooches it away from the desk. "All I'm saying is that if they wanted to kill us, they would have done it by now." Scraping a dried white splotch on the side of her thumb, she hums softly to herself. "I don't think that's what they're after. It's not their end goal."

"Then why kill Alejandro? Why kill anyone, at all?"

Tilting her head to the side, she considers my question for a few silent seconds. "I don't know." She meets my gaze as she pushes herself out of her chair and picks up my shirt off the floor. After inspecting it for a moment, she hands it to me. "But maybe we should ask."

I roll my eyes, and she pinches my side. "I'm serious! Maybe they'll tell us!"

"Maybe they'll *lie* to us." Shaking my head, I crumble my shirt into a tight ball. "Whatever, Mercy, if you want to ask, go ahead. But I don't think they'll be honest with you. We'll have to figure them out on our own." I hate the idea that pops into my head, but I say it out loud anyway, hoping that Mercy will say no. "We could invite them out, or something. Observe them up close."

The last thing I want to do is hang out with Reaper and his brother, but if it helps Mercy make them fall in love with her... I clench my jaw and quickly rewrite that sentence in my head.

If it helps us convince them not to kill us... then *fine.* I'll try anything.

"That's not a bad idea," Mercy admits, actually fucking agreeing with me. Great.

At least let me turn this into something for me, too. "Does it count as a date if they're third and fourth wheeling?"

"Who says it's a date?"

I bend at the waist to reach Mercy's height. "I do. I want to take you on a date."

Mercy quickly averts her eyes. "You don't have to do that."

Puzzled, I gently cup her chin and turn her face back towards mine. "Do what?"

"Pretend that you like me." Sighing, she takes a step backwards, putting distance between us. "The hand job was nice—thank you for that—and you can still come over to hang out after practice, but we don't have to play the game with each other. You don't need to fall in love with me."

I tap the hollow of her cheek with my fingertips. "Mercy. That wasn't part of the deal." I brush my thumb across the seam of her lips. "I'm supposed to make *you* fall in love with *me*, remember? And I'd like to try. Won't you let me?"

Her eyes shimmer like crystals in the sunlight. "Why would you want to?"

Sighing, I try to hide my smile. "Because I actually like you, Mercy. I didn't kiss you last year by accident. I wanted to date you then, and I still want to date you now." I link our hands together and press a gentle kiss to the edge of her lips, tempted to take more, but knowing that I shouldn't. I don't want our second first-kiss to be in an empty office in some stuffy campus building.

I want to kiss her on a real date.

"Go out with me," I insist, "and let me prove it to you."

She looks like a deer caught in headlights, and it's so fucking cute. "Okay. We can... date."

If I'm being honest, I don't know if she's ever had a boyfriend before, but I hope that I make the cut. I'd love to brighten her life the same way that she's brightened mine. As long as those other two men keep their dicks in their pants and their hearts to themselves, I'll go as slow as Mercy needs me to.

But the minute either of them tries to take her from me, I can't risk going slow and steady. I'll have to dive in and drag Mercy under with me. It's the only way I know how to survive.

CHAPTER 11

ZANE

THE GRAVESTONES on the Morningstar property are set in uneven rows that curve along the natural slope of the mountain. Whoever first dug them—likely long dead by now—had the impossible task of breaking ground in a terrible location. By the looks of it, no one has ever tried to correct the original owner's mistakes, choosing to keep to the lines crooked, curving, and completely fucking annoying to look at.

I take a pull from my cigarette and blow the smoke into the air. If Kane were here, he'd call the entire property *art*, declaring that it holds humanity's very essence within its soil. Imperfection, as he puts it, is part of the whole *being human* experience. We aren't meant to create flawless works of art. We're only meant to live in these imperfect moments and somehow be happy about it.

Scoffing, I walk the rows of graves for the third time, aimlessly giving my feet something to do while my mind wanders. As I move between the narrow paths, I fiddle with the cameras in my pocket. They're small enough that no one should notice them planted around the house. Getting to know Mercy's habits when she thinks no one is looking will tell us everything we need to know about her to make her fall for Kane... and I can keep an eye on her to make sure she keeps her promise.

Not a promise, I remind myself, frowning. The condition I set for the game. Refusing to sleep with Kane.

I scrub my hand down my face and crouch in front of a newer headstone, brushing off its face to read the engraving. The name and dates don't mean anything to me, but I know they meant something to someone, once upon a time. I brush the remaining dirt and debris from the stone before turning to the plot itself. The grass is overgrown, the autumn leaves are threatening to take over, and the scent of natural decay hangs in the air. Someone's been neglecting their groundskeeper duties.

It's easy to find a shed off to the side with a rake and a dust brush. I start by clearing the tombstones of dirt and cobwebs, then I move on to the leaves, raking them into tall piles along the far edges of each row. This isn't why I came here today—but it's a good distraction from my thoughts.

Are Kane and Mercy together right this very second? Is he flirting with her, or is he actually going to take things slow for once? With Mercy, I feel like my entire world has been flipped upside-down and turned inside-out. The normal rules don't apply with her, and it leaves me feeling like a boat being tossed around in a stormy sea.

At the mercy of things beyond my control.

So, I clean up at least half of the property on my own and avoid facing my problems. The cameras and bugs in my pocket jangle against each other as a constant reminder of why I'm here at all, and when I finally wipe a layer of sweat from my brow and lean against my companion, the rake, for a spell, I stare across the lot at the dilapidated church.

That would be a cool location for some footage.

After returning my tools to the shed, I enter the church and scope out locations for my cameras and mics, placing half a dozen in various shadowed corners, along tall pillars, or beneath the pulpit. The stained glass windows are covered in grime, but multicolored light still filters through in muted tones. Kane would have a fit if he knew that the lighting could be even better, so I make a mental note to clean the windows, too, eventually. Sunlight fills the room from a hole in the ceiling, and a bird's nest sits on one of the beams crossing the rafters. String lights would help the ambience. Maybe a bundle of pillows or a mattress on the floor...

I take a few pictures of the space and guess the square footage so that I can make a few online orders once I'm at my desk. We could kill Mercy here. I don't think Kane would oppose changing our usual venue for a place as hauntingly ethereal as this.

Shuffling footsteps sound at the door, and I turn to find an old woman peering through the shadows at me.

She smacks her lips and places her hand on the nearest pew to steady herself. "Thought I saw you come in here," she murmurs, exhaling softly. "After all that work, I was worried you'd leave without saying hello." She motions for me to follow her. "Come on inside and have a glass of tea."

I watch the woman disappear through the doorway before making my decision to follow. Being invited inside their home makes it easier to plant cameras. I won't have to sneak around. As we walk across the property at her slow pace, she talks to me, pausing at various points for me to comment. Not having anything to say, I stay silent for the entire journey.

I never asked for an overview of the land or a history lesson on its owners, but she provides anyway, seemingly happy for the company.

After telling me about the soil quality and number of graves on the property, she begins telling me more about her family. "The Morningstars have lived on this property for generations," she regales, looking appreciatively out across the landscape. "Mercy's the fifth generation... or was it the sixth?" She subtly shakes her head. "Did you know she was born right here, in this very house?" Granny hobbles up the front porch steps and holds open the screen door for me. "Do you like your tea sweet or unsweet?" Leading me into the kitchen without a moment's hesitation, she reaches into an upper cabinet and grabs two glasses. Her hands shake like she's about to drop them.

I swoop in and take them from her, grabbing the

glasses and taking them to the fridge. I don't know *why* I'm helping this woman. She's the host here—I'm the stranger wandering onto her family land in the middle of a random November morning. "I like sweet," I finally answer, relieved when she plops into a chair at the round breakfast table.

"Red lid. Pour me some, too, dear."

I set the glasses down on the counter, fill them with ice from the tray, and generously pour sweet tea from the red-lidded pitcher into our cups. Handing her a glass, I take the seat opposite her and survey their kitchen. It's small, which is expected for an older home, and cluttered. Spices in unlabeled jars sit out near the stove, with herbs dangling from the chandelier over our heads. The cabinets are paneled with glass, allowing me to see even more clutter buried within. Layer upon layer of dried pasta, canned sauces and jellies, round containers filled with bleached flour and three types of sugar. Thrown around in complete disarray. The flour isn't even sitting next to the sugar; they're in separate cabinets entirely. If there's an organization method to the madness, I'm not picking up on it.

My eye twitches, and I have to force myself to look at something else. The breakfast table wobbles to the right and its face has long since lost its protective seal, the stain faded in patches.

Kane would *love* this shit.

Granny hums to herself while she sips her tea, staring at me like she's sizing me up. "You were here the other night," she muses, pulling up the edge of the table to reveal a hidden compartment. She retrieves a deck of cards and starts shuffling them in her hands, surprisingly agile for a woman so old. "Want a reading?" Before I can answer, she flips three cards onto the table and hunches over them, tutting to herself as she reads them.

One thing becomes immediately clear: they're not normal playing cards—they're tarot cards.

I try not to snort aloud. "I don't believe in that stuff, Granny."

She grunts, flicking her gaze up for a split second before returning to her cards. "Whether or not you believe doesn't change the reading." Touching each of the cards, she mumbles something under her breath.

Curiosity gets the better of me, and I lean over the table to get a look. A handsome, shirtless man holds out his hand for the viewer in the first card, then in the middle card, a girl sits in front of a mirror, her reflection tied up and blindfolded, and the last image is of two lovers embracing as they stare deeply into each other's eyes, a red string tying their bodies together. Instinctively, I think of Kane and Mercy. He's the shirtless man offering her his hand, then she's the girl all tied up in knots over him in the second card, and then they're obviously the lovers embracing at the end.

Granny Morningstar slides the cards closer to me and studies my face. "What do you see?"

"They're just cards, Granny."

She tuts. "Your perspective is important when reading the cards."

"I didn't ask for a reading."

Tapping the first card, she takes a quick breath. "This is The Devil. He often represents temptation, overindulgence, and obsession. But when we are surrounded by shadows, we can finally see the light." I won't pretend to understand what she means, so she moves on quickly. She taps the next card's face, the one with the girl and the mirror. "This is the eight of swords."

I stare at the picture, and the girl's features easily morph into Mercy's, her skin turning white as snow and her hair dark as ink. "There aren't any swords." Rather, crows tie the girl up with a thin strand of string coiling around her body. The blindfold is a simple black strip of cloth tied over her eyes. It's not what I would have imagined a sword card to look like. "Not a very good depiction, if you ask me."

"I didn't ask you," Granny says gruffly. She stares at my face while I stare at the cards. "The eight of swords represents feeling trapped when you're the one tying the knot. You can't see the truth because you're too wrapped up in your own lies." Pointing to the final card, she continues, "The Lovers is often considered self-explanatory. Many people believe that it means love is coming into your life, but I'm not sure that interpretation fits here. I think you need to let go of something you've been holding onto. A belief? A fear?" Her eyes narrow as she leans closer. "Maybe a secret?"

Leaning back in my chair, I sip my tea. "I don't know what you mean."

Granny holds my gaze for a long moment before stacking the cards in order and sliding them towards me.

"Place these under your pillow." She reshuffles the rest of the deck and returns them to the secret compartment in the table. "Maybe in dreams, your mind will quiet enough to listen." A pack of cigarettes appears from her stash, and after pulling one for herself, she holds the pack out to me. I pull one from the pack and light the tip before holding the lighter up to hers. Once hers has started to burn, she takes a drag before speaking again. "Ever since my grandson went away, no one spends any time in the fields. My husband used to keep the spirits company. Malachi takes after him." Her gaze grows distant. "He was a good man, my husband. My grandson, too, although troubled in his youth. I hope he returns home. We all miss him."

Mercy has a brother? I don't remember seeing that in any of her records or online profiles.

Granny's mouth twists wryly. "Not many remember Malachi. He left, oh, years ago now." Her tired eyes wrinkle around the edges. "I miss him."

I didn't come here for a heart-to-heart, so I merely grunt and finish my cigarette in silence. But then I wonder... is Mercy as upset about her brother's absence as her grandmother? "Why hasn't he come to visit?"

She waves her hand dismissively. "Oh, you know how it is. Always up in the clouds."

Okay, Granny is a dead end.

Pushing my chair out, I stub my cigarette on the table, drain the rest of my glass, and set it in the farm-house sink. "I'll wait for Mercy upstairs." But first, a self-guided tour of their home. The walls are exposed wood, dark from age and repeated finishings. In fact, I'd say this house was originally a log cabin that has been redesigned a few times over the decades. Pictures dating back centuries line the hallways, from grainy black and white images to clear as day modern ones. I look between the photos and pinpoint where Mercy gets her looks from; all of the women in the family have the same haunting beauty. Thick, dark locks, pale complexions, and vibrant eyes like autumn bonfires. Mercy's mother, in fact, is an absolute knockout. Her smiles are full of life and laughter, especially in candid shots with her husband. The two are head over heels for each other.

After placing a camera along the edge of one frame, I move into the den and immediately sneeze from the stale air. Dust covers most surfaces and the curtains are drawn shut, casting the room in an eerie gloom. For a couple so in love, their home is staggeringly devoid of warmth. I flick on the overhead light and peruse the built-in shelves. They're as cluttered as the kitchen cabinets—all except for one. Not a single speck of dust covers its surface, and a familiar wooden box with a golden lock sits in the center. Mercy's mother is smiling at me from a framed photograph sitting beside it.

Mrs. Morningstar is dead.

From the looks of things, she's been gone for years. Did the son succumb to depression and disappear? Attempt suicide? I consider the idea that he's also deceased, but I'll have to look for an obituary to be sure. Granny says he's in the clouds—so he very well could be dead.

Maybe Mercy's doorstep has been graced by more tragedy than I realized.

I merely glance inside Mercy's father's bedroom, unwilling to step inside his grief, and don't bother with Granny's. When I make it around to the front of the house again, Granny is sitting in a rocking chair near the front door.

"She won't be home for a few hours," the old woman mutters, fanning herself with a paper fan. "Mercy likes to linger elsewhere." She holds out her hand to offer me the three tarot cards from earlier. "You mustn't forget. Under your pillow." Placing them in my palm, she pats the back of my hand.

"Sure, Granny." I slip the cards into my back pocket. "I'll do that."

As if.

I follow her gaze out the window and find nothing of interest. The graves I cleared earlier appear brighter in the morning light than their dingy counterparts, and a sense of accomplishment stirs inside my chest. "Thanks for the tea," I tell Granny, but she doesn't seem to hear me. Her brow pinches as she stares out the window, suddenly focused on thin air. I pat her shoulder before moving up the stairs, carefully setting a bug and a camera at the top. I put another pair in the upstairs bathroom once it becomes clear that Mercy's the only one living on the second floor. Her brother's room is covered in nearly as much dust as the den, with various athletic trophies and memorabilia left to tarnish. A newspaper clipping of his mother's obituary, however, catches my eye.

Ingrid Morningstar was only forty when she died.

Doing the math, that puts Mercy at… fifteen or so when she lost her mother. I try to empathize for the briefest possible moment, but nothing stirs inside my heart. Not unexpected, but perhaps unfortunate. I find myself scowling at her mother's obituary, but I'm not sure what I was expecting. To suddenly burst into tears at someone's sob story? To feel bad for the young girl and her family for losing a true light in their lives?

People die all the time, and there's nothing anyone can do about it.

I ignore the flicker of emotion that comes when I think of one day losing Kane, knowing that if I travel down that path, the dam I keep locked up tight will burst. It's better to feel nothing at all than give in to the flood beyond the gates.

For good measure, I place one camera in Malachi's room before retreating to Mercy's bedroom and closing the door behind me. In the daylight, her room appears messier than it did the other night. Art supplies are scattered across the floor in what resembles organized chaos, with various brushes, paint types, and drawing pencils lying in piles. Easels and sketchbooks are a dime a dozen in here; most are open, and I flip through the closest ones before moving to the sketchbook laid out on her desk. This one is filled from front to back with only a few blank pages remaining. Loose sheets of paper with various stages of design linger outside the sketchbook, like she wasn't sure what she was drawing at first and didn't want to commit it to the permanence of her sketchbook. My eyes linger on the topmost page where a man's face, featureless, stares blankly up at me.

Heat licks a nasty path up my arms and legs, burning deep enough that I feel like a dragon about to spit fire. I quickly turn away from her desk and get to work rigging the room with cameras, putting most of them here rather than scattering them around the house. If Mercy can't sleep, I'll know. If she dreams in fits and screams, I'll hear her. And if she brings anyone to her bed at night, I'll be watching.

Kane knows of my video feeds and usually leaves them alone, but if he finds out that I've rigged Mercy's bedroom this extensively, he'll demand access to the footage. This needs to be kept a secret or he'll fall for her faster and harder than he already is. I drag my bottom lip through my teeth and slump into Mercy's desk chair. The candle on her windowsill has been replaced after I knocked it over the other night, and I light it with the matches set beside it. The flame flickers but can't compete with the natural light pouring through the curtainless window. Even at night, I bet it fights against the silvery moonlight, desperate to keep the viewer's attention. But a single candle can only do so much. It would have to grow into an inferno to have a chance at beating something as powerful and compelling as the moon.

Sometimes, I wonder why I even try.

As I wait for Mercy to return home, I idle away the hours flipping through the thickest sketchbook on her desk—the one that's nearly filled. Every single drawing is done in unforgiving charcoal, the thick, black lines a testament to either her confidence or her stupidity. The passage of time within those pages is evident only by her wandering focus. She'll start sketching a flower that eventually wilts a few pages down, or the tree overlooking a grave will lose its leaves as a wintry snow blankets the page. Sometimes she'll start sketching a figure and then cross it out with angry slashes. A few torn edges cling to the book's spine, but their contents are lost, undoubtedly crumpled in the trash heap.

Grabbing the edges of the sketchbook, I lean back and prop my feet up on her desk, grabbing the closest charcoal pencil and flipping to the final page in her sketchbook. What no one knows is that while Kane paints, I draw. Messy sketches, full of scratchy lines and wacky shading, but it's drawing nonetheless. I picture Kane at first, but he's quickly joined by Mercy, the two of them holding hands as they lean into each other and threaten to kiss right in front of me. I draw what I see in my mind's eye, keeping Kane's hair a light gray and Mercy's the darkest shade of black, carefully drawing in the details from memory. As the minutes pass, Kane's visage shifts. His hair darkens. His muscles are less defined. The slant of his lips is flatter, and his hand isn't on Mercy's waist, it's tangled in the thick strand of raven hair grazing her neck. An open window with a candle on its sill sits just beyond their silhouette, and she peers up at him with a subtle curve to her lips and her hand resting on his throat.

I'm so absorbed in getting Mercy's expression *just*

right that I don't notice the sun crawling across the sky or the cooling temperatures as morning shifts to afternoon then quickly slides into evening. I'm fixing the shading on her combat boots when I hear them coming up the stairs. I jolt out of my trance and slam the sketchbook shut only to tilt too far back in my chair. I catch the barest glimpse of Mercy pushing open her bedroom door before I topple over and slam into the unforgiving hardwood.

She's on me in seconds, tossing her bag to the ground and stepping on my throat.

This isn't quite how I imagined my evening going.

"Zane," she growls, pressing down harder against my windpipe. "What the hell are you doing in my room? Or having tea with my grandmother?" She shakes her head with one short, jerky motion and forgets to breathe, a vein in her neck appearing with her distress.

I relax my body and grab her ankle, the leather of her boot worn thin enough that it fits like a second skin. Her body heat radiates into my palm. Grinning up at her, I dig my fingers into her Achilles heel and enjoy her full-bodied flinch. She doesn't move, so neither do I, the two of us locked in a stalemate. I would tell her that she needs to be careful before I slit her tendon with my knife, but I can't speak until she lets up on my throat.

Too bad, not very sad.

"Answer me," she hisses, glaring twice as hard.

If I actually hurt her, Kane will blow up at me. *It's too soon*, I can hear him whine, and I have to stop myself from rolling my eyes. If she's bad enough to stomp on my fucking neck, she can handle a little pain. I ease up my grip on her Achilles tendon and tap the toes of her boot instead. After a moment's hesitation, she eases up enough for me to breathe. The inhale burns. I use the pain to keep me grounded. "Needed to check something." Grabbing the ridiculously flowy fabric of her skirt, I wrench it aside to check that her panties are still in place.

She shrieks and slams the heel of her boot into my nose. "You fucking pervert!"

The *crunch* hurts—that shit's gonna fucking bruise—but at least I have my answer. If Kane had slept with her, he'd probably have torn her panties off or taken them with him as a trophy. The fact that they're still on means that she survived her first day with him unscathed.

That is, until I notice the hickey on her fucking throat.

"What the *fuck* is that?"

Mercy backpedals, jumping off of me to grab the baseball bat leaning against her shitty metal headboard. Its wood is worn and chipped on the side. I doubt it's hers. Maybe her brother's? She wields it like a weapon and bares her teeth at me. "Get the fuck out of here, Zane!"

I roll onto my feet and close the distance between us, grabbing the middle of the bat when she tries to swing. Wrenching it from her grasp, I toss it across the room and shove her against the wall. "Did he do this?" I grab her chin and force her head to the side to get a better look at the bruise. It's hickey-shaped. Reddish purple. Exactly where Kane likes to leave them. "I told you not to let him fuck you."

She sputters, blowing her hair into my face. "I didn't! *He* didn't!"

Mmm. "You sound guilty."

She flushes bright crimson, and my anger flares.

"One day," I murmur, feeling the bitterness rise like bile in the back of my throat. "One *fucking* day, and you couldn't keep your hands off of him." I've known Kane for over a decade, and when he wants something, he goes after it without an ounce of hesitation. I'd expected Mercy to fight him, but perhaps that was naive of me.

It's hard resisting Kane's charms.

Mercy's eyes lock onto mine as she tries to turn her head, but I don't let her, too angry to let her win.

"It's not from him! It's from Sam!"

Some of the hot air in my chest escapes. "You're lying."

"Sam and I—" Her flush trails down the side of her neck.

Maybe she *isn't* lying.

"We were intimate today, okay?"

I force myself to breathe. "Explain. In detail."

Her eyes nearly bug out of her skull. "Excuse me?"

I wrap her hair in my fist and tug until she winces. "I said, *explain.* Paint me a goddamn picture." I can tell that she doesn't want to. Her tongue ties in knots the first few times she tries to form a coherent sentence.

"We—we were at the Registrar's office—"

"Weird hookup spot, but go on."

She glares. "Fuck you."

Smirking, I rub my thumb across her jaw. "You wish, Kitten. Keep going."

In the end, her tale is boring. They were in the Registrar's office for God knows what reason, and they ended up kissing and mutually masturbating. But it doesn't make sense. Who the fuck gets each other off without actually *fucking*?

I stare into her eyes for a long, long time, trying to determine if she's lying or not. "Why didn't you have sex? It would have been faster if you'd let him blow his load inside you." Hand jobs are tough on the best days. Dry, unsatisfying, boring.

Mercy won't meet my eyes, and I quickly reach beneath her skirt to touch her pussy. She fights me, but I'm already sliding my fingers through her folds by the time she grabs my arm. Gasping, she pushes up onto her tiptoes as she tries to retreat, but I pull her hair until she cries out and gives up.

She's wet, sure, but not *that* wet. If she had gotten off, she'd be soaked. Swollen. *Needy.* Her body twitches as I explore, rubbing her clit with the pads of my fingers before I slip one inside. She's tight as *fuck*, sucking me in like a greedy little whore.

I search her face as I finger her nice and slow, analyzing every shallow breath and muscle spasm. She should be riding my hand right now, not acting like a scared—

My eyes widen as it hits me. "You're a virgin."

Her eyes flutter closed as she bites her bottom lip, not saying anything to deny it. She shakes her head, but I can't tell what she's objecting to. The accusation, my touch, or this entire situation.

What it is, is fucking bullshit.

"You can't be a virgin," I snap, rubbing her clit with the heel of my palm. Kane will lose his goddamn mind if she's a fucking virgin. Mercy whines loudly, and I quickly cover her mouth with my other hand. She's too sensitive. Too *fresh*. Growling, I bury my face in her hair so that I don't have to see how flushed her cheeks are. The only solution is to make sure that she's experienced enough to throw off Kane's trail until she loses her virginity. If she sleeps with Sam—her alleged lover—the problem will be solved. "Stop squirming," I order, unable to ignore the way her body presses against mine. Heat stirs deep in my gut, and it takes every ounce of my being to ignore it.

But none of this is about me. It's about *her* and how goddamn inadequate she is.

I lessen the pressure on her clit and rub her sensitive nub with my fingertips. She exhales harshly against my palm. "That's it," I coax, "relax. It'll feel better." Taking a deep breath, I steel my resolve and press my lips against the shell of her ear. "I'm going to make you come on my fingers, Kitten."

She grips my arm so tightly that her nails dig into my skin, but she doesn't actually protest. Her hips rock in a subtle, slow roll, and her breath catches in her throat.

"What a dirty little virgin you are," I rasp, chuckling.

"You *want* to come, don't you? Sam couldn't get you off, huh?" I click my tongue. Figures that lover boy sucks in the sack. "Don't worry, this will be our secret." I drag my fingers through her slick folds before sliding two inside her heat. She gasps, and I clench my jaw as I bury my fingers to the hilt.

I haven't fingered a girl in a *long* time, but Mercy's inexperience works in my favor, because she can't tell that I'm nearly as inexperienced as she is.

She mutters something beneath my palm, but I have no interest in listening. "Shh," I murmur, closing my eyes. *Fuck*, she's still so tight. "Relax, Mercy." I drag my nose along the curve of her neck and inhale the scent of her sweat and what little remains of her sweet perfume. "Don't think. Just feel." It takes a minute, but I find the spot I'm looking for. As soon as I rub it, she gasps and claws at my shoulders. Shit, that's gonna leave a mark.

"Doesn't that feel good?" I groan as her pussy gets wetter.

It *does* feel good.

Foolishly, I let myself enjoy the moment, building her pleasure slowly and making it last. By the time she clamps around my fingers and comes, I'm drenched in sweat and trembling nearly as much as she is. I slip my fingers from her core and hold them up for us both to see. They glisten with her desire, the pads pruned, my entire hand slick from her needy pussy.

Our eyes meet, and I'm suddenly weightless.

She gently detaches from my shoulders, and I slam back into my body long enough to realize how much of a necessary mistake this was. Kane wouldn't be able to stop after that, but *I* can. Swallowing hard, I take a step away from her and run a hand through my hair. *Shit*, that's the hand I touched her with. I can smell her pussy all over my body, which means that Kane will, too.

Without another word, I retreat to the shared bathroom in the hallway and scrub my hands—my arms—my neck—every visible surface of my skin. When that isn't enough, I pull my shirt off and dunk my head in her shower, grabbing her shampoo to scrub myself clean. The memory of her lingers, but the physical evidence is gone. That'll have to be good enough.

Mercy stares from the open doorway, her lips pinched and her eyes angry.

I flick water from my hair and frown back at her. "What?"

"Glad to know my pussy's so *disgusting*." She scoffs haughtily. "If it's good enough for your brother, why isn't it good enough for you?"

My brain processes her words at half speed. Is she... *upset*?

Fucking virgins.

Rolling my eyes, I towel dry my hair. "Get over yourself. Me fingering you has absolutely nothing to do with me."

She fumes. "I'm sorry, since when does getting a girl off mean that you're not interested in her sexually?"

Jesus fucking Christ, she even talks like a virgin.

"I'm not like most guys." I throw the towel at her

and put on my t-shirt. "Not everything is about getting my dick wet."

Her gaze travels down to my crotch. Yeah, I'm half-hard, but that doesn't mean shit. It's not a compliment or an insult. "I'm built differently," I try to explain, growing frustrated. I've never had to explain myself to anyone before. No one's ever needed to know. "Look, I won't have sex with you. It's not about you or your body or anything. Don't take it personally."

Blushing furiously, she wrings the towel in her hands. "How can I not? The first guy to touch me didn't even enjoy it." Tears pool in the corner of her eyes, but she holds her breath to keep them at bay.

Sighing, I drag my hand down my face.

Yeah, still smells like pussy.

"It's complicated." When that answer doesn't suffice, I grit my teeth and try to force myself through the other half of the truth. "I didn't *not* enjoy it. You're a beautiful girl, Mercy, and my half-chub is a testament to that. I don't..." I growl in frustration. I don't owe her an explanation, so why do I feel the need to give her one? "I don't sleep with women, okay? I don't sleep with anyone." Avoiding her gaze, I shrug. "So when I say that I'm not going to have sex with you, it's not about you. Really." I can feel her gaze burning into my skull.

"You're not joking."

I wince. "I wish I were."

She turns around and walks back to her bedroom. I don't know why, but I follow her. A thread of anxiety wraps around my lungs. "Are you... okay?"

A tiny laugh passes her lips. "I don't know how to answer that."

"I guess that's fair." After an awkward silence, I clear my throat. "So, I'm gonna go."

Spinning around, she grabs my arm. "Hey, wait, I need to ask you something. It's, um..." Mercy lets go of me and crosses her arms. "It feels really stupid now, but uhh, do you want to... go out with me?"

I stare blankly at her. "What?"

Her blush never really disappeared, but it comes back in full force. "Sam and I are going on a date later this week, and I wanted to invite you and Reaper."

You have *got* to be shitting me.

"You're asking me to go on a double-date with my brother?"

She clasps and unclasps her hands together repeatedly. "Um, well, you're not really related, right?" Laughing awkwardly, she continues, "It doesn't have to be romantic. We just wanted to ask you guys some questions—"

"No." I shut her down before she can run with the idea. "I'm not going on a fucking date." Kane will be obsessing over Mercy the entire time, leaving me as the third—fourth?—wheel. "If you have something to say, say it. Don't be all—" I wave my hand in front of her. "Cute about it."

"I'm not trying to be cute!"

"That's not—" I pinch the bridge of my nose. That's not what I meant. "I'm not going on a date with you, Mercy. Not even a platonic one. You—" I grab her chin.

"—are a means to an end." Tilting her head back, I stare at the hickey on her neck. I still don't know if Kane or Sam left it there. Brushing my thumb over the mark, I hum in the back of my throat. So what, if it was Kane? He clearly didn't fuck her, or she wouldn't even be here right now. She'd be locked up in the studio until he filled every one of her holes.

Mercy doesn't even flinch. "What does that mean?"

A smile curves on my lips. "That's for me to know, Kitten, and for you to never find out."

Chapter 12

Mercy

Over the next few days, my life goes back to normal. Sam is too busy to hang out, citing football practice for the upcoming championship game, and Kane doesn't attend class again. If I'm lucky, he'll stay away for good, but I have a feeling that his absence is only temporary. Zane also keeps his distance, disappearing into thin air after our last meeting.

It's like I'm boy-free again.

I should be happy. No more imminent threat of death or orgasms or anything else remotely dramatic. I'm back to being regular old Mercy Morningstar, college senior without any friends.

So why does it feel like my chest is filled with lead?

When I text Sam, his replies are short and to the point. He insists that yes, we're still on for our date Friday night, but he can't come over before then. I don't have a way to contact Kane or Zane, but I keep looking for one of them to appear from around every corner.

I'm disappointed every time I expect one of them to show up.

The worst part is that when I toss and turn at night, my body's on fire from the inside. I'm used to having trouble sleeping. It's why I've invested in my lavender essential oils and a sleep mask. They don't always work, but I like to pretend that they do. Even still, when sleep evades me, I usually sketch or paint or sit outside on the front porch to watch the stars sparkle in the night sky.

Lately, all I've wanted is for someone to touch me again.

Who it is doesn't seem to matter. My mind flits between Sam's guttural groan as he comes to Reaper's massive cock in his hand, and worst of all, Zane has slipped into my fever dreams, his voice rasping in my ear as he tells me what a dirty little virgin I am. I throw my bedsheets off and hook my thumbs into the waistband of my panties, nervous to take them off. The cool breeze flowing through the open window makes me shiver, but it does nothing to satiate the raw need burning through my system.

I glance at the window, remembering how Zane broke in before. He could do it again. I guess any one of them could if they really wanted to. Zane tore Sam's old baseball bat out of my hands before I could even take a swing. It's not like I could fight any of them off.

But would I even want to?

Clenching my fists, I toss my head back onto my pillow. I don't know what I want anymore. The lack of sleep and inability to talk to anyone is driving me insane.

What are they doing? Is Kane still mad at me for what happened in the cemetery? Is Sam having second thoughts about our date? Does Zane regret touching me?

The thought of Zane sends another wave of heat through my body, and I can't take it anymore. Pulling my panties down my legs, I flatten my heels on the bed and slowly slide my hands down my stomach. I don't touch myself that often. Something about it doesn't feel right, like I'm doing it wrong. It feels good up until a point, and then it's like... there's a block in my brain, or there's too much pressure down there, or I feel like I have to pee. None of which makes me feel like a goddess of her sexuality.

But if I pretend that my fingers are Zane's—

A gasp escapes past my lips as I slide my fingers over my clit. *Whoa.* That's... wow. Biting my lip, I rub up and down slowly, closing my eyes to picture Zane better. The stubble on his chin tickles my neck, and his hot breath crackles in my ear. Something electric zings up my spine, and I muffle my cries as my hips start to move on their own.

This is wrong. Wrongwrongwrong. Zane doesn't want to have sex with me, so I shouldn't—

I'm going to make you come on my fingers, Kitten.

I whimper. Liquid heat spills from my center, and I gently glide my fingers across my entrance. I've been burning up every night this week, ever since all three of those men showed me something new.

Kane let me grind on him, and then he masturbated because *I* turned him on.

Sam not only showed me his dick, but he let me stroke it with him and showed me what he likes.

And Zane—I curve my finger and try to hit the same spot he did. My heart races as I plunge my fingers inside my pussy, desperate for the same friction, the same tingling pleasure, the same crescendo—

I grind on my hand, but it's not the same. Frustrated, I try different positions. Arched back. Curled on my side. Lying on my stomach. Ass in the air. Hips flat to the mattress. But nothing works. The pressure and heat build, but there's nowhere for it to escape. I can't release it. I don't know how.

Tossing and turning becomes an understatement. Sweat pools beneath my back, wetting my sheets. My pussy throbs, and I grab my breasts in a desperate attempt at relief. Nothing works, and I don't know what to do.

...but I know someone who might.

Grabbing my phone from my nightstand, I pull up Sam's contact info. He was nice enough to teach me about how he finds pleasure, so... maybe he can tell me how it works... for women? Even that sounds ridiculous in my head. I might as well call my sister, but it's two A.M. I can't bother her with something like this. She'll *know* what's going on, and that's embarrassing!

Then again, if I text Sam...

He'll probably figure it out, too.

I'm between a rock and a hard place, and neither of them are going to get me off.

Just when I'm about to give up, my phone vibrates.

Can't sleep?

I stare at the text message for a long time, not knowing who it's from. My thumbs hover over my screen, but I decide not to answer. They probably have the wrong number.

Neither can I, but it's your fault.

Someone's being a very bad girl.

My breath catches as I read and reread the messages. I must read them half a dozen times, and I'm still stunned. Who's texting me?

Who's watching me?

Jumping out of bed, I cover myself with my bedsheet and cross to the window. Moonlight covers the yard with clouds blowing past to obscure its light. I stare out the window for a long time, looking for whoever is spying on me. But I don't see a flicker of light or any signs of movement. It's like I'm alone...

But then my phone vibrates again.

I unlock my phone with shaking hands.

Tell me how wet you are, and I'll help you.

Help me what?

Come

You want to come, don't you?

> You've been trying for hours.

> I've been waiting patiently.

> But I can't wait any more.

> Let me help you.

When I take too long to reply, another message arrives.

> We can come together.

I shut my bedroom window and climb back into bed.

> Ok. What should I do?

> Touch yourself. Tell me how wet you are.

Nerves flutter in my stomach. I must be crazy to sext a stranger, but if this week has taught me anything, it's that I'm tired of playing it safe. Once I lie down on my back, I lift my knees and spread my thighs. Already, I can feel my desire dripping from my slit. It coats the groove where my pelvis meets my thighs, and I rub my fingertips over my folds, unable to stop my body from trembling.

> Beautiful, Mercy, fucking beautiful

> How wet are you?

Dipping my middle finger inside my pussy, I whimper. Using voice to text, I tell him that I'm dripping down my thighs. The message sends, and I close my eyes to play with myself a little more.

> You fucking tease

What? Squinting at my phone, I nearly scream at the little speaker icon.

I didn't send a voice-to-text message.

I sent a *voice* message.

> Don't stop now
>
> Turn your microphone on
>
> I want to hear you moan as you slide your fingers inside your pussy

My core clenches, turning my desire into a deep ache. I hesitate to record anything else. The first one was an accident—but any more means that I'm okay with this.

I'm okay being a bad girl.

A dirty little virgin.

I turn on the voice recording feature before I can talk myself out of it. Swirling my fingertips over my clit, I let myself moan. Pleasure rocks my body, and I catch myself panting as I curl my fingers deep inside of me. I almost forget to hit *send*.

> Fuck, you're gorgeous
>
> Do you want to see me?
>
> I'm rock hard for you, beautiful

Before I can reply, a picture pops up. A huge, veiny dick fills the screen, its tip shiny in the flash. The hand grasping its base is wrapped tightly around the shaft, the hair at the base neatly trimmed.

Dirty blonde.

A massive cock.

Enough confidence to sext me in the middle of the night—no, to *watch* me first. I glance around the room for cameras, but I don't see any of those dome things or a webcam anywhere.

> video message

Oh, God.

My heart skips a beat as the video plays. The man strokes his cock with slow, steady movements, his breathing fast as his palm glides from the very base up past the tip. I watch, fascinated, at the subtle curve to the left and the way his skin pulls up over part of the head before he strokes back down. The video ends, and I watch it for a second time.

> Don't stop

> I won't come without you

> Slip your fingers back inside your pussy and use your other hand to play with your tits

> Rub your nipple with the tips of your fingers and thumb

Or you can pinch it

Whichever feels better

Let me know

I follow his guidance and slide my right hand between my legs while reaching up with my left. At first, I don't feel much from rubbing my nipples, but once I pinch them between my fingertips, my back arches off the bed. I quickly turn on my microphone and record my next moan, whimpering as I think about him jerking off to the sound of my voice.

Is this something Zane would like, too, or is he simply not attracted to me at all?

My bubble of happiness deflates, and I let my nipple go and remove my fingers from my clit. I still ache, but only part of it is from my pussy.

Is Zane asexual?

It's okay if he is. It might even make me feel better.

No. Did he tell you that?

Not in those words, but...

I wasn't sure.

He said something about not having sex with people. I thought guys like him had sex all the time.

Unlike virgins like me, but I leave that part out.

Guys like him?

You know. Hot. Dangerous. Bad boys.

Like you.

Sex means different things to different people.

It's not the same for him as it is for me.

Why are you curious?

I think about my response.

He says that he doesn't want to have sex with me. I guess I'm used to that. But I got mixed signals. I'm probably overthinking it.

Forget I said anything

I'll never forget anything you say.

Do you want to have sex with him?

I don't know. Is that a bad thing?

No, it means you're human.

Want to know what I think?

Sure

I think

Anyone would be lucky to have sex
with you

Because it means that you trust them
to take care of you

It's the same with Zane.

Closing my eyes, I picture Zane towel-drying his hair in my bathroom. He trusted me enough to take his shirt off and come into my bedroom. Or maybe he's just not scared of me. But he shared something about himself—something personal. Isn't that a type of trust?

Do you trust me, Mercy?

Am I talking to Kane or am I talking to
Reaper?

Three pulsing dots appear on the screen, then disappear. A minute passes before they appear again.

What if I'm both Reaper and Kane?

Then I don't know how to answer.

Probably not.

After all, Zane or Reaper bugged my bedroom. I don't want to guess what could come next.

No more texts come through, and I turn my phone on

silent before putting it on my nightstand. I'm still warm and wet between my thighs, but now I don't know how to turn my brain off. My thoughts circle the drain, spinning from the concept of trust to what it could mean for Zane, back around to Kane and his sexual advances, then all the way to Sam and our upcoming date. If I asked, I know that Sam would have sex with me. I trust Sam. He'll be good to me. He'll be gentle and sweet and treat me like a princess.

But I don't know if I want to be someone's princess anymore.

I might want to be someone's dirty girl.

A fucking tease.

Or a little bit of all three.

CHAPTER 13

KANE

I WANTED to hear my Siren sing for me, and instead, I'm cockblocked by my best friend. I fist my angry dick and will it to deflate, but it's useless once it gets to this point. If I let it sit unattended, I'll have blue balls from hell. Rubbing one out is my only option.

But *man*, did Mercy take a left turn in that conversation.

My thoughts swirl round and round between Mercy's ragged breaths to the video feed of her masturbating, aaaall the way back to a few hours ago when I discovered Zane's hidden cameras. He thinks he can keep secrets from me, but I know him like I know the feel of my cock in my fist. *Really fucking well.* I'm an expert in both, even if Zane doesn't realize it.

After this morning, I already know that Mercy's a virgin.

Just like I know he got her off before me.

I'll let it slide only because the man deserves some

action, and I want to see him let loose a little. Not to mention, I'd love for him to be happy for once. In all the years I've known him, it's like he doesn't know how to embrace life to the fullest. I try to show him—feeding him my favorite beef jerky or lifting him off the ground to prove how much weight I can carry—but it's like we operate on different wavelengths.

Sometimes, I think he only tolerates me because we're all each other has.

But then I see *this*.

Rewinding the recording from a few hours ago, I watch as Zane pins Mercy to the wall and shoves his hand beneath her skirt. Pride swells inside my chest, but not nearly as strong as the blood pooling between my thighs. I grip my fat cock in my right hand and turn the volume up with my left, watching the scandal unfold for the dozenth time. He whispers something in her ear, and she blushes like the pretty virgin she is, grinding all over his fingers until she comes.

Fucking breathtaking.

Then he has to go and ruin the moment by running away.

I know that Zane doesn't operate by the same rules that I do, but Mercy was ripe and ready for the taking. By rejecting her, he's bruised her ego. Otherwise, I would have been able to make her come tonight. But Zane got into her head, and now she's not sure about her value. I don't want her because she's a virgin—I want her because she's *Mercy*.

My Siren, who's too scared to sing for anyone other than the dead.

I rewind the video again and switch to another camera until I've successfully pulled up two separate feeds of the same few seconds, splitting them amongst two monitors. Mercy's body is in perfect view on one screen while the other is focused on Zane. I can't see nearly enough of Zane's face because of how he's folded over Mercy's body, but I catch the red flush burning down his neck and over the tips of his ears, and from this angle, I can see how he uses both his wrist and his arm to get her off. The skirt is another obstacle to the show, but Mercy's blissed out face more than makes up for it.

Fisting my cock, I stroke slow and steady, prepared to take in the moment as best I can without having been in the room when it happened. My gaze travels between the two of them, and my mind starts wandering from the recording of them together to fond memories I have of them apart.

Mercy grinding on top of me this afternoon.

Zane fucking his fist to a video of me topping a guy a few years back. I only walked in on him masturbating once, and I'm pretty sure that scarred him for life, because I haven't seen or heard him jerk off since. The man is sexually repressed, and I feel like I'm to blame.

Man, tonight is not my night.

I stop stroking my cock and close the videos. Leaning back in my office chair, I take a deep breath and try to come up with a plan. The desire to kill Mercy gets stronger every day, but that's only because I can't wait to watch her unravel. She's like a painting that gets better and better the more you work the canvas. I'm eagerly awaiting the finished piece.

In fact, the past few days I've spent away from her have given me time to compose a few pieces. None of them are quite right—I'm missing an element that I haven't figured out yet—but I know that it'll come to me in time, and I'll finish all of them in a sprint to the finish line.

Zane will be ecstatic that I've moved on from Alejandro.

Shaking my head, I put Alejandro out of my mind and focus on Mercy. Watching her ask Zane on a date was goddamn adorable, but the way he refused her hurts.

Not just for her—but for *me.*

Why the fuck wouldn't he want to go on a date with me?

I grind my jaw as I stew over that little detail. I know he's attracted to me. We don't have the same hangups that he has with Mercy. I trust him with my life, and I know he feels the same about me. We're bonded. Brothers. Friends. No matter the title or how you phrase it, that's just what we are. Together. Through thick and thin, heaven and hell. Always have been, always will be.

Mercy won't change that, no matter what happens.

I just wish he would trust in our bond more, but the fucker has issues even I can't solve.

Shoving my still-hard cock into the waistband of my sweats, I stand from my chair and leave my bedroom. Zane's room is two doors down, separated by a guest room no one fucking uses, and I march right on over. Without knocking, I turn the door handle and push inside. "Zane," I call out, flicking on the light. "Man, stop being a prick and go on a double date with me and Mercy. You don't *have* to kiss me, but if the 'kiss cam' turns our way, pucker up because—"

I stare at Zane's empty bedroom for a moment before I sit down on his bed. Smoothing my hand over the sheets, I lean back and kick up my feet, burrowing my arm under his pillow and lying on my side. Something scratches the back of my hand, and I fumble around until I pull a playing card from out of nowhere.

A really weird playing card.

A shirtless man—a *ridiculously hot* shirtless man—offers his hand out to me. The curved script along the bottom edge reads *The Devil*, and I can't help but grin. Yeah, Zane's always been into men more than women, and here's the proof. Flicking the edge of the card, I shove it back under his pillow for safe-keeping.

What a childish thing, keeping a porno card beneath his pillow.

I snicker to myself about it while I wait for Zane to appear. But the longer it takes, the more restless I get. My dick twitches just as impatiently, ready to go off at a moment's notice. Sighing, I rub it a little through my pants, knowing that I'm stoking the beast rather than putting it to bed. Another few minutes pass, and I use Zane's computer to print off a few male and female models' photos. Once they're taped to the wall next to his bed, I stand back in triumph.

Maybe a little nudie incentive will get his pump flowing again.

I bet if I printed my picture—or better yet, a picture of me and Mercy together—it'd work. But I don't have a picture of us, clothed or otherwise, to use, and I sure as shit can't photoshop.

What I *can* do is paint something.

Inspiration takes over immediately, and I'm running down the hall before I can think to leave Zane a note or text about the date with me and Mercy.

Because we're fucking going.

There's no way in hell that Sam is winning my Siren's heart *or* pussy before me or Zane. In fact, we're already winning. She watched me come for her today, and then Zane finished her off after I turned her on. She's wet right this very second because of us, too, likely shoving her fingers as deep inside her pussy as they'll go.

If that's not winning, I don't know what the fuck is.

Chapter 14

Sam

Alejandro Carerra disappeared on Wednesday, September 16th. He finished his shift at his family's auto shop and walked home, but according to his roommates, he never made it. To the casual observer, this seems like your everyday crime against people of color. A story to briefly mention before the local news channels move on to something else. It doesn't look like anyone has fought for Alejandro or helped his family find peace.

It's a goddamn injustice.

I stare at pictures of Alejandro with his family—smiling parents, two younger brothers, and a darling youngest sister. This specific picture of them at the beach is a few years old, before their daughter was taken from them, too.

Drunk driver.

The blow hits me square in the chest, and I have to take a deep, steadying breath. It's fucked up—everything about the situation. Their auto shop is still in business, but the weariness in the father's eyes has easily aged him by a few decades. The two remaining sons, older now, smile stiffly at the camera.

It doesn't take long to transfer an anonymous donation from the Wright Foundation to their banking institution, but even that feels like mediocre compensation for their hardship.

I could, instead, bring Alejandro's killers to justice.

My gaze lingers on Alejandro's Missing Persons flyer on my computer monitor. I'm not home in the frat, having spent the past few nights at my father's house. He's never home, making a collision with him low risk, but he keeps his web browsing encrypted and all outgoing calls routed through proxies. Doing research here is better for my psyche in terms of hiding my search history, but everything else about the experience is a drain on my mental stamina. This office is pure white and sterile, kept immaculately clean by the staff, and I absolutely fucking hate it. But what I hate more is knowing that people like my father don't give a fuck about anyone outside of the upper echelons of society. They don't bat an eye when a man like Alejandro goes missing. He was twenty-five with dreams of taking over the family business someday. Now, he's dead.

And I know who killed him.

I rub my tired eyes and glance at the clock. Two-thirty A.M.. Way past my bedtime if I'm going to make it through my eight o'clock practice. Sighing, I drag my body down the hall to my bedroom. This, too, is in pristine condition. If my father could have cleaned me up like this house, he would have turned me into a perfect replica of himself no matter the amount of anti-depressants and hair dye it would take. I've been to every top-tier shrink in the city, and they all say the same thing.

He's not broken, Samuel, he's just human.

Human and grieving.

As I lay in bed, my mind inevitably drifts back to the day I met Mercy. It was a last-ditch effort to "fix" me. Grief counseling with the general population. He attended the adult group and met Mr. Morningstar while I attended the youth group and met Mercy.

If there's one thing I'm grateful to the bastard for, it's that he inadvertently introduced me to Mercy... or I guess we could say that my mom did.

Thinking of her doesn't hurt as much as it used to, but not having a mom doesn't suck any less. She never got to meet Mercy.

"I think you'd like her." I stare up at the tiered ceiling and rub the ache brewing inside my chest. "She's got pretty eyes and a killer smile. A lot of things don't bother her. Like how I only eat hot dogs with relish or can't watch scary movies. She likes the gory ones more than the ghost ones. I think it's because of her family's affinity for dead things." Grandma Star offered to conduct a seance for me once, but I could never muster the courage to go through with it. I'd rather speak with my mom like this, where I don't have to wonder what she'll say back.

I tuck my hands behind my head and wonder, like I do every night, if Mercy is having trouble sleeping.

Staying the night to hold her is purely selfish, however, no matter how much it helps her dream sweetly. It helps me, too. Sighing, I close my eyes and allow my mind to wander, but all it does is spiral around Mercy. Her infectious laugh. The way her eyes sparkle in certain slants of light. How skilled she is with her artwork. Inevitably, my thoughts drift back to the first night I kissed her.

If I could do things differently, I would. I'd tell her that I'm not kissing her just because I think she's pretty or we've been friends for a long time. She isn't a convenient hookup or a means to pass the time.

"I messed up," I admit aloud. "I know that. But I'm going to make it up to her." We lost a year that we could have spent together because I didn't have the balls to admit how I felt. I let her slip through my fingers.

But I won't make that mistake twice.

Sitting up, I rummage through the nightstand drawer for the burner phone my father insists I keep in case of *special* emergencies. When I turn it on, it's fully charged and ready to use. I roll my eyes despite how convenient it is to have it ready and waiting for me. I stall for a few minutes, playing around with the burner, checking my phone for texts I know aren't there, before finally dialing the number for my dad's "fix it" guy.

I don't know the extent he goes to take care of things, but from what I've gleaned over the years under my father's roof, if you need a job done and have the money to pay for it, you call Grey.

"Yo," he answers on the first ring. "What's up, Wright?"

I hesitate for so long that Grey shuffles on the other end of the line. "Hello?"

"I'm here," I reply, running a hand through my hair. It's not too late to back out, but I've come this far already. "I want you to look into something for me."

"Little Wright. Rock on. Always wondered when you'd call." Grey chuckles. "What's daddy got you into?"

"I'm not—he's not—" Sighing, I pinch the bridge of my nose. "I just want you to find out everything you can about a set of brothers. They go by Kane and Zane, but Kane also goes by the name Reaper on campus. He's a fifth-year and up to some shady shit." I know that Mercy doesn't want me to go to the police, so I'll use the other channels I have to dig a little deeper into Kane and Zane's lives. "Cross reference a man named Alejandro Carrera or any other missing persons within the past decade."

"Got it, Boss. You wanna pick up or order delivery?"

"Delivery." I won't have time to venture across the city with the championship game around the corner. "I need this fast, Grey. As soon as possible."

"That'll cost double."

"Add it to my tab." Depending on what info Grey digs up, I'll be calling him for a follow-up job, anyway. "And hey, tip yourself generously."

Although I can't see Grey's smile, I can hear it in his voice. "Happy to be of service. Anything else ya need, kid?"

"Yeah." I pray that my mom covers her ears for this. "I need a gun. Something easy to hide. Have it delivered to the house overnight."

"I'll throw in some ammo," Grey muses, grunting. "And a spare. Didn't Samuel give you one years ago? I'm surprised you don't have an arsenal."

We do, in fact, have a gun safe that might as well be a walk-in closet. But I don't want my dad to stick his nose where it doesn't belong, and if I take one of his guns—even the one he gave me when I turned fifteen—he'll have an excuse to breathe down my neck.

Grey's pitch lowers. "If you've got a problem, kid, I can send someone to handle it."

"That won't be necessary." I glare into the darkness, picturing Reaper's smug smile. "I'm a good shot."

By the time the sun rises, I'm locked and loaded and practicing my aim in the range hidden beneath my father's ground floor. I skip morning football practice intentionally, knowing that I won't be able to focus, and give up my chance of playing Saturday's game. For something I've worked so hard for, I'm not as upset as I imagined I would be.

All I can think about is keeping Mercy away from those men.

With my father's resources, I could spirit her away. Go into hiding. No one would be able to find us. We could disappear today without a trace. Be free from all of this bullshit.

I could have Reaper killed. Zane, too, if he becomes a problem.

And Mercy would be mine.

I put a few more bullets into my target as I mull the idea over. I've never been a man for extremes. Pissing my father off by ignoring his life plans for me has been fun, but I've never wanted to go nuclear. I've merely wanted to be left alone to live my life the way I want. Money or no money. Wright legacy or no legacy. None of that shit has ever mattered to me.

But if that's the only way I can keep Mercy safe...

I could always lean into becoming Samson Wright, heir to the Wright family fortune. I might not be happy about it, but if I can come home to Mercy every night, if she'll be happy to see me and run into my arms, then maybe—

Maybe the rest of it doesn't matter.

As much as I hate being under my father's thumb, I stay in his house for the rest of the day to get a feel for what my life could be like if I stay. My skin crawls every time I imagine my dad walking into the room to lecture me or order me to join him in a business meeting. But when I picture Mercy swinging her legs on a stool in front of the kitchen island or sketching in the sunroom, the tension roiling in my gut dissipates. I like the idea of having her around.

If I'm honest about how bad Kane and Zane are for her, I don't think she would run away from me. Especially if she has nowhere to run to... The only hitch in the plan is her family, but I could house Grandma Star and her dad somewhere safe. We could visit. I doubt her brother is coming back anytime soon, so he's a nonfactor as long as he's out of town and out of range. Lilith will throw a fit if I take Mercy away, though, so she's an issue to deal with. I don't want there to be collateral damage if I can avoid it.

I guess we'll see what Grey digs up first and go from there.

I'm running on next to no sleep and a gallon of caffeine, but I get ready for my date with Mercy with meticulous care. Hair slicked back. Rolex in place. Cologne dabbed on my wrists. A white button-up I know she likes and a pair of form-fitting jeans that are easy to take off. If she wants. If she *asks.* My dick hardens at the thought of her touching me again, and I quickly tent hard enough for my dick imprint to show. Groaning through my teeth, I try to think of something else. Anything else. But imagining Mercy's hands sliding down my chest to grab my cock—

Fuuuuck.

The gun strapped to my thigh is gonna have to go. My muscles bulge as I remove the holster and toss it onto the bed. I need to keep it on me in case Reaper shows up to collect Mercy's life early.

Or mine.

It hasn't slipped my mind that I'm in on this, too, but thankfully, he doesn't seem too interested in my life. It's only Mercy that's caught his eye. As I grab my swollen dick and beat off, I can't keep my frustration under wraps. I picture the two of them together—his mouth on her throat and his hands roaming her body— and I see red. With a hiss, I slam my fist into the wall and grit my teeth. I *hate* picturing the two of them together. It doesn't matter that Kane can probably get her off with his pinky finger—I can do better.

I need to prove to her that I can do better.

Squeezing the base of my shaft, I take deep breaths and try to calm down. I won't waste a load in my fist. I'll hold it for her. If she wants it. *Please* let her want it.

My phone chimes, and I quickly pick it up and unlock my screen. Mercy's contact photo appears beside the text message icon, and I click the image rather than the text. I took this picture last year when we were fooling around. She's lounging back on her elbows, eyes closed, shirt unbuttoned and her tits perfectly cradled in a black bra. Smiling. For me. *Because* of me.

I open her message before I can think twice about my no-jerking-off decision.

MERCY

I'm ready

Are you still picking me up?

She's early. Maybe she's as eager as I am.

ME

Of course. I'll be there in twenty minutes.

As I'm grabbing my keys, another message pings.

MERCY

You might want to hurry…

> Kane just showed up.

> I don't know what he wants.

Shit. Of course he's going to ruin our date. I shouldn't have stayed away this long, but I wanted to make sure that I had enough information against Reaper—

A video pops up on my screen.

Hey, Sam. Don't worry about picking up our girl. I'll take it from here.

Reaper's cocky grin pisses me the fuck off. Mercy's trapped under his arm, a bouquet of white roses clutched to her chest. Her eyes are wide as she stares at him instead of the camera, her lips parted in a precious little *o*. Hair straight. Deep red lipstick. A little black dress that would turn a preacher's head.

I hit the call button, and it goes unanswered. I try again. And again. The entire drive over, I barrel through red lights and keep calling. Every time it goes to voice-mail, I hang up and redial.

By the time I storm into the Morningstar's house and up to Mercy's bedroom, I'm seething with rage. No one's ever been interested in Mercy enough to steal her from me. I spot her phone on her desk, along with her purse. The sketchbook on the table is flipped to the back where a drawing of Mercy pushed up against the wall—with a man I recognize as Reaper's brother—burying his face in the curve of her neck.

Maybe Reaper didn't give her the hickey like I thought... and maybe there *is* another threat with Zane, after all.

Cursing loudly, I take the stairs two at a time and burst outside into the evening air. Gravel's been kicked up on the driveway, a single track cutting a trench all the way up to the mortuary's paved lot.

"She went with that tall fellow." Grandma Star's sudden comment damn near makes me shoot her. She nods to herself as she rocks in a chair on the front porch, a smile tugging at her lips. "So many suitors, so little time."

"What do you mean, Grandma?"

She nods again, this time towards the church on the far end of the property. "That other one's been here every night fixin' up the old church. Don't need a church to get married, though." She rocks slowly, her gaze distant. "He seems nice. He cleaned up the graves until my husband gets back."

Mercy's grandfather's been dead for at least half a decade.

"Did they say where they were going?"

Grandma Star hums to herself, not sensing the urgency of the situation. I'd never hurt the old woman, but it's tempting if it means getting Mercy back. But if I hurt her, Mercy would never forgive me, so as Grandma starts muttering to herself, I consider her a lost cause and jump back into my car. Taking a deep breath, I put my phone on speaker and make another call.

"Hey, it's me again."

"Little Wright," Grey greets cheerily. "Rock on. What do you need?"

"I need to track a vehicle that just left the Morningstar Mortuary's lot. It might be a motorcycle. Can you pull up the traffic cams?"

Grey is silent, but I can hear him typing on a keyboard. "Black hot rod, yeah. It's headed across town by the looks of it. Want me to—"

"Send me the feed, yeah. Can you lock on and send me updated coordinates?"

"Sure, Boss. Need backup?"

I consider it for half a second before shaking my head. "No, I want to handle this myself."

Because if Reaper hurts a single hair on her head, I won't hesitate to pull the trigger.

CHAPTER 15

ZANE

I'M HANGING STRING lights in the rafters of the ancient church when I hear a roaring engine tear down the Morningstar driveway, kicking up dust and rocks without a second thought. Peering out the hole in the roof, I damn near fall off my ladder as Kane swings his leg over the seat of his motorcycle and bounds up Mercy's front porch steps. I've told him to sell that thing a dozen times, but he refuses to listen, citing that he's here for a good time, not a long time.

He's going to send me to an early grave before he's even dead.

Sighing, I abandon my task and descend the rungs of the ladder, making it outside the church just in time to witness Kane present a bouquet of roses to Mercy. From my vantage point through her window, it's hard to discern her reaction, but Kane's smile is pinched.

Something is bothering him.

They spend an exorbitant amount of time in her

bedroom before he picks her up, tosses her over his shoulder, and bounds down the stairs and out of the house.

"Zane!" He's back to grinning as he smacks Mercy's ass atop his shoulder. She yelps like a dog and slams her knee into Kane's collarbone. "You're just in time for our date."

Date?

Dropping her onto his bike seat, he grabs the spare helmet and gently pulls it over the top of her head, then snaps it in place. "Hold onto me," he instructs, "and lean into the turns."

Mercy slams her hands against Kane's chest. "I'm not going anywhere with you!" Her gaze flicks from Kane's face to mine, and I catch a glimmer of fear in her eyes. "I—I already have a date."

Don't you dare—

"With Zane." Forcing a smile, she uses Kane's stunned silence to slip from his grasp. "He agreed to go out with me and Sam tonight." She unsnaps her helmet and tosses it to the ground at Kane's feet before coming to stand beside me. Resting her forearm on my shoulder, she tosses her curtain of hair over her shoulder. "Sorry, you weren't invited."

"She's—she's lying!" I sputter, alarm bells ringing in my head. "I never agreed to go out with her!"

If Kane gets jealous, I'm fucked. Royally fucked. In the ass. With no lube. Torn right down the middle of my cra—

"Zanie," Mercy whines childishly, frowning a little

too dramatically to be taken seriously. "I know you're shy, but you don't need to lie. What we have is real." She takes my hand and links our fingers together, smiling cheekily at Kane as he finally turns around. "The least you can do is take me to dinner now that we've been to third base."

Jesus fucking Christ.

Kane's a little too relaxed, his smile matching Mercy's. Fake as hell. "Alright, beautiful. I'll tell you what. Why don't you go out with both of us, and we'll decide who gets to take you to home plate over dinner."

No, no, no!

"I'm not sleeping with her!"

Neither of them is listening, too content with grinning viciously at each other to pay any attention to me. Like wolves, they size each other up like they're eying pieces of meat and neither of them has had a meal in weeks.

Kane has spent the past three days ignoring Mercy, and now, all of a sudden, he shows up with roses and demands for a date? "You saw the video feed," I surmise, pressing my lips together into a firm line. The fucker gets off on breaking through my security measures and gloating about it. I'm surprised it took him this long to show his hand.

"Bingo."

Mercy's the only one out of the loop. "What video feed?"

"The one that Zane set up in your bedroom." He not-so-subtly adjusts his growing hard-on. "It's how I knew you were fingering that needy pussy last night." Licking his lips, his gaze travels down her body. "Does she still need attention?"

She flushes bright pink and averts her gaze.

What the hell did I miss last night?

"Take me to dinner," she says after a moment, "and we'll discuss who's having dessert."

Kane's eyes flash dangerously. "Yes, ma'am."

"But I want Zane to drive me."

The grin on Kane's face disappears. "Don't play with my heart, Siren, or you'll have to pick up the pieces when it breaks."

Biting her lip, Mercy glances at Kane's motorcycle. "I'm, um, scared to ride one of those."

"All the more reason to give her a spin." Kane picks up the discarded helmet and moves to put it on Mercy's head, but before he can succeed, I grab her hand and pull her into my side. The way Kane's face falls cracks my heart into pieces.

"Can't ruin her hair and makeup before we've had a chance to enjoy it," I explain lamely, wrapping my arm around her waist. "I'll take her to Lucio's. Meet us there?"

Kane glances between the two of us before stiffly nodding. "Fine. But when dinner's over, she's riding with me." Stepping into our personal space, he places his left hand directly over mine on Mercy's waist and the other on my hip. He pecks her cheek before turning his face towards mine and doing the same, tenderly pressing his lips against my cheekbone. Warmth radiates from that simple point of contact, and when Kane pulls back, I know that I'm blushing just as much as Mercy is.

Shit.

Why the hell would he do that?

He meets my eyes for the briefest moment before turning and walking back to his motorcycle. Once he's slung his leg over the side and adjusted the kickstand, he revs the engine and speeds back up the driveway, tearing a rut into the gravel.

Mercy drops the act as soon as Kane's out of sight, and we separate immediately. "Where's your car?"

"I'm not going on a date with you," I growl, feeling frustrated and confused and—

"You don't have a choice." She swings her arm out towards the road. "Kane's going to be waiting for us. Do you really want to stand him up?"

"Why the hell are you insisting on this fucking date?" Regardless of the reason—even if it *is* simply picking our brains like she claims—it's a waste of fucking time. Glaring at her, I cross my arms over my chest. "I'm not dressed for dinner at Lucio's. I won't make it through the door." The cobwebs and dust sticking to my sweatpants sure don't scream *fine dining.*

Rolling her eyes, she grabs my wrist and drags me inside her house and across the main floor to her father's closet. His clothes are vintage and well-loved, but we manage to find a dress shirt that's only a few sizes too large and a pair of slacks that I don't have to suck my gut in to fit. "There. Now you're dressed."

I curl my lip in the bathroom mirror. "I look like a

goddamn renaissance man." Now that the shirt is buttoned, I realize the sleeves have ruffled cuffs. Un-fuck-ing-believable. While I tear off the frill with my bare hands, Mercy steals a pair of her father's shoes and sets them down in front of me.

"Hurry up."

I don't know why, but her tone pisses me off.

Grabbing her hair as she tries to walk away, I pull her into my arms, spinning us until we're both facing the mirror. Her makeup is flawless, but her dark locks fan out across her face and catch on her scarlet lips. The dress cuts over her knees and hugs her body like a glove, accentuating her curves.

She's pretty when she dresses up, I'll give her that.

I brush the hair from her eyes and open my mouth, but a door behind us slams. I cover her mouth and listen as heavy footsteps pound up the stairs, lingering for only a moment before they storm back down and out the front door. "Expecting company?" Our eyes meet in the mirror, and she tries to wiggle free. Holding her tighter against my chest, I *tsk-tsk*. "You weren't waiting for Kane, were you?"

Part of me thought that they had set this up to force me on a date with them, but Kane seemed surprised to see me. He would have carried Mercy off like a caveman claiming his mate. I bet he'd intended to rut her into the dirt, too, on a cliff somewhere or against the rough bark of an evergreen, ripping her dress from her body in his haste to get inside of her.

He might pretend to be a gentleman, but when his

patience has worn out and a target's time is up, he turns into an untamed beast. Scaring them. Fucking them. Making them scream themselves hoarse. "You're lucky I stopped him from taking you," I tell Mercy, speaking honestly. "If he gets his claws in you—" I drag my fingernails across Mercy's throat, enjoying the way she flinches. Red scratch marks slice across her porcelain throat. "You'll be begging him to stop."

Mercy glares at me and opens her mouth.

I prepare myself for her muffled screams.

She bites down on my palm hard enough that *I* yell, quickly shoving her away from me. "Fucking *bitch!*" My hand throbs as she truly screams, running from the room before I can grab her.

"Sam!"

I follow her trail, catching up to her as she passes through the front door. Tackling her on the stairs, we slam into the grass, one on top of the other. My bones rattle as she kicks my ribs with her combat boot and tries to scramble away, aiming her next kick at my face. I dodge, growling as I grab her calf and drag her body back to mine. "You stupid bitch!" A laugh cracks in my chest. "*God*, I should have killed you that night. Then this whole thing would be over!"

"Get off of me!"

Using my body weight to my advantage, I grapple her and lock her head in a chokehold. "He wants you." My chest heaves as I hold her in submission. "God knows why." The truth grates on my nerves like a nail file, tearing my flesh open after so long spent in denial.

Mercy is a beautiful woman. Her eyes hold the warmth of the setting sun, and her skin—I press my cheek against hers—is softer than velvet. Wrapping my legs around her ankles, I hold on until she whimpers, the fight draining from her body. But it's more than her appearance that draws Kane in—it's the way she sits at her desk for hours, staring out the window long after the sun sets, a forgotten pencil tucked between her fingers. The lingering loneliness on her bedroom walls. Not a single picture frame hangs on nails or sits on a shelf, like she doesn't have a single memory worth keeping. How she sings to the dead in a mausoleum on Halloween night, unafraid of the spirits she summons with her voice.

Kane is the most observant man I know. He'll take one glance at a person and pinpoint their core wounds in the span of a few heartbeats. It's how he picks his targets. They make perfect art pieces because of how much weight they carry on their backs.

If I ruin Mercy before Kane has a chance to paint her, I destroy his only outlet for all of the feelings he can't contain within his body. They'll spill over, and we'll backslide into even worse habits at a breakneck pace. It'll break him from the inside out.

But watching him obsess over this girl is breaking *me*.

I thought I could lessen the blow by taking away the pieces of her that appeal to Kane the most. All of the shiny new experiences she has yet to have call to him like the sweetest song. I could claim them one by one until there aren't any left for him. Then, he'll realize that she's nothing special, and we can move on with our lives.

I'd thought that Sam would have handled the physical parts by now, but it seems like lover boy has dropped the ball. He's moving so slowly that he's inadvertently making room for Kane to steal Mercy's firsts.

"Shhh." Tightening the headlock, I wait for her body to slump. As soon as she's unconscious, I lie on my back on the grass and stare up at the darkening night sky. The closer we move to winter, the shorter the days are, and tonight feels especially dark. I catch my breath and ignore the aches in my body, but a light breeze flutters the ends of Mercy's hair across my arm, and her head suddenly lolls onto my bicep. I stare at her smudged lipstick, then the gentle slope of her nose, the thick scratch of brows over her eyes, the bright red scrape along her hairline.

I hate how goddamn pretty she is.

I hate how inadequate she makes me feel.

I hate how I curl my body into hers and weep for all the things I can't control.

The ghost of her breath tickling my cheek.

The curl of her fingers in my shirt.

The way she doesn't leave even though she should.

KANE

THE FACE that walks through the door of Lucio's Italiano isn't the one I'm expecting. Either one of them.

It's Samson fucking Wright, the frat boy with a pretty mouth and a whole lot of daddy's money burning a hole in his pocket, according to Zane. His eyes scan the room until they snag on mine, the scowl on his face downright *mean* as he ignores the Maitre d' and takes the seat directly across the table from me.

"Sam." His name sounds foreign on my tongue, but it's such a boring name that I doubt many people have to suffer it.

"Where's Mercy?"

I sip my drink with an air of nonchalance. Truthfully, I'm wondering the same thing. Zane should have been here by now. It's not like him to detour—that's *my* thing.

"Avoiding this happy reunion, if I had to guess." I signal to our server, and they quickly bring Sam a glass of his own. "You like gin?" Before he can answer, I pour a generous amount over ice and slide it over to him. "You look like you want to kill someone." My smile is genuine. "Can't say I disapprove. Who's the lucky bastard?"

Oh, if looks could kill.

Glee makes my personality louder, and I smack my hand on the edge of the table. "See, that's what I'm talking about. That fire burning in your chest? The need to just—" I mimic stabbing, twisting my waist for the full swing of motion. "Nothing like it."

Sam scoffs, but the way his emerald eyes smolder gives him away. He doesn't disapprove nearly as much as he pretends. "You're insane."

I clink my glass against his. "Makes life more interesting, doesn't it?"

"I don't need interesting." The cut of his jaw is sharp enough to snap glass. "I need to know what you've done with Mercy."

Holding my hands up, I try to show a little good faith. "I haven't done anything, or you'd already know about it. I'm not above sharing home videos with interested parties."

His lip curls, but I think if a video of Mercy sucking me off graced his presence, he'd jerk off like the rest of us degenerates.

"She's on her way here," I say, extending an olive branch. "Zane is bringing her since she didn't want to ride on my bike. Sit down and wait like a good dog."

Despite any misgivings he may have, Sam actually sits. "If you're lying—"

"I'm not."

There he goes with that murderous glint in his eye again. He maintains his composure, though, actually gracing me with a fake smile. "If you or your friend hurt her, we won't have to play this stupid game anymore. That, I can promise." Settling into his chair, he slings his arm over the back and glances at the nearby mirror to check the front door. Mercy and Zane still haven't arrived, and he's right to be antsy.

I'm getting nervous, too.

But I have no reason not to trust Zane. He's always had my back. Yeah, he wanted to kill Mercy that first night, but he wouldn't... Not without me. Then again, something's different this time. I can feel it in the air when he looks at her. There's a crackle of tension that's usually missing when it comes to our targets. Normally, Zane keeps his distance because he doesn't want to get involved with the romantic parts. This time, he's not only bugging her bedroom, but he's fingering her afterward. He's lingering in shared spaces and pretending that he doesn't care.

Something's up with him, but I'm not sure how it involves Mercy.

I'd hoped that the peck on the cheek would prompt him to say something, but I must have shocked him. He looked like a deer caught in headlights, frozen solid and immobile. Unable to think past the blindingly obvious implication.

I don't just want to take Mercy out on a date. I want to take him out, too.

Logistics for these kinds of things don't matter to

me, so it's not like we have to put a label on it. I'm happy so long as we're all happy. Why make things complicated? I swirl the ice in my glass, enjoying the way the cubes clink together. They slowly melt before mixing with the alcohol, and I imagine that Zane and I are much the same way. I have to warm him up, get him comfortable, before he'll melt in my hands.

The past few years have been a kind of slow, agonizing foreplay where no one wins. Not my kink—could be his.

Ignoring his drink, Sam cuts his gaze across the mirror to glare at me. "Seriously, Reaper, where are you hiding her? She wasn't at home, she's not here—are you fucking with me?"

Grabbing his knee under the table, I lean over the short distance between us, unable to keep a wolfish grin off my face. "You'd know if I was fucking with you, Samson, because you'd be on your knees worshipping my cock right now. I can be very persuasive." I glance at his lips, mildly curious. Sometimes the most pent-up ones are worth the explosion. "I've baited more than one man away from their home team."

"Fuck you." He rips my hand off his thigh, rudely knocking my knuckles against the underside of the table and jostling our silverware. "There's no way in hell I'm interested. Back the fuck off."

"Just your girl, then. Got it." Sam doesn't say anything, so I continue. "We could share, you know." I've been toying with the idea over the past few days. Zane and I already get along, so it's a no-brainer with us. Sam is the odd man out. If he wants in on the action, he has to join the winning side, otherwise, he'll end up going home alone. "You might even enjoy it." I study his expression, looking for any sign that he's curious. He sits perfectly still, which could be a tell of its own. He's trying too hard to remain neutral. But then his fingers twitch, and he takes a slow, steady breath, filling his lungs to the brim.

"Don't talk about her like she's—" he laughs, the sound cracking like glass, "like she's one of your whores." Dragging his hand through his chestnut hair, he shuts his eyes. "She's important to me, Reaper, and I—" He swallows. "She deserves so much more than *this.*" Snapping his eyes back open, he gestures between us. "We're sick fucking bastards, aren't we? Fighting over her like children."

My mouth curves up. "Speak for yourself." I can see where he's coming from, but I'm not about to water myself down for Mercy's sake. "She can handle it. I even think she can handle *more.*"

Oh, have I thought about it.

My paintings usually start out tame. Smiles. Flowers. Beachside bikinis and tan lines. The condensation dripping down a forgotten iced coffee. Hands linked together. They're cute little vignettes that tell a story of two people falling in love. These sell, of course, to basic bitches who want their homes to feel warm and inviting.

The *real* art comes later.

With Mercy, however, I've traded simple paintings depicting hand-holding and daisies for impassioned clutching. Wrists. Fingers. Thighs. I've only been able to imagine snippets—nothing overtly sexual—but I know that it's coming. That's usually stage two. The physical intimacy. But we've flipped the script, and I don't know what comes after.

I'm eager to find out.

Sam sits up straight and damn near topples over his chair as Mercy and Zane suddenly appear in the doorway. Zane's arm is slung over her shoulder in a show of confidence that's unlike him, but then I realize why. He's limping and trying to play it off.

What's more, she's *helping* him.

They approach our table and do a good job of pretending everything is normal. Despite the low lighting, I can see the scrapes and bruises on Mercy's skin, a few of them mirrored on Zane's. They got into a tussle and didn't think to forewarn either me or Sam before showing up.

Grabbing Mercy's wrist, Sam stops her from sliding into our oversized booth. His eyes bore into hers, and she shakes her head. But that doesn't stop him from grazing the back of his hand over the bump on her forehead or kissing the scrape across her knuckles. "I tried to pick you up."

"I know." Her mouth twists. "I heard you." She sighs but doesn't explain any further. "I need a drink."

Taking Mercy's other hand, I gently tug her into the booth, wrapping my arm around her waist to pull her the rest of the way in. Nestling her against my side, I hold my glass of gin up to her lips. As she greedily gulps the clear liquid, I admire the drop that breaks free and slides down her chin. With a groan, I move the glass out of the way and claim the droplet for myself, licking its trail back up to her lips.

Sam kicks my shin under the table, and I flick my gaze over to him, smirking as I kiss the corner of Mercy's lips. "Someone's jealous," I rumble, chuckling from the depths of my soul. I love a jealous bastard, even if it *is* Sam. Grasping Mercy's chin, I turn her face directly towards him as I kiss a path down to her neck. "Show him how good it feels." I thumb her pulse point as I kiss a tender spot on her neck, and she gasps appropriately, suddenly clutching my thigh with her kitten claws. Her nails scratch the fabric, leaving little room for imagining how it would feel against my skin, and I am *living* for it.

Exhaling across her neck, I murmur in her ear. "Good girl."

By the time I sit back up and pour myself another glass, I realize that it isn't only Sam who's fuming at the sudden PDA—Zane is, too, only he's handling it better.

"Relax, boys," I chuckle. "There's more than enough of us to go around."

Mercy's warm eyes widen. "You want to…" She trips over the word *share*, so I let go of her waist to grab Zane's shirt. I tug, delighted when he fails to catch himself and quite literally slams into her other side. In all of two seconds, we've boxed Mercy between us, and lover boy across the table is *livid*.

"Get your hands off of her," Sam hisses, slamming the heel of his shoe into my toes. He grinds down as hard as he's grinding his teeth. "Or I will fucking *kill* you."

I lift my hands so that they aren't touching Mercy. "Alright, alright, let's play nice." Sliding a hand over the nape of Zane's neck, I play with the ends of his hair and keep my drink in my other hand. "Satisfied, pretty boy?"

Zane stiffens again, but I work some of the tension out by deliberately kneading his muscles. Man's tense as shit. He needs to fucking relax.

We *all* need to relax.

I snap my fingers and call the server over. "Another round for my friends. Mercy, baby, what do you want?" She orders a red wine while Zane chokes out a *vodka tonic*—fucking disgusting—and Sam gets a goddamn soda. I roll my fucking eyes. "Live a little, *shit*."

He crosses his arms over his chest, inadvertently showing off how tightly the fabric cling to his body. Yeah, the guy's a linebacker, alright. Yummy. It's no wonder Mercy likes him, because it sure as shit ain't for his personality. "One of us should stay sober."

"Couldn't be me." I take a hearty gulp of my gin. Weirdest fucking dinner date ever, but I kind of dig it.

Mercy's quiet as a mouse, having some kind of tele-pathic conversation with Sam from across the table. They stare at each other without blinking, and then she tilts her head towards Zane. "I kicked him in the face, so we're even."

"You *missed*," Zane snorts, finally contributing to the group convo. "The only reason you got so banged up is because you fucking *bit* me."

I snicker into my glass. "Kinky."

Elbowing my ribs, Mercy huffs. "Don't turn every-thing sexual!"

"Like there's more to him than his dick." The insult arrives faster than I expect, the malice in Sam's eyes making it hurt.

Frowning, I lift my middle finger off my glass to point it at him. "Fuck you, Wright. There's plenty more to me than my dick."

Our drinks arrive, and we place our food order. Silence falls over the table, and Mercy's the one who breaks it with a tinkling little laugh that soothes some of the tension brewing between the four of us. "If I'd known that asking you three on a date would be this bad, I never would have suggested it!"

"Why *did* you suggest it?" Zane leans into my touch, and I eat that shit up, idly scratching his scalp. "And don't say some bullshit about 'getting to know us' better."

"But it's true!" She wiggles like she's trying to get some room but quickly gives up once it's clear that neither Zane or I are moving. "Guys, can I have some space?"

"No," we answer simultaneously. I meet Zane's eyes and smile at how they soften just enough for me to know that he's actually going to be okay. That silent brooding shit gets old fast. But then I notice his shirt—some kind of billowy pillowcase thing I've never seen before—and laugh in his face. "Ha! What the fuck are you wearing?"

He blushes, a bright stripe of pink across his cheek-bones. "I didn't plan on going out! I had to improvise!"

Mercy links her arm through his and leans away from me to smile sweetly at him. "I think he looks dashing."

This time, Sam and I exchange looks. What the *fuck* did we miss with these two?

"If I knew you liked it rough, sweetheart, we could have traded blows days ago." Cheekily, I press my tongue into the pocket of my cheek until she gets the reference. "But there's still time. My lap's open."

Sam looks between the three of us like he can't believe this is happening. I'm likely to agree. Shit's wild. Didn't expect this in my wildest dreams.

But.

It makes the prospect of sharing even sweeter.

"I have a proposal," I announce. Our food arrives in record time, cutting me off and making me wait while Mercy asks for red pepper flakes, Sam requests a steak knife for his chicken parm, and Zane gets another drink. While Mercy waits for no man before tucking into her pasta, I mull over how to phrase my idea... before deciding, *fuck it.*

"We should pop Mercy's cherry together."

Mercy herself moans, the sound going straight through my body from my heart to my balls. They draw up instinctively, and I spread my thighs for even the slightest relief. My dick's on standby for another one of those.

She flushes the prettiest shade of deep red, matching the smudge of lipstick just below her bottom lip. "I, um, that wasn't—it's so good!" Her hand shakes as she lowers her fork.

To my complete surprise, Zane takes her fork from her and spears a penne noodle on the tip before lifting it to her lips. "Blow," he instructs, staring just as intently as I am as Mercy obeys, puckering her lips and blowing gently.

A choked sound catches in Sam's throat, and the three of us watch as she wraps her lips around her fork and pulls, closing her eyes the second the flavor hits her tongue. "Mmm." She swallows and licks her lips. "I've never tried this before. It's really good!"

"Neither have I, but I'm *really* enjoying it."

Sam clenches his eyes shut and tilts his head down like he's in prayer, but I'm not sure if he's thanking God for this moment or condemning the devil for tempting him with it. His arm muscles twitch, and I have zero doubt that he's just as turned on as I am.

"Mercy, baby..." Sam trails off, swallowing hard. "Did you hear what Reaper just said?"

"That he's enjoying his food?"

My plate sits untouched in front of me.

"No, gorgeous." I wipe off the sauce clinging to her lip with my thumb. "I want to share you. With them." I nod towards each man, knowing that they're both unsure about it, but I think it's a great fucking idea. I'd rather we share her now than strangle each other—or her—when we don't get our way. None of us is getting our ideal scenario, but that doesn't have to be a bad thing.

It could be fucking beautiful.

Her forehead crinkles. "Like, take turns or something? Create a schedule for dates?"

Shaking my head, I press my lips to her ear. "I want to share your body with them, Siren." I slip my hand between her thighs and spread them apart, gently teasing her soft skin. "If you're really good, we won't make you wait." Someone grabs her knee and widens her stance, and within seconds, my knuckles brush another man's. I'm not sure if it's Zane or Sam, but frankly, I don't care either way. My cock throbs with need, and I move Mercy's hand off the table so that she can feel how eager I am. I cup her palm over my length and groan.

Her eyes widen as I rub her hand over my crotch, but then her breath catches and she sinks into the seat, grabbing my cock with a whimper.

Someone's helping make my point.

"I—I don't know," she murmurs, barely able to catch her breath. "What's in it for me?" Her eyes flutter, and she pinches her plump bottom lip between her teeth. "*Ooh.*"

I arch my neck to peek into her lap. Her dress has shimmied up her thighs, and Zane's rubbing her clit over her panties. Two more hands grip her knees tightly, forcing them open. Sam's staring her down hard, the clench of his jaw making *mine* ache.

"Look at me, Mercy," he rasps, his Adam's apple bobbing on a swallow. "You don't have to do this." He's practically begging, but without any real heat to it. It's not convincing in the slightest. "We can go home right now. You and me. I'll—" His voice catches. "I'll do whatever you want, Mercy, just say no." Softer, he adds, "Tell me that you don't want them over me. Please."

She stops rubbing my dick, and I nearly weep right alongside Sad Boy Sam.

"I want you to kiss me."

My eyes meet Zane's, and we both look up to find her staring directly at Sam. A wave of confidence washes over him, painting over the stupid puppy dog look, and he quickly stands. "Of course, baby, let's go—"

"No," Mercy interrupts, smiling sweetly. "I want you to kiss me here." She taps her lips. "And here." Her neck. She trails her fingertips over her breasts before sliding them into her lap. "And *here.*" Patting the table like she's waiting for one of us to move, she turns her smile on the rest of us. "So who's getting on their knees, gentlemen?"

CHAPTER 17

MERCY

MAYBE IT'S the way that Sam barely hesitates, maintaining eye contact as he drops to one knee, then the other, lifting the tablecloth before disappearing underneath.

Or it could be how Zane pulls my leg over his thigh and tips my head to the side, giving him unfettered access to every inch of my neck.

Better yet, it could be how Kane grazes his knuckles down the side of my cheek before slipping his fingers into my hair. He pulls the thick curtain off my shoulder just as Zane descends, his lips brushing over my skin. Heat spreads like wildfire everywhere these men touch me, growing hotter as Sam kisses each of my knees before settling between my thighs, easily reaching up and hooking his fingers inside the waistband of my panties.

"Lift your hips," Kane murmurs, pressing a gentle kiss to the shell of my ear, "so he can take those off, pretty girl."

Biting my lip, I lift my ass the barest inch off the seat, and off my panties go, lost somewhere in the shadows beneath the table. Sam squeezes my inner thigh before his warm breath ghosts across my center. As he pulls my folds apart, he curses under his breath and nudges my clit with the tip of his nose, murmuring something that I have no hope of hearing.

Any number of these actions could be the reason for my inevitable downfall, but it's when the three men work in tandem that I realize how silly trying to separate them into parts is.

The whole is *so much sweeter.*

Any embarrassment at being kissed *down there* quickly dissolves into a puddle of pure want.

As Sam buries his face in my pussy and licks a wet stripe along the seam, Zane latches onto the side of my neck, panting as he grabs my hand and sets it over his crotch, going further than Kane did earlier and thrusting into my palm. The sound that leaves my throat is half-whimper, half-moan, and Kane grins like a madman as he swallows it, hungry and impatient for every single note that tries to escape past my lips.

Stimulated from all sides and overwhelmed by the sudden onslaught of pleasure, tension, and *need*, I let all three men take what they want from my body. In the end, I made the suggestion, but they're the ones that run with it—refusing to come up for air even if it means drowning. Kane's groans rumbles in his chest, but it does little to drown out the smack of our lips or Zane's heavy panting in my ear. The worst offender by far, however, is Sam.

Every time he flattens his tongue over my clit, I squirm against his hot mouth and he moans, very quickly adjusting his strategy and cupping my ass and pull me to the very edge of the seat. A few more inches of my body disappears under the table, and I yelp as I bang my knee. Someone's hand—Zane's, I think—rubs the impending bruise before lowering my leg back down to the floor. The rubber sole of my boot screeches across the tile as my leg spasms.

"Relax, Kitten," Zane breathes, rubbing circles into the small of my back. "Or you'll get us kicked out."

Kane smiles against my lips, pulling away just long enough to tease. "Don't be so obvious."

Our server appears shortly thereafter, and I hide my face in Kane's chest. He runs his fingers through my hair and assures them that we're fine, our other guest took a business call outside, and we don't need any refills at the moment. Sam slows his pace while we have company, but his mouth never leaves my pussy, licking into my core with slow reverence that makes me tremble from head to toe.

As soon as our server's gone, I reach blindly under the table to find him. "S-Sam," I stutter, catching my breath as he presses a quick kiss to my palm before suddenly diving back in, scraping my clit with his teeth. My fingers wind in his hair as I see stars. A tremor courses through my body, and I clench my eyes shut against the full-bodied moan that threatens to break free. I can't—I *can't*—

I crack open my eyes to find Zane staring back at me. A thin layer of sweat forms where his forehead meets his hairline, and his cheeks are flushed nearly as much as mine. "Such an eager kitten," he rasps, smirking, "desperate to come all over your best friend's face."

A needy whine passes my lips. The sound is muffled in Kane's shirt, but I can feel him laugh, the vibration in his chest seeping into mine.

Zane's right. I'm a dirty little virgin, after all, asking three men to kiss me in public. Letting one of them eat me out under the table while the other two are forced to sit and listen as my pussy gets wetter and wetter. I pant as the pressure builds, clinging to whoever is holding my hand, scraping Sam's scalp with my nails, unable to stop the cry tearing from my throat as my pussy spasms. Kane smothers my face in his chest while Sam laps up my release, eventually lowering my dress over my thighs and reappearing at the other end of the table, the lower half of his face glistening.

He licks his lips and carefully wipes his mouth on his shirtsleeves, taking a deep breath as his eyes burn with lust. "Any other special requests?"

I pick my head up and straighten my posture, swallowing a mouthful of wine before I can summon my voice. Within seconds, all four of us have gone back to eating and drinking like nothing happened. Shame burns inside my chest as Sam stares at me, still waiting for an answer. I can't tell if he's upset with me or not.

He practically begged me to decline Kane's suggestion of sharing, and instead, I demanded it. It's one thing to ask Sam to kiss me—we've been down that road before. But it's another thing to ask that of Zane, who explicitly denies having any interest in me. Yet when the opportunity arose, Zane chose to participate just like the others.

For a long time, Sam was the only person vying for my attention, but now, there are more players on the board. I know that I could ask Sam for anything and he would give it to me. But part of the thrill of having Kane and Zane's attention is that I never know exactly which version of them I'm getting.

Salty or sweet. Bitter or broken. Love or hate.

Sam feels safe. Kane and Zane don't.

"No, that's—I'm fine, thank you."

We spend the rest of our meal in silence, but I catch Kane adjusting his dick more than once, Sam glowering at his plate instead of eating it, and Zane sitting as far away from me as possible, leaving enough room between us for an entire person to fit.

Unable to stand the tension, I set down my silverware and push my plate away. "Did I do something wrong?" I look between the three of them and cross my arms over my chest. "*You're* brooding." I gesture across the table to Sam. "You're back to extremes." I glare at Zane, unable to keep my annoyance under wraps for him in particular. "If anyone has a complaint to file against someone," I huff, "it's me! You tackled me down the fucking stairs!"

Flinching, Sam turns his ire onto Zane. "You *what?*"

He stands from his seat and reaches for something behind his back, but Kane beats him to it, pulling a gun from God knows where and pointing it directly at Sam's head.

"Sit down," Kane rumbles, smiling maliciously. "I have a dozen reasons to shoot you, Samson Wright, and I'll gladly pull the trigger for any one of them."

I gape at Kane and reach for his gun. "You'll do no such thing!" I grab the barrel, but I'm no match for Kane's strength. I can't move it a single inch. "Stop it!"

"Tell your boyfriend to keep his gun behind his back, Mercy, or his brains are gonna splatter all over your pretty dress." Kane slips his finger beneath the strap of my dress and tugs it down. "I'd hate for him to ruin our evening because he can't keep it in his pants."

"Kane!" I smack his hand away. "Knock it off!"

"It's okay," Zane interjects, throwing his napkin onto the table. "I'll leave." He looks between me and Kane, his gaze lingering on where our shoulders touch. "It's not like I have anything to gain from staying."

Groaning in frustration, I scoot out of the booth after Zane. "Why are you all so fucking complicated? Zane, wait!"

Sam grabs my wrist before I can leave. "Don't follow him, Mercy." His eyes turn steely as he scans my body, taking in the tiny bruises and scrapes from my scuffle with Zane in my front yard. "He hurt you. A man like that doesn't deserve you."

I pull my arm free from his grasp. "I'm not some prize for you to win, Sam, and you can't make me want you. We're *friends*," I reiterate, hating how hard he flinches. "Maybe we should leave it at that."

Kane whistles, and I flick him off. "Stay out of this, Reaper."

He pushes the table back, spilling our drinks as he makes room for himself to stand. "No, no, Siren. I told you to call me Kane." The gun is still in his hand, but at least with Zane gone, he's not aiming it at Sam. "*Kane*," he emphasizes, stepping around the table and pulling me into his arms. The barrel of the gun presses against my temple and he grins at the sight. "You're going to scream it when I'm balls fucking deep inside that sweet pussy of yours, beautiful." Dragging the gun down the side of my face, he taps it against my lips. "Kiss it, and I'll forgive you."

"You're a fucking psycho."

"I'm crazy about you."

The *click* of a bullet loading into the chamber makes my heartbeat stutter. But Kane hasn't moved—it's Sam, his gun suddenly buried beneath Kane's chin. "Move the gun," Sam orders calmly, "and you can keep your head."

"How generous of you." Just when I think he's going to listen, Kane pushes harder, knocking the metal against my teeth. "Kiss it, Mercy," he rasps, his head tilting back from the pressure of Sam's gun. He stares at me down the bridge of his nose. "Or your boyfriend's going to die. Zane will drag you from his arms and force you to watch as he buries a dozen bullets into his body— *after* he skins him alive." Smiling, Kane chuckles darkly. "People think that I'm the scary one, but Zane... He doesn't give a fuck how badly it hurts. I'm merciful compared to him."

Police sirens sound in the distance, and I quickly kiss the tip of Kane's gun to end this idiotic stalemate once and for all. He grins, putting his weapon away and backing off. "See? Was that so hard?"

The loud *crack* of Sam pistol-whipping Kane in the face makes me scream. Before I can process what's happening, Sam's suddenly kneeing Kane in the gut and dragging me out of the restaurant.

Kane's maniacal laughter follows us out the door. "Keep her warm for me, Sam."

We've barely made it a few steps out of the restaurant before Sam pulls me into an alley and pins me against a brick wall. His chest heaves with each breath he takes as he buries his face in my neck. Trembling, he puts the gun in my hands and squeezes my fingers around the handle. "I need you to promise me something," he rasps, digging the barrel into his gut. I try to pull it back, but just like with Kane, I'm outmatched when it comes to strength.

"Sam, don't—"

"Promise me that if I ever—" His voice cracks. "If I ever hurt you, Mercy—"

"You won't!"

"Promise that you'll kill me." His body trembles as he drags in a shallow breath. "*Please.* I can't—I can't live with knowing that I've hurt you."

The answer is so simple that I'm astounded Sam doesn't see it. "Then don't hurt me." I grab the back of his neck and pull him in for a hug, the gun wedging painfully between us. I keep my fingers off the trigger, but alarms ring at how close he is to pulling it himself. "Okay? It's that easy."

"It's *not.*" He sighs into my hair. "Just promise me."

If it gets him to move the gun, then I don't have a choice. "I promise."

"Say the whole thing."

Sighing, I repeat the entire phrase. "If you hurt me, I promise that I'll kill you. But you won't hurt me, Sam. I trust you."

He exhales harshly and drags his mouth across my ear. "I'm good enough to eat your pussy, but not good enough for anything else, is that it?"

Anger and frustration boil in my blood. I dig the gun deeper into Sam's stomach, knowing it has to hurt, but being *so fucking tired* of this bullshit. "I thought you were okay with being friends!"

"I thought so too!"

Our voices echo against the bricks, drowned out by the police cars screeching to a halt by the curb. Sam lifts me up off the ground and carries me deeper into the alley, then through a parking lot until we get to his pickup truck. He opens the passenger door one-handed and sets me down on the seat before sprinting to the driver's side. The gun's disappeared from sight, but I have no illusions that it's gone for good.

He starts the car and drives off, speeding down the road and weaving through traffic. "I thought I was okay with being friends." Running a hand through his hair, he chuffs. "Until I saw the way he looks at you."

I watch as conflicted emotions cross Sam's face, each one more tortured than the last. "I don't want him to have you, because *I* want you. I thought I could take things slow and give you the kind of dating experience you deserve, but—" He grips the steering wheel tightly. "We don't have that kind of time. Now he wants to *share* you."

My body ignites at the mere mention of being shared, and I press my thighs together. "You seemed like you had fun."

Sam clenches his jaw. "Yeah. You did too."

We cross half of the city in silence. It gives me time to think, but I don't trust the thoughts running through my head. Kane's mouth was greedy and insistent, but so was Sam's. Zane's was—

Complicated.

I woke up on my driveway to the sound of him crying. Felt his tears on my chest and witnessed the cracks in his heart. The man is bleeding for his best friend, and I don't think Kane realizes how bad it is.

"You'd tell me..." My voice carries like a whisper on the wind, so soft that I can barely hear it. "You'd tell me if I hurt you, right?"

Sam's answer is immediate, his eyes locked firmly onto the road ahead. "Of course."

For the first time since I met Sam, I'm not sure that I believe him.

CHAPTER 18

SAM

THAT NIGHT, I fix the locks on Mercy's bedroom door, changing out her doorknob and adding three sliding locks—two across the top and one at the bottom. "You have to use them," I tell her, glancing at her for the thousandth time since we arrived. She's been sitting at her desk for the past hour, either staring outside her window or at that drawing of her and Zane in her sketchbook.

Every time I see the drawing, a cord of anger tightens inside my chest.

Setting my tools down, I cross to Mercy's chair and grip the backrest. "Why did you draw that?" The man—dark hair, lean build, clearly not me or Reaper—mocks me with the level of intimacy displayed on the page.

Mercy's legs are pulled up in front of her, squished between her torso and her desk. She taps a dull pencil against her knee. "I didn't."

I grab the sketchbook from over Mercy's shoulder and tear the drawing out, the harsh *riiiiip* satisfying a lesser demon throwing a tantrum inside my heart. Crumpling it in my hand, I toss it outside the open bedroom window, wishing it would crash into the earth and shatter, but it merely floats down to the dewy grass and gently tumbles another foot before rolling to a stop.

Mercy snatches the sketchbook from my hands and snaps it closed. "Don't touch my stuff."

I scoff aloud. "What, are you upset? I fixed it." Something ugly scratches inside my chest, clawing to get out. "I'll fix everything, Mercy." On the drive home from Lucio's, I came up with a plan to leave the city. It would take a few weeks to set everything up, but I could have fake IDs and a safe house set up for us. Mercy would be my wife, the two of us fresh off our honeymoon and looking for a new start in another town—another life— while Grey gets rid of both Kane and Zane for good.

I don't need to see their dossiers to know that they're better off six feet under, where they won't have a chance in hell of dragging her down with them.

If I'm being honest, I don't even need Mercy's permission. I'd *like* it, obviously, which is why I have to be delicate about how I propose the idea to her. She can't think that we're running away for good, or she'll never agree to it. Her family means too much to her.

Spinning her chair around, I meet the flare of indignancy in her auburn eyes, and my proposal for a two-week getaway vacation dies on my lips. "Why are you—"

So stubborn!

"—mad at me?"

She huffs. "Because it's like—" The frantic *tap tap*

tap of her pencil on her knee makes my eye twitch. "It's like I don't even know you, Sam." Her jaw clenches as she looks me up and down. "I didn't even know you *had* a gun."

"I didn't until yesterday." Wincing, I admit, "Well, okay, my dad gave me one for my birthday once, but I don't ever use it. I specifically brought one to dinner last night because I don't trust them. And clearly, I was right!" The memory of Mercy with a gun pressed to her lips nearly tips me over the edge from *moderately calm* to *I'm going to shoot that fucker.* "Kane's a fucking psycho, Mercy. I tried to tell you that, but you wouldn't listen."

"So this is my fault?" She shoves my arm. "Poor little Mercy Morningstar, so desperate for attention that the only men she pulls are murderers and psychos!" She lifts her chin. "So what does that make you, Samson Wright? A murderer or a psycho?"

"Neither," I insist, planting my hands on her knees. "I'm the only one who's good for you. You *have* to see that by now."

She laughs, the sound catching in her throat like a bitter pill. "God, it's like you're trying to convince yourself. Wake up, Sam!" Her smile turns cruel, the corners of her eyes watering. "No one's good for me."

I stop her from spinning her chair back around. "You don't honestly believe that." A silent tear falls down her cheek, and I gently brush it away. "You're not destined to be alone, Mercy."

"Everyone ends up alone." She blinks through a wave of tears, barely holding them back. "I've seen thousands of people come through the funeral home, Sam, and every one of them walks away emptier than before. Being alone is our default. We're the ones fighting against it when we shack up with other people. Make friends. Take lovers." A broken laugh spills past her lips. "Not that I have either."

I've seen her talk this way before when her depression gets bad. It's usually seasonal, but we should be coming out of it instead of driving into the dark. "Have you been taking your meds?"

She purses her lips.

That would be a no.

Sighing, I reach around her to open her desk drawer. "You shouldn't skip them—"

"Like you care."

"I *do* care, Mercy. I want you to feel better."

The pill bottle is half full. By now, she can take them dry, but it still sucks. "Let me get you a glass of water."

"I'm not taking them."

I swallow my sigh this time. "You're not thinking clearly, Mercy." No wonder she's been letting those two darken her doorstep. It's all that she thinks she deserves. "You need to take them." I place two in her hand and curl her fingers over them. I guess the water's a no-go. "Please. For me."

Glaring, she unravels her fist to stare at the two little white pills. They practically glow in the moonlight. "It doesn't change anything. I'm still The Dead Girl. I might as well *be* dead."

Panic mixes with dread. I can't let Mercy out of my

sight if she's talking like this. As much as I hate to admit it, maybe having Kane and Zane stalk her is a good thing if it keeps her breathing. "If you die, Mercy, then take me with you." It's not what I should say, but it's the most honest thing I have right now. "Because I don't want to know what life is like without you."

She avoids my eyes. "You don't mean that."

"I do." Slipping my hand into hers, I lace our fingers together, the pills pressed tightly between our palms. "So don't make me find out." Gently, I turn her face towards mine. "I love you, Mercy. No matter what you think about yourself, know that I think the world of you."

Bathed in moonlight, Mercy always takes my breath away. It doesn't matter the time of year or what she's wearing—she was born for the night, and even the most shadowed parts of her don't scare me away.

Finally, she relents, slipping her hand from mine to pinch the pills between her fingers. She offers one to me, pushing it past the seam of my lips, before slipping the other into her mouth. As she swallows, I slide my fingers into her hair and slant my lips over hers, gently licking into her mouth. The pill she gave me passes between us. "Swallow." I cup her throat, unable to stop a full-bodied shudder as she obeys, swallowing like a good fucking girl. Sighing against her lips, I kiss her as gently as I can. This is all I've wanted. Tender moments with the girl I never want to live without.

Her arms wind around my neck, and she deepens our kiss. My heart seizes inside my chest, begging me for more, and I greedily oblige. Lifting her into my arms, I carry Mercy to her bed and lay her down. She stretches her arms over her head and parts her lips, the tears catching on her lashes shimmering like diamonds.

I don't ask her what she wants, fearing that she'll tell me *no*.

Instead, I pop open the front of my shirt and tear it off my body.

She does the same with her dress, tugging it over her hips, then her breasts, lifting it over her head before tossing it to the floor. Her pussy glistens in the soft, silvery glow of the moon, the bundle of curls framing her entrance still damp from earlier.

My cock stands at full mast and I groan at the memory of her taste bursting on my tongue, sweet and succulent and *filthy*. She may not realize it, but she rocked her hips all over my face when she came, her innocence quickly fading as she chased her release.

Stepping over the friendship line is something I've yearned for, and now that it's close, I'm desperate. My need for this woman soars, and I undress in record time, kicking off my shoes and shucking my pants, carefully tucking the gun away beneath them. When all that's left are my boxers, I catch her eyes as I pull them down. "You can tell me to stop."

Please don't.

I watch for the subtlest shake of her head. An aversion of her gaze. A flicker of doubt. When none arrive, I climb onto her rickety bed and wind my fingers in the waves of her hair, sealing my lips over hers. I groan into her mouth as she reciprocates, kissing me like she used to.

Back then, she was nervous but eager, the two of us stopping because she didn't want to ruin our friendship.

Tonight is a different story. She lifts her legs to trap me between them, eagerly locking her ankles around my waist. Our hips align like they were made for each other, my cock nestling against her curls as she drags her pussy over my length, a needy whine catching in her throat. If she's not careful—

I clench my entire body to keep from moving as the tip slips inside her sticky sweet center. Mercy tries to angle her hips to go deeper, but I fight against her vice grip. Every vein in my body threatens to burst from how hard my heart is pumping, spurring me on, begging me to claim her before any other man has the chance.

But I have to be sure that she wants this with me. That she won't wake up tomorrow full of aches and pains and... regrets.

Dragging in a lungful of air, I taste her lavender spray on my tongue and know exactly where we are—in my favorite dream and my worst nightmare. "Mercy." I grab her hip to keep her from grinding against me. She's *so* close to sliding right in, her pussy soaking wet and ready. So fucking ready. "Please be sure." I bury my face in her hair and pray that she is. "I won't—I can't go back after this." Kissing her neck, I borrow time, shaking like a leaf and just as fragile. My muscles scream at me to give in, to let loose and plunge my entire being into this woman. But with Mercy, nothing is ever simple. It's not just my body that I'm giving her—it's my heart, too.

I need her to understand that.

Her voice is softer than her skin. "Don't you love me?"

Holding my breath, I push up onto my elbows and stare into her eyes. "I do." But something isn't right. The tears from earlier are back, freely falling down the sides of her cheeks.

"Then you can have it." She hastily wipes away her tears. "If you love me, Sam, you can have it. I won't mind. I want you to have it."

I press our foreheads together and cup her cheek, unable to look away from the agony painted on her face. "Then why are you crying?"

"I don't—I don't know." A sob catches in her chest, and she slams her eyes shut. "Just do it, okay? Please." Grabbing my shoulders, she tries to force me inside of her, using all of her body weight to drag me down. "Please, Sam."

Fuck.

I want her more than anything, but not like this.

"I can't, baby," I whisper, breaking my own heart as I kiss the tip of her nose, the swell of her cheek, her trembling bottom lip. "Fuck, I want to." Indulging the fantasy, I slide an inch inside of her molten core, gritting my teeth against the needy sound she makes as she clings to me, trying to make it a reality. I pull out and collapse on top of her, pinning her body to the mattress so that she can't move. "But I can't risk you hating me for it."

When I make love to Mercy, I want her to love me back.

"Kane would do it!" Her voice cracks like a whip,

striking where it hurts. "He wouldn't be such a fucking pussy about it!" She smacks her fists against my back, taking out her frustration on me. "He wants me more than you do!"

Pain lances through my heart. "That's not true." Grabbing her face, I kiss her hard, feeding into her frustration. Being with her shouldn't feel this way. It shouldn't hurt. "You know that's not true," I growl, breaking the kiss to glare at her. Rosy cheeks. Swollen lips. Teary eyes. None of this is right.

I roll off of her and stand, my frustration skyrocketing. This is all Reaper's fault. He's confusing her. Twisting things in her head. I run my fingers through my hair and pull the ends, knowing that all of my problems go back to that fucking guy. I need to get rid of him. Grabbing my clothes, I get dressed as quickly as possible.

"Where are you going?"

Flinching, I keep my gaze on the floor. "I have to take care of something."

"But you won't take care of me?" The accusation in her voice stings.

"Mercy—" I freeze the minute I turn around, unable to tear my gaze off of her body. The flush trailing down her neck makes me salivate, but it's her hands that do me in. She covers her pussy with her fingers, slowly dipping them inside. Precum weeps from the tip of my cock, and I have to force myself to look away.

In the next instant, Mercy is standing directly in front of me. "Why can't you look?" Shoving me, she bares her teeth, clearly hurting and putting up a front.

She's like a wounded animal trying to fight against whatever is causing her pain.

I guess she thinks that's me.

"Am I so unattractive that you'll only fuck me if you can't see me?"

My restraint snaps into pieces. "Shut the *fuck* up." Spinning us around, I slam her against the wall. I know that she's hurting. I know that she's lashing out. I know that it isn't her fault. But *damnit*, does it piss me off. "Stop questioning my intentions!" Pinning her hand beside her head, I force her fist open so that I can interlock our fingers. "I will *make love* to you, Mercy Morningstar, when you're ready to accept that I want more from you than sex."

I've told her that I love her, but I don't think she understands what that means. I'm not saying it to get in her pants. I'm saying it because I mean it.

"What I won't do is fuck you because you think that's all anyone wants from you. I want so much more than your body, Mercy." I press my palm flat against her chest and feel her hammering heartbeat. "But if you can't give me anything else right now—" I slip my hand between her thighs and bury my fingers inside her pussy, hating how the beauty of the moment is ruined by that *fucking* drawing of her and Zane. I grit my teeth as I grind her clit against my palm, desperately hoping to replace that *stupid fucking image* with this one. "—I'll manage."

Mercy cries out with pleasure, greedily rocking her hips as I finger her. Tearing at my shoulders, dragging her nails against my scalp—it's almost everything I wanted, but without the satisfaction of knowing that *I'm* the one who turned her into a rabid animal. She could be thinking of Zane right now, pretending that he's the one making her come. Or Reaper, even—she keeps bringing him up. There has to be a reason.

Dropping to my knees, I hook her calf over my shoulder and bury my face in her pussy, groaning as she gushes, filling my mouth with her desire. I lick every inch of her and slip my fingers past her entrance to go even deeper. She bucks, gasping, and I don't let up, quickly finding the rough patch of flesh and curling my fingers, driving her wild. She claws at my hair and grinds on my face.

"*Ah, ah, ah!*"

Music to my goddamn ears.

I'm drowning in her desire, and it's exactly where I want to be.

Well, close enough.

My cock leaks like I'm getting paid by the ounce. I groan as I grab my shaft and pull, needing to fight against the fire burning in my chest. She can't give me everything yet, and I don't want only half of her.

I want it all.

She comes with a feral scream, and I follow her, painting the floor, coating my fist, hating that it's wasted but loving how I grab her ass and rub it into her skin, marking her as mine. Lifting her up, I carry her boneless body back to the bed and lay her down, just like before. Only this time, I steal a greedy kiss while her taste is on my tongue, ensuring that the memory sticks.

The next time she draws someone kissing her, it's going to be me.

When I pull back, she licks her lips, her eyes half-lidded and dazed. "Get some sleep," I murmur, pressing a chaste kiss to her forehead. "I'll call you tomorrow."

She mumbles sleepily, already closing her eyes. "G'night."

I wait until her breathing has slowed to leave. Rather than leave her door unlocked, I climb over her desk and out the window, grunting as my feet slam onto the front porch. The wood creaks, threatening to give way, and I make a mental note to offer to pay for the repairs again. Mr. Morningstar has refused at least three times, but maybe if he knows that I'm dating his daughter, he'll finally relent.

As I stand up, a slow clap echoes around me.

Reaper steps out from the shadows, his grin feral. "Samson Wright, good for something after all. I told you to keep her warm for me, but I didn't expect you to deliver so... *exceptionally.*" A shiver rolls down his spine as he looks up at Mercy's bedroom window. "I could have done without the cum on her ass, but hey, I get it." He steps up and claps my shoulder. "I'll be sure to fill her up extra for you."

Grabbing his arm, I throw him off of me. "Stay the fuck away from her, Reaper."

It's like he enjoys the challenge. He licks a stripe

across his top teeth, his voice rumbling like a wolf's when he speaks. "Why? Because you *love* her?"

How the hell did he hear that?

"I don't usually fuck other people's girlfriends, but for you, I'll make an exception."

Fury roars in my ears, making it hard to see straight. I clutch the handrail and block the path to Mercy's front door. "Over my dead body."

"See," Reaper exclaims, snapping his fingers. "That's the beauty of it. I can kill you *and* fuck your girl. Hell, I can even make you watch as I pop that pretty fucking cherry." He groans, palming the dick imprint on his jeans. He's fucking *massive*, hung like a beast.

It'll tear Mercy to shreds.

"I bet she'll bleed all over my cock."

I grab the gun hidden in the waistband of my pants and aim it at him. "Back the fuck up." Gritting my teeth, I tell myself to do it. Shoot. Get rid of the fucker before he hurts Mercy.

Reaper doesn't back up—he marches forward, slotting the barrel against his neck. He swallows, the bob of his Adam's apple pushing against the metal. "I don't think you have the balls to kill someone, Sam." Shaking his head, he chuckles. "Or else you would have buried a bullet in my gut a long time ago."

The front door creaks behind me, and all of a sudden, something much larger than a pistol presses against my spine.

"Get out of here, boys." The shotgun cocks loudly, making me sweat.

"Mr. Morningstar—"

"I don't want to hear it, Sam," Mercy's father replies calmly, "unless you can explain why my daughter is crying her eyes out."

What? She was sleeping a moment ago—

I try to turn my head, but he digs the barrel harder into my back.

"Go on, both of you. Before I shoot you for trespassing on private property."

Reluctantly, I follow Reaper off the front porch. Both of us glance back up at Mercy's window, her sobbing muffled but audible.

Shit. Is it my fault? Did I hurt her?

All of a sudden, Reaper hooks his arm across my shoulders and drags me up the gravel driveway. His motorcycle sits beside my truck, the two of them as polar opposite as their owners. "I like you, Samson," he says cheerily, taking the gun from my hand while I'm distracted. He unloads the chamber, releases the magazine, and hands it back to me. "I was serious about sharing her."

Every muscle in my body screeches to a halt. I throw him off of me, annoyed when he laughs. "Why the hell do you keep saying that?"

"Because it's true." He kicks the bullet magazine into the bushes before turning back to me. "You saw how she responded at dinner. I think she'd enjoy it. I think *you* would." Shaking his head, he keeps grinning like he's some kind of mastermind. "Live a little. You can have sex without it meaning anything."

"You indulge too much," I counter, frowning. "If it doesn't mean anything, what's the point?"

He looks at me like I'm stupid. "Do I really need to answer that?"

"Actually, yeah." I clench my fists, feeling my resentment towards him rise. "You fuck people like you're aiming for a world record. Your body count is astronomical." I can't even begin to fathom how many people he's slept with. "How can you still enjoy it?"

For a long moment, Reaper doesn't answer. He stares at me like he's seeing me for the first time. "Because it's not about the sex."

I didn't expect him to answer honestly, so I'm at a loss for words.

Sighing, Reaper pinches his lips together and stares up at the moon. "It's not about the sex, Sam. It's about the experience." Something in his gaze softens, and I nearly have a stroke.

Is he opening up?

To *me*?

"I've slept with hundreds of people—"

This isn't making me feel any better about letting him touch Mercy.

"But that gives me hundreds of new experiences." His gaze cuts across the sky to find mine. "How many have you had, Sam?"

I stare dumbly as the man I hate more than anyone smiles at me. Rather than wait for my answer—because it's a rhetorical question—he puts on his helmet and kickstarts his bike, driving off before I have a chance to do anything about it. I spend ten minutes searching for the gun magazine and another ten minutes waiting for Mercy to stop crying. When she finally settles down, I slump against the bed of my truck and slam my fist into the tailgate. The throbbing pain doesn't make me feel any better.

At this point, I don't know what will.

SLEEPLESS NIGHTS AREN'T new for me. After my mom passed away, I would lie awake and pretend she was sitting beside me. Braiding my hair, watching me draw, singing a lullaby—whatever small comforts I gave myself, I attributed to her. It worked for the most part. I could pretend that she wasn't really gone and that everything was still okay.

But tonight, absolutely nothing feels okay.

The ache between my thighs throbs with its own heartbeat, the release Sam inevitably gave me only making my heart hurt even more. It's not what I wanted, merely a cheap imitation. If I'd had my way, he would have taken my virginity—that I finally offered him!—and held me while we slept until daybreak, the two of us wrapped around each other so that we don't have to face our demons alone.

I shut my eyes and cover my ears, but nothing drowns out their screams.

You're so pathetic that even your best friend won't sleep with you. He got you off so that you'd shut up about it.

Reaper's only interested in you because you're a virgin. As soon as you give it up, he'll disappear, just like Sam.

Zane doesn't want you—he's priming you to take Reaper's cock, and then he's going to kill you for taking it so well.

Such a dirty little virgin, letting three men kiss you.

Round and round the thoughts spiral, chewing me up until there's nothing left but dust. I try to stifle my sobs, but even my pillow is worn out, tired of my bullshit. A knock on my door barely registers in my brain, and it takes me a millennium to undo the new latches that Sam installed.

Not like they matter for keeping people out. I might as well lock myself inside.

Once I finally manage to unlock and crack open the door, my father's face appears. Tired, wrinkled, with streaks of gray that didn't used to be there. He brightens upon seeing me. It's been a few days since our paths crossed.

"Hi, Daddy."

"Hi, Pumpkin. Can I come in?"

I clutch the door handle and quickly glance behind me. My room is a mess—it usually is, but after Sam left, I tore up an entire sketchbook and threw the papers around the room. They litter the floor like ash, scattering with every gentle breeze through my open window. "No," I murmur, closing the door another inch. "I'm fine."

"You're not fine." He sighs. "I called your sister. She'll be here in the morning."

"Okay." I scrub my hand down my face and take a breath. Having company keeps the shadows from crawling out of their corners of the room. Lilith will be a welcome distraction. But I can't ask my father to step inside my perpetual den of sadness. It isn't always this gloomy, but tonight, it feels suffocating. Before he can leave, I reach through the crack in the door and grab his hand. "Dad—" I swallow my hesitation. "Um, when you and Mom..." I think of how to phrase my question. "When you fell in love, did you know it wouldn't last?"

My father used to be an upbeat man. He would sing with the songbirds and paint with my mother in the sunroom. They were so, *so* in love that it followed them everywhere, bringing comfort to grieving hearts that wandered in their path. Lately, he's been so buried in work that I haven't seen him smile. I rarely see him at all.

Sometimes I wonder if he could take it all back, would he?

"Are you asking if I regret marrying your mother?"

I shrug. "I don't know. Do you?"

His resounding exhale blows past the streaks of gray in his thick mustache. "Of course not, Pumpkin. Your mother—she was the light of my life. I still love her dearly." He squeezes the tips of my fingers. "But you have your own light, too, you know. All of you kids do. In all different shades." A small smile graces his features, making him appear a few years younger. "I'll never regret a single moment with your mother. I only wish we had more time together..." His voice trails off. "But, that's what makes every moment precious. We can't go back and rewrite the past, so we need to enjoy the present. Your mother brought me so much joy, and she will always mean the world to me. Why would I want to erase that?"

I try to shrink in on myself, suddenly feeling very small. "Because it's so much harder without her."

My dad sighs. "It is harder, yes. But it's because of your mom that I know how to keep going. She made me stronger. She's made you stronger, too."

"I don't know about that."

Sometimes, I feel like I'm drowning.

"I do." He places something in my palm. "You have all the power in the world, Mercy. You can keep going on this path, or you can pick a new direction. It's up to you where you go, and... who you go with."

My nose crinkles. "You saw Sam."

"It was hard to miss him." My dad rubs the back of his neck. "But it's the other one I'm more concerned about. He seems... rough."

Talk about an understatement.

"You don't usually hang out with those kind of boys, Mercy."

"I don't usually hang out with any kinds of boys," I sigh, rubbing my eyes.

"Right... " My dad sighs. "Your grandmother spoke with him before I came around. She seems to like him, despite his... differences." My father has no idea how much he's sugarcoating Kane's personality. "She fed him a cookie, too. You know how she is about her superstitions."

Grandma and those damned cookies. "I wish she wouldn't get involved."

"It's her house, too, Mercy. She's allowed to know who's coming and going. As do I." Dad raps his knuckles on the door frame. "Just be safe, Pumpkin. That's all I ask."

When my older sister Lilith arrives at dawn, we spend an hour staring at the ceiling and listening to music, and then she flutters around my room picking up my drawings and pinning them to the wall with thumbtacks. It's like I'm watching a mirror image of myself—a little older, a little more confident in herself—fixing up my space so that I can become her in a few years' time. We share similar tastes in style, preferring lace spider webs and striped stockings to the typical clothing you'll find in a department store. Our brother does too, actually, but I haven't seen Malachi in years.

I wonder if he's doing any better than me at military school.

By the time Lilith has finished tidying up and pinning things to my wall, charcoal sketches fill an entire section from top to bottom—or at least as high as she could reach. I stare at them for a long time while she sweeps the floor, dusts my empty bookshelf, and gathers my dirty laundry into a basket.

"I'm not usually this pathetic." Lying back on my bare mattress—because she's also washing my bedsheets —I cover my eyes with my forearm. "I haven't been sleeping."

Lilith spritzes my pillow with the lavender spray and hums appreciatively. She's always loved lavender. "Wanna talk about it?"

No. I wouldn't know what to say. I've never had boy problems before. Or, I don't know, played life-or-death games with my pussy.

I start with the simplest topic. "Sam told me he loved me."

My sister sits on the creaking bed beside me. "How does that make you feel?"

I twist my lips, unsure how to answer. "Happy. Sad. Confused." Sighing, I kick my feet against my metal foot-board. "We decided to remain friends a year ago, you know. He kissed me, and I liked it at first. But then I got scared." What if I like Sam a lot, and he breaks up with me? Then I'd have no one. "I didn't want to ruin our friendship."

"Are you still friends?"

"Yeah... maybe a little more than friends." Remembering the greedy way he ate me out makes my body hot all over again. "He wants to have sex with me." I bite my lip. "Even though I want it, I cried before we could... do anything. And then he backed *way* up."

Lilith takes my hand and squeezes. "Sex can be overwhelming when it means change. But change doesn't have to be scary or bad. It can be really, really good."

"I don't need a therapist right now," I grumble, "I need a sister." I smack her with my pillow. "I cried because... because I *want* to want him. He's my best friend. I know he'll take care of me. He *loves* me. If anyone gets my virginity, it *should* be him!"

"...but?"

I cover my face with both of my hands. "There are these other guys." Thankfully, Lilith doesn't comment. "One of them wants to share me." Still, nothing. Some of the tension in my body relaxes, and I peek over at her. She's listening intently, her eyes closed and her lips pursed.

"I'm worried that if I have sex with Sam, that's it, we're a couple. It'll close the other doors."

"But you don't love Sam."

"I *do* love Sam. He's funny and charming and caring. He makes sure I take my meds—" I blush at the memory of his tongue inside my mouth. "And he's always there for me. Of course, I love Sam. But I also..." I take a breath. "I like this other guy. He's different. Crazy and chaotic and powerful. He wants to have sex with me, too, but he doesn't want more than that. For him, it's just sex."

And murder, but I leave that part out.

"I *should* date Sam." If I fall in love with Sam, he and I win this stupid game, and we all walk away with our lives. I should be happy with that.

So why doesn't it feel like it's enough?

The ache in my chest grows when I think of all three men arguing over me. Who gets to kiss me. Who gets to fuck me. Who gets to kill me. A shiver rolls down my spine at how easily they turned on each other. Zane was the only one who didn't seem to care, opting to walk away instead of argue. I haven't figured him out yet, and I'm not sure if I ever will.

If he gets a chance, he might kill me before I have sex with anyone.

"I just don't know what to do," I say finally. "Someone's going to get hurt no matter what."

"This is your life, Mercy," Lilith reminds me, turning on her side to meet my gaze. She taps my forehead. "You make the rules. So what if the other guys want something from you? What do *you* want?"

That's the problem. I don't think I can have everything I want without losing Sam.

"And," she continues, "what are you willing to do to get it?"

CHAPTER 20

ZANE

AFTER WHAT CAN ONLY BE DESCRIBED as a dinner date from hell, where I not only gave into my baser instincts but watched the man I lo—

Like.

Watched the man I *like* make out with the girl who is insufferably frustrating, the only logical next step is to fuck off. I'd buy booze, but then I wouldn't dare drive home. Sleeping on the beach sounds miserable.

But not as miserable as admitting that I'm jealous every time Kane touches Mercy.

Groaning, I lie back on the sand and blow cigarette smoke towards the stars. They twinkle overhead without a care in the world, mocking me for my problems. The older I get, the more I seem to have. Such bullshit.

My phone pings, and I'd ignore it if I weren't so strung out for my best friend. Pinching my cigarette between my lips, I hold my phone over my face and squint at the screen.

KANE

Hey, check the cams

Sam's gonna fuck her

If he can get it up

Frowning, I close my messages and hold my thumb over the surveillance app. I don't think I want to watch Mercy being dicked down, but part of me is curious. Another part knows that Kane is watching, and that's enough for my cock to warm. Blowing out a breath, I tap the icon and stare at the video feed.

Mercy's voice, breathless and begging, fills the air.

My dick stands at full attention. I don't even turn down the volume; I turn that shit *up*, gluing my eyes to the screen as Sam and Mercy tangle in the bedsheets. Except neither of them are moving, and then I hear the softest, most broken whisper of my life.

"Don't you love me?"

"Fuuuuck me," I groan, raking my hand through my hair. Sam's got it just as bad as me. Our situations suck. Although, being sweaty and naked with Kane would be leagues better than cold and alone on the beach in November. Even then, I don't know if I could go through with it.

Judging by how hard Sam is clenching every single muscle in his body, he may have the same dilemma.

We don't just want sex—we want love, too.

I see the truth clear as day, and my heart goes out to the man.

My phone chimes again.

KANE

Fucking hell, he's a goner. There goes her sweet cherry.

Keep watching

KANE

You don't think he'll do it?

Fucking pussy

I'd shove my dick so deep—

I stop reading and toss my phone into the sand. Kane's always been a sexual man. Hearing about his exploits comes with *best friend / foster brother* territory. I was there when he lost his virginity, and I've been here ever since. He's toned down on talking about his sexcapades over the past few years, but with Mercy, it's like the filter's been removed.

He can't wait to bury himself inside of her.

And I can't stop picturing it.

What I have instead of that explicit fantasy, however, is a live video of Sam *not* fucking Mercy. I wipe off the sand from my phone and open the video, unable to believe my eyes. He's not gonna do it.

Mercy's virginity lives to see another day.

KANE

Would you do it?

I stare at Kane's text message. What kind of a question is that?

No

But I'm not pining after her like Lover Boy

KANE
You might enjoy it

Even if you don't like her

I never said I didn't like her

I also never said that I did. She's a complication that's twisting my heart and my head into knots. I don't know how to feel about her.

KANE
You seemed to like kissing her

You were rock hard

Frowning, I check my dick and confirm that it's still, surprisingly, hard as hell. I bite my lip and type out a message, hitting send before I can delete.

Still am.

KANE
That's hot

Send a pic?

My cheeks burn. Why the hell would he want to see my dick?

You've seen it before

KANE

Not like this

Don't make me beg

I huff, a laugh catching in my chest.

ME

You, beg?

I'll never see it

KANE

Please

My heart skips a beat.

I like it when you let loose

I want to see it

A picture arrives, but it's terrible quality. The flash is just bright enough for me to make out a POV shot of Kane's lower half, his jeans undone and his swollen cock peeking through his open zipper. The tip shines like it's wet, but the rest is a mystery. He's outside somewhere, casually taking his dick out to snap a pic.

Unbelievable.

But it makes me sweat.

My cigarette falls from my lips and disappears, long forgotten as I rub my cock over my jeans. Pleasure shoots down my spine. Fuck, I haven't jerked off in months. My balls ache. Quickly glancing around to make sure I'm alone, I undo my pants and heave a sigh of relief. Mr. Morningstar's got shit taste, and his clothes are uncomfortable as hell. I shouldn't jerk off in them, but—

I can't help it when I'm staring at Kane's dick.

Grabbing my shaft, I tentatively stroke up, gasping as electricity rumbles like rain down to my toes. They curl as I stroke again and again, the sigh passing my lips curving into a moan.

My phone vibrates on my chest, and I pause everything to open my texts.

KANE

You're touching yourself

Aren't you

Please let me watch

I'm contemplating what to do when another barrage of messages comes through.

KANE

Fuck

Gotta go

See u at home

Don't cum without me

The whine that leaves my lips is as pathetic as I feel

when I shove my dick back into my pants. Telling me not to come without him is ridiculous, but what's worse is that I actually listen! I pull my knees up and light another cigarette, glaring at the waves rolling across the shore. "That's fucked up," I tell myself, rubbing my forehead. "*You're* fucked up."

I came to terms with having a crush on Kane a decade ago. What I didn't anticipate was that crush never going away. It deepened, burning hotter and harder until all of a sudden, I was in love with a man who wouldn't love me back.

It's not that Kane *couldn't*. It's that he won't give up his lifestyle to go steady. Monogamy isn't exactly his thing, and neither is commitment. It's a miracle that he's stuck around with me for as long as he has.

Especially when I love the fucking bastard.

I try to keep it under wraps. I *really* do. Half the time, I'm convinced that I'm not in love at all—I'm merely Kane's keeper, ensuring that he stays out of prison and in my life.

But the other half of the time, it fucking hurts to see him with women like Mercy. That's why I need her out of the picture. Everything would be so much better if Kane would hurry up and graduate, leave the bitch behind, and run away with me.

Scoffing aloud, I flick ash off the end of my cigarette.

As if *happily ever after* really exists.

Pulling up the security app, I open Mercy's bedroom feed to find that Sam's gone. Mercy is curled up with her pillow, probably sleeping off the disappointment. I pinch my cigarette between my teeth, knowing exactly what that kind of disappointment feels like. She's in for a long night.

I frown at my dick as it twitches, eager for some action that's not fucking happening.

Yeah, I'm in for a long night, too.

People like us don't have happy endings.

CHAPTER 21

KANE

THERE'S a certain calm before a storm that I usually ignore. Running and gunning my way through life—through people—means that I don't pay attention to signs if they get in my way. If I want something, I go after it. End of story.

But with Zane, I've been waiting for him to make the first move.

I'm not stupid or unobservant or cruel enough to lead him on. The man needs to learn to buck up and nut up. I thought that over time, he'd get so sick of watching me flirt with and date other people that he'd explode, charging at me with his fists until I could calm him down and reassure him that I'm not going anywhere.

And that, yes, I love him too.

But with each passing year, I get less and less sure that he wants anything from me other than the pain. The hole in his heart is self-inflicted, a festering wound that he can fix if he just—

Stops being so goddamn stubborn.

I stare at my phone for the hundredth time, rechecking his location to make sure that I'm not seeing things. He's home. He's just not inside. Sitting in his car, no doubt, frozen to the spot.

Is it fear? Is it regret? Does he not want to rock the boat because I could rock *his* boat? I snicker at how witty I am, but my levity dies in an instant as the deadbolt on the front door unlocks. Standing from the couch, I wipe my palms on my thighs and wait for Zane to enter.

Any second now.

He'll walk through that door and finally admit how he feels.

I sigh, dragging my hand through my hair as another minute passes without any change. Maybe he really does regret it. Maybe I pushed him too hard. Maybe I should have focused on his emotional well-being instead of the physical, but I'm better at the latter. Groaning, I shuffle to the front door and rap my knuckles on it. "Zane," I call out, "I know you're there."

A moment passes before he responds. "Yeah."

Pulling open the door, I give him a once-over, pausing at the heavy flush on his cheeks and the hint of tears in his eyes. The bastard's gonna psych himself out from coming home. Fuck. Maybe I *did* push him too hard.

But there's no going back.

I grab his hand and pull him into my chest, cradling the back of his head and holding on tight. "Welcome home, idiot." He relaxes instantly, a choked sound catching in his throat.

"You're just horny," he rasps, grabbing my hips. "That's all this is."

Yeah, I'm damn near always horny, but—

"That's *not* what this is." Walking backwards into our apartment, I kick our front door shut before pinning Zane against it. Grabbing his chin, I force him to meet my eyes. "Zane Hunter," I growl, using his full name, "you are so fucking stupid."

He scoffs, grabbing my wrist with both hands. "Get off of me."

"No."

A silent tear tracks down his cheek. "What do you want from me?"

"I'd settle for honesty."

Grinding his jaw, he doesn't say anything, clamming up once again.

Fine.

Fuck it.

I'll make the first move.

Crashing into Zane feels like being hit by a tidal wave, both of us suddenly lost at sea. Most people would claw their way to the surface, desperate for air, but we cling to each other and forego oxygen so that we drown. He gasps as our lips meet, his entire body reacting to mine like a live wire, twitching at the slightest touch. I let go of his chin to cup his cheek, sighing into the kiss and trying to take it slow.

Really trying.

But then he rakes his nails against my scalp and moans, the neediest little sound I've ever heard pass his lips, and I'm a goner, grabbing his hips and grinding into him. We gasp in unison as our dicks touch through our pants.

He stares into my eyes and suddenly says the sweetest thing. "Is this really happening?"

Chuckling, I press our foreheads together and lift him off the ground, eager to feel him wrapped around and beneath me. "Fucking finally," I laugh, carrying him out of the foyer and into his bedroom. I lay him down on the bed and try to admire the sight, but those stupid fucking clothes *have* to go. "Take off your clothes." I rip my shirt off my shoulders, tearing the buttons clean off. "And let me worship you."

He flushes prettily, exhaling like he doesn't believe me. "Kane—"

I stop tugging my belt through the loop and raise an eyebrow. "Do you want to go slow?" I wait for him to answer.

"No."

"Good." I unbuckle my belt and strip, pulling my boxers off with my dress pants and kicking my shoes out of the way. "Any slower and the glaciers would fucking melt."

Throwing a pillow at my face, Zane cracks a smile. "Shut the fuck up."

"Get the fuck naked," I growl, climbing onto the foot of the bed. I pull off his ugly ass shoes and help him out of his pants, tossing those as far away as possible.

When I grab the band of his boxers, I slow down, meeting his wide eyes. My heart's beating fast, but I can only imagine how hard his is pumping. "Tell me if I need to stop." His pubic hair tickles my knuckles as I pull his boxers down, grazing his dick as it bounces up and smacks his stomach.

Fuck, that looks tasty.

I whip off his boxers and slide between his thighs, wrapping my palm around his shaft and admiring the view. I rest my head on his thigh and exhale over him. "Fuck, you're pretty."

Biting his lip like that.

Mmm.

"I'm not supposed to be pretty," he chokes, moaning at my first stroke.

"You're fucking pretty," I assure him, smiling. "All wound up over me. Prettiest fucking thing I ever saw." Kissing his thigh, I groan. Damn, I never knew it would be this good, and we've barely begun. My cock is leaking like crazy, and we haven't even touched it. I jump up to steal a quick kiss from his lips before hunkering back down over his cock. "Ready?"

His chest expands on a deep breath and he nods, quickly biting that plump bottom lip again. I'm tempted to make him beg for it, but I'll play nice tonight. After all, we've both been waiting long enough.

I kiss the tip first, flicking my tongue against the salty slit, and Zane's entire body trembles as he moans. Responsive as fuck, and I'm *here* for it.

I'm also here for *this*.

Popping open my jaw, I take him inside my mouth in one fluid motion, going as deep as I can without choking. I'll be fine after a warm-up, but I also want to take things slow and enjoy every one of Zane's reactions.

The man is falling apart.

Arching his back, grabbing my hair, whining as I drag his cock over my tongue. A sweaty, hot mess, hardly able to catch his breath and unable to decide if watching is better than closing his eyes. He tries to stare, but then I'll grab his shaft and stroke on the upswing, and he's tossing his head back with a moan.

This is what I've been missing. All of those times I've had sex with other people, it's never been this intense. I've been looking for something that was right in front of me the entire time.

Zane's dick throbs, swelling as he gets close. "K— Kane," he pants, struggling to breathe as I take him even deeper, relaxing my throat as I get ready to swallow.

I'm a pro, after all.

He comes with the neediest fucking whine caught in his throat while I've got his dick pumping into mine. I let up after the first few spurts so that I can roll his cum over my tongue and taste it, swallowing greedily as even more spills into my mouth. Zane's hips jerk with each pulse, and I have to hold his hips down. "Easy, boy," I rumble, kissing his shaft. "You'll wear yourself out."

Covering his face with his hands, he groans. "You should *not* have swallowed that."

I nip his abdomen, enjoying the way his muscles twitch. "I always swallow."

"I'm sure you do," he huffs, peeking at me through his fingers. "I just never thought—" There he goes, biting his lip again. "I never thought you'd do that for *me.*"

Sliding up his body, I kiss his cheek and throw my leg over his, idly grinding my cock against his thigh. I'm okay taking things slower than I usually do, but that doesn't mean I'm a saint. "I'd do anything for you, Zane." Turning his face towards mine, I stare into his eyes for what I have to say next. "I love you." Seeing him smile makes me so happy that I have to kiss him again. I've missed the way he lights up the room.

He's been way too fucking moody and broody lately. Speaking of—

We need to talk about Mercy, because I'm not willing to let her go. I love Zane. I want Zane. But I also want her. Having both of them would make me the happiest man alive. But I know that Zane doesn't think the same way I do. We run on different wavelengths and at different speeds, and getting him involved with Mercy could take time. After all, it's taken us *years* to get to this point. I don't want to fuck this up, but I'd be lying if I said that this was all I wanted.

This is only the first piece of the puzzle falling into place.

Zane's quiet and contemplative, gently stroking my hair. "You'd do anything?"

I hum in response, not sure where this is going.

He takes a breath and exhales slowly, blowing air across my forehead. "Stay with me," he murmurs after a moment, rolling onto his side so that he can smother me.

I have a feeling that he's choosing the safer path, because this is an easy ask.

"Alright," I promise, "but we *have* to do something about my dick, or you'll wake up covered in cum." Cupping my balls, I hiss at how hot and heavy they are. "Between you and Mercy, I've been ready to bust all damn day. I'm gonna explode." I grab my shaft and lazily tug, seriously needing some relief. "I don't expect you to—"

He smacks my hand away and takes over, grabbing my dick and stroking *hard*. Hissing, I thrust into his palm and let him take out his frustration on me. Yeah, I know that talking about Mercy, even in passing, is going to rile him up, but that's what I want. I *want* him to work himself up into a frenzy. I need him to break out of his goddamn box. I need—

Shit, I need to come.

Zane pants in my ear and kisses my neck, sending heat straight down my spine. "You're such a fucking slut," he growls, gripping me tighter. "Can't wait to come for your best friend, huh? For your *brother*?"

We aren't related, but *fuck*, that's hot.

Grabbing Zane's face, I drag him on top of me and grind against his body, sealing our lips together and panting into his dirty fucking mouth. He *is* my best friend. We *are* brothers. But we're so much more than that. "Don't insult me," I laugh, winding my fist in his hair and pulling his head back. His Adam's apple bobs as he swallows, giving me a perfect view of his neck. "*Lover*." He whines, and I quickly cover his mouth with mine, greedy to claim the sound. Releasing his hair, I grab his ass and wedge my cock against his cheeks, greedily thrusting between them. Lube would be killer—fucking his tight little hole would be better—but I'll settle for whatever Zane can give me, because the look on his face is priceless.

Lidded eyes, mouth open, pink from his hairline to his chest.

I suck on his tongue just to hear him moan, and I come so fucking hard that it hurts. Thick ropes paint Zane's ass, his sheets, his back, dirtying his bed but filling my heart. We collapse onto his pillow—*one* pillow, needs another—and catch our breath, smoothly transitioning into cuddles and comfort, like we always do when we're in bed together.

Only this time, I'm not afraid to hold him closer, spread kisses across his shoulders, or whisper that I love him, knowing that when he's ready, he'll say it back.

CHAPTER 22

SAM

MERCY IGNORES ALL of my phone calls and texts over the next week. I go to her house, but her father won't let me in. I leave hand-written notes on her car windshield and fold a few into paper planes that get stuck on her roof, but they all go unanswered. The seasons change quickly, and apparently so does my relationship with my best friend.

I may have royally fucked myself over by turning her down for sex.

So much for proving to her how much she means to me. She won't even give me a chance. My only saving grace is that Grandma Star has been keeping track of Mercy's medication for me. Every time I stop by the house, she tells me how many pills are left.

That's the one good thing to come out of that night. Mercy's taking better care of herself.

Football practice helps give me an outlet for the turmoil inside my heart, but even that is short-lived. The season is nearing its end, and we only have one or two more games before that's gone, too. Classes for this semester will be over, breezy fall will turn to chilly winter, and I'll spend another holiday season hopelessly alone. Truthfully, I've been attending the Morningstar Holiday Banquet every year, but if I don't patch things up with Mercy, I doubt I'll be invited unless Grandma Star throws me a bone.

Her father sure as shit won't invite me after what happened the other night.

Blowing out a breath, I kick an empty can down the curb as I walk from campus back to the frat house. It's only a few blocks, no big deal. But I walk the same path that Mercy and I took when we went to Papa Joe's Pizzeria and she first told me about Reaper's stupid game, and my mind drifts back to her for the millionth time.

I miss my friend.

Reaper better be keeping his hands—and every other appendage—to himself. I've texted Mercy to ask about that, too. If she's keeping up with them. If she's seen them. If they text her.

I already know the answer, but I want to hear it from her.

After I left her house the other night, I had Grey connect her call log and messages to my phone so that I can make sure she's safe. When I'm not on the practice field or running drills, I'm glued to my screen to check on her. She doesn't call or text people often, and what little has passed between her and Reaper has been mild at best.

KANE

Good morning, Siren.

Thinking of you, beautiful.

When are you coming to class? I can't
cover for you forever.

Surprisingly, even Zane has been messaging her...
And I happen to agree with everything he's saying. It's a
knife to the heart that she's texting them instead of me,
but maybe that's what I deserve. Maybe I got too
comfortable with the idea of being with Mercy that I
didn't give her any other choice.

Maybe she genuinely only wants to be friends.

ZANE

Just tell him that you're sorry.

You are sorry, right?

Even if you're not, is it worth all this?
You're backsliding.

Hey, answer me.

Did you take your meds?

You've been sitting for two hours.
Time to stretch.

It's like he's watching her twenty-four seven. I itch
for the same unfiltered access. I want to know when she
sleeps. Was it enough? Does she need more? Did she skip
breakfast again, or did Grandma Star bring her scrambled
eggs and toast with strawberry jelly? Is she getting
enough steps in every day, or does she sit in her room

with a pencil tucked behind her ear? Has she showered this week, or is she lying in bed crying?

The worst part of all is knowing that if something's wrong—if she's sad or lonely or spiraling into a bout of depression—I'm the one to blame. I can't even fix it, because she won't let me. If Reaper or Zane gets close to her, it's my fault for breaking the door off its hinges and giving them a clear path to get to her.

I've been so focused on the physical part of our relationship and making her feel like my girlfriend that I took what we had for granted.

That's on me. But it doesn't make watching her befriend the enemy any easier. I *hate* that they're winning.

"This is stupid," I yell, kicking the can so hard that it skids across the road, tumbling to a stop in front of a sorority house. Their yard is immaculate—lush green despite the season change—and I frown at how stupid *that* is, too. Everything feels pointless. Even going to class, knowing that it won't amount to anything if my father snaps his fingers and forces me to start working for the family business, is a chore. Classes used to give me something to focus on other than my impending doom as the sole heir to the Wright fortune and every million-dollar expectation that comes with it.

Now, all I think about is her and how badly I fucked up.

"Sam? Is that you?"

I try not to flinch as Abby bounces over from the sorority house, cheery despite our last meeting. "I thought so! Walking home?" She links her hands behind her back and leans towards me, pushing her tits in my direction. I blink as her cleavage comes into view, frowning at how tan she is compared to Mercy. Tanned and freckled. Nothing like Mercy at all.

Sighing, I pinch the bridge of my nose and close my eyes. "Yeah. On the way." The last thing I want is another girl butting her head into my business, but thankfully, Abby doesn't bring up Mercy at all. She falls into step beside me, content with walking the few blocks to the frat house in silence. I didn't want company, but now that she's here, I don't have the heart to turn her away.

"The boys said that you've been really stressed lately." Abby's shoulder brushes mine. "Is it about the Championship game? Everyone knows that you're going to win." With a smile, she loops her arm through mine and leans into me. "I'll cheer you on, okay? Better look for me."

"Yeah. Okay."

Her smile falters. "Hey, did something happen with..." After a few seconds, she stops trying to guess Mercy's name. "You and that girl?"

I guess the peaceful silence was short-lived.

Confiding in strangers has become normal ever since I started therapy and group counseling, but confiding in Abby is new territory. Still, I've been cagey with the rest of the team and everyone in the frat; they're walking on eggshells around me because they can tell something's up. If they've brought up my sour mood to Abby, they're probably trying to hook me up with a rebound.

Everyone knows that I've got a thing for The Dead Girl.

I stare at the sidewalk. "You could say that."

"Sooooo..." Abby perks up. "You need a date to the party tonight?"

The party. Shit. I completely forgot. I'm supposed to pick up the president's beer order with my truck. I turn around so fast that Abby stumbles, nearly toppling the two of us over. She catches herself by wrapping her arms around my waist and burying her face in my chest, giggling the entire time.

"Oops, sorry! I'm really clumsy."

Yeah, okay. A varsity cheerleader is *clumsy*.

"Look, I'm not interested—"

"If you need to unwind—"

We both stop talking at the same time, but she's the only one of us smiling. "You're a good guy, Sam. I know you have a thing for that other girl, but if she's not interested in you, then it's her loss. You need to move on. We had fun Freshman year, didn't we?"

I'd nearly forgotten that Abby and I dated for a semester. If I'm remembering right, she dumped me for not taking her out enough or paying for her manicures every few weeks.

"I don't really remember," I answer honestly, "and I'm not in the mood, Abby. Sorry." I detangle from her octopus arms and walk faster down the sidewalk, the sound of her annoyed *huff* following me.

"At least try it before you say no!" She jogs to catch up to me. "If you want to make her jealous, I can help!"

The *last* thing I want is some other girl clinging to my arm, especially at a party that Mercy won't attend. I know that technically we're not dating, but it still feels like cheating.

"Go away, Abby."

"If you take me to the party—"

"No."

"It's *your* frat's party! You can't go alone! I'm doing you a favor!"

A laugh bursts from my chest. Abby just won't give up. "I can do whatever the hell I want," I snap, grabbing her wrist. Letting out some of my frustration, I squeeze until she whimpers. "If I wanted to fuck you, Abby, I would, because you wouldn't hesitate to get on your knees, would you?" As much as I have a reputation for being a nice guy, Abby has a reputation for being a pretty girl —a slutty one. "But I already told you, I'm not interested, so back off." Releasing her, I turn around and pound the pavement, eager to get the fuck away from here.

I don't even care about the frat or the parties or the women. Hell, I hardly care about my *degree.*

Once I'm around the corner and Abby's out of sight, I pull my phone from my pocket and check everything again.

My texts and calls. Zero.

Mercy's texts and calls. Six. Two from Kane and four from Zane. Kane sent her a cryptic picture of a painting he's working on and asked her to guess what it is, and

Zane asked her about her plans for the upcoming holiday break.

It's like the events from our disastrous dinner date never happened.

MERCY

We don't really celebrate Thanksgiving. We save up for our annual Christmas party instead.

ZANE

Kane and I rent a cabin every year. Want to come?

What.
The.
Fuck.

MERCY

I don't know…

Who's going?

He better say that they invite the entire goddamn neighborhood—

ZANE

Me and him

Hopefully you

That's it

Did you want to invite someone?

Say my name. *Mercy*. Tell him that you want to invite me. I clutch my phone so tightly that my case creaks.

MERCY

Maybe. Let me think about it.

I curse under my breath at her noncommittal answer. She could be thinking about inviting her sister. Her father. Hell, her *grandmother*. None of which are good answers, but hey, if it keeps either of them from kissing her at this romantic cabin, she can invite the goddamn Pope for all I care.

My phone suddenly vibrates in my hand.

MERCY

Hey, can we talk?

My lungs collapse as I stare at the three little dots on our text chain. She's typing something. Texting. Communicating.

With me.

MERCY

I want to apologize… and ask for a favor.

Can I come over?

Rather than write a reply, I hit the call button and pray that she answers. After the third ring, her voice rumbles through the speaker, scratchy and hoarse, like she either has a cold or she hasn't been using it at all over the past week. It wouldn't surprise me if she's been avoiding talking to people. "Hello?"

"Mercy," I breathe, my heartbeat stuttering. "Hey."

"Hey."

There's a beat of silence that I'm desperate to fill. "How are you? I left you messages." I wince, knowing that it's stupid to bring that up. Of course, she knows that I've left her messages. "Nevermind. You wanted to ask me something?"

"Can I—" She takes a small breath. "Can I come over? I'd rather ask you in person, and... there's more I want to say."

"Of course you can come—"

A car whizzes by, the passenger *whooping* loudly as they see me in my letterman jacket. "Gonna get smashed, Harlot!" He sticks his hand out the window and flicks me off as they drive away. Their bumper sticker proudly supports the opposing team for next week's game.

Shit, the pregame party's tonight. All Greek life has to be there to continue the annual *Harlots'* traditions of getting wasted and pretending we like it. My house will be trashed. It's the last place I want to bring Mercy.

"There's a party at my place, though," I backtrack, kicking myself for it. I'd love to lock her away in my room for even an hour or two so that I can apologize for everything I've ever done wrong in my life. "Can I come to yours?"

"I need to get out of the house," Mercy admits sheepishly. "I don't mind the party. Do I need to bring anything?"

Is she seriously coming to a frat party?

"Uhh—" I quickly file through everything people

usually bring to parties. Condoms. Alcohol. A designated driver. A pack of friends. A change of clothes. Sensible shoes.

"Sam?"

"Just yourself!" Pounding my fist against my forehead, I internally scream. I'm such an idiot. I need to steer her away from coming. "It's a big party, so everything's taken care of. Wear closed-toe shoes. And pants." There's no way in hell I want anyone trying to look up her skirt tonight. "And maybe pin your hair back."

She sighs. "Any other requests, Your Majesty?"

"Don't leave my side." This is the most important part. "And don't set your drink down. Only drink what I give you. Don't take anything from strangers."

"Got it. What time should I be there?"

"I'll come get you." That way, I can check her outfit before she comes over. If it's too revealing, maybe I can convince her to change without her getting pissed off about it.

We hang up after confirming the time, and I stare at my phone for a solid minute, unable to believe my eyes.

MERCY

Looking forward to it :)

I run the rest of the way to my truck, eager to pick up the beer and sprint home to clean my room before tonight. Mercy's never been inside, and I have to make sure that everything is perfect. I won't mess this up. At the least, I'm getting my best friend back, and at best...

I'm getting back into the race to win Mercy's heart.

CHAPTER 23

MERCY

I don't get invited to college parties. To be invited, you have to have friends who are either going or hosting, and that's never applied to me. Technically, Sam didn't even invite me. I invited myself. But I need to get out of the house after a week of stagnation.

A party will ensure that we're not alone.

Sighing, I braid my hair over my shoulder and fiddle with the ribbon at the end, wondering if it looks silly or too girlish. It's a bright crimson, tied into a bow, which I quickly undo. Then I rebraid my hair and weave the ribbon in the strands, tying it into a knot at the end. That could work. I don't feel nearly as girly without the bow.

My phone vibrates in my pocket.

KANE

You're not in pajamas

Where are you going

> Need a ride?

Ever since the revelation that Kane and Zane put cameras in my bedroom, I've been changing my clothes in the bathroom and trying not to be nude at all. The thought that they saw me and Sam—I blush, quivering at the memory of the *heat*. I've made out with Sam before, but I never knew how hot two bodies could get when they're coiled around each other like that. My heartbeat trips as heat pools between my thighs.

I've had to ignore *that*, too, with the boys watching me. Neither of them would object to a little show, I'm sure, but I can't bring myself to do it, knowing that it'll be lackluster compared to the sparks of someone else touching me.

I type back a quick *no* and run my hands down the front of my dress. It's a high-collar neckline, so I forego a necklace for smokey quartz earrings and trade my combat boots for strappy flats my sister gave me for my birthday. As I'm buckling the first strap around my ankle, my phone goes off again.

KANE

> You look good, Siren

> Tell me that you're coming to see me

> It'll make my day

I shake my head with a smile. "I'm not coming to see you," I say aloud. "I wouldn't even know where to find you."

KANE

That's an easy fix

Ask me where I am

I play with the ruffles of my skirt, admiring the soft champagne color. Lace butterflies are sewn into the fabric, matching the black button-up bodice. This dress was also a gift, but from my sister's best friend Celia. She works in fashion. She might have even designed this. I stand up off of my bed and take a quick picture to send to her, including a thank you.

KANE

Send that to me

Rolling my eyes, I slip my student ID into my pocket and dab perfume on my wrists. "You're seeing the outfit now. Isn't that enough?"

KANE

No

I need to save it

I'm changing my wallpaper

To a pretty girl

If she'd send me a picture

Sam's truck rolls down the driveway, and I watch him hop down from the cab. Our eyes meet through the window, and he smiles warmly, looking as handsome as ever. Normally, his green eyes sparkle in the summer, but in the fall they pop with color. Even from this distance, I can make out their exact shade of emerald.

"See you later, Kane," I call out, heading for the door. "Don't wait up." Ignoring the rest of the incoming messages, I carefully descend the stairs and say goodbye to the house, knowing that my grandmother is here somewhere. "I'll be back soon."

The crisp fall air refreshes my senses as I step onto the front porch. The wood panels creak more than usual, a testament to how badly they need replaced, but I barely hear it over the sound of my hammering heart.

Sam meets me at the stairs and takes my hand without asking, leading me to his truck. He gently squeezes my fingers. "You look great, Mercy."

I run my hand down the length of my braid. "Thanks. It's new."

The skirt isn't exactly short, easily brushing the tips of my knees, but he stares at the curve of my calves anyway, practically mesmerized. After a hard swallow, he turns his gaze away. "Let's get going."

"Wait." I pull him to a stop before he can get too far away. I've rehearsed what I've wanted to say in my head, not wanting Kane or Zane to tease me for it, but now that Sam is standing in front of me, the words die in my mouth. I part my lips, and no sound comes out.

I've known this man for years. We've had countless sleepovers and one-on-one bonfires and movie nights and strolls through the endless rows of graves. He's held me at night when I can't sleep, and I've talked him out of bad dreams. I *know* Sam.

But stepping into a new light with him almost feels like letting something go, and I'm not sure how to handle that.

"You don't have to say anything," he murmurs, tugging on the end of my braid. He slides his fingers across the braid, a pensive crease between his brows. "If you need forgiveness, then you have it. For today. For tomorrow. For anything. You don't have to ask, because no matter what, I'll always give it to you." Our eyes meet, and warmth blossoms in my chest. "I guess you could say that I'm..." He searches for the right words. "I'm so far gone." Chuckling, he looks away, the pink tint to his cheeks spreading to the tips of his ears. "I'm lost without you, Mercy. This past week has been shit. So whatever I have to do to make sure that never happens again, I'll do it. We don't have to be anything you don't want us to be. I'm sorry that I pushed you and made you uncomfortable. I don't ever want you to do something unless your heart is one hundred percent in it."

A flicker of guilt crosses his features before he schools his expression. "I'm sorry, Mercy. That's all I wanted to say."

Well, shit.

"I'm supposed to be the one apologizing." I clasp my hands together and sway in place. "I, uhh, I wanted to..." That's not quite right. "When we were..." Taking a breath, I close my eyes and start again. "I'm so tired of feeling like I'm going to make a mistake. I don't want to ruin what we have, but I *do* like you, Sam. And when you said that you loved me, I thought, 'this is it.

This is what I'm supposed to do.' But then we were kissing and you were really into it—*I* was really into it—"

Sam places his hands on my shoulders. "Mercy, it's okay, you don't have to—"

"I love you." My hands shake. "I do. I love you, Sam." I open my eyes to find him frozen in place, like I've shocked him to the core. "And I want to be more than friends." Biting my lip, I power through the next part. "But I also... I think I like Kane." Wincing, I wait for Sam to blow up. Storm off. Rage and rant and curse Kane to hell.

"I know I shouldn't," I continue, desperate to fill the silence. "And I don't understand it. He's—he's—" There are a lot of ways to describe Kane, but his confidence is infectious. It's what draws me to him. While I've been distant with Sam this past week, I've been texting Kane. He's rough on the surface but soft on the inside, surprisingly romantic and in touch with his emotions. Even Zane, who I'm pretty sure hates my guts half the time, has been nice to me.

"You like Kane." Sam's expression flatlines, but his eyes smolder with a hatred unlike any I've ever seen. "You love me, but you like him." He lets go of me to run a hand through his hair and look off into the distance. "You *like* him. Mercy, he's trying to kill you."

"I know."

"He's a murderer."

Wincing, I repeat myself. "I know."

"He's a *man whore*." Clenching his jaw, Sam growls,

the sound rumbling between us. "Mercy, he's slept with hundreds of people. He fucking told me so!"

"And I've slept with no one, unless we suddenly count the tip." I glare at Sam, flicking my gaze to his crotch. "So, what? Does a person's experience level make them any less of a person? Maybe I'll like sex so much that I sleep with a hundred people! Would you hate me then?"

Sam's face falls. "Of course not. I'll never hate you."

"Then why does it matter who anyone's slept with? You'll judge Kane but you won't judge me?"

"Yes." The fire in Sam's eyes burns hotter. "I don't care what you've done, Mercy, or who you screw. I will always forgive you. I will always be here for you." He pinches my chin and tilts my head back. "So if you want to fuck Reaper like one of his whores, fine. Go bounce on his dick. But when he's done filling you up—"

I flinch, but Sam doesn't let go. He leans closer, eyes wild and body quivering.

"Stretching you out—"

"Stop, Sam—"

He scoffs. "That's the thing, Mercy. You can tell me to stop, and I will. But Reaper? It'll turn him on to hear you beg. You'll be crying from how hard he's pounding your pussy, and he won't stop until he's wrung you out and left you to dry. Is that what you want?" Pressing the pad of his thumb against my lips, he frowns. "Think long and hard about it, because I may have the restraint to pull out, but he won't."

"You're trying to scare me." Grabbing his wrist, I tear

his hand off my face. "But it won't work." Cupping Sam's cheek, I pray that he hears me when I say this. "I didn't want to tell you, because I knew how you would react. I kept my distance this week because I wasn't sure if I was going to tell you at all. But I missed you." I brush my thumb across his cheekbone, and his eyes flutter closed. "I missed my best friend."

Taking a deep breath, Sam wrestles with himself. "I missed you, too." He opens his eyes, unable to clear the agony hiding in their depths. "But I don't agree with this, Mercy."

"I know." Lifting onto my tiptoes, I kiss his jawline. "But I'm not asking for your permission. Or your blessing." This is the hardest part, and I don't know if he'll say yes, but—

"I want you to be there."

Leaves cascade all around us as a gust of wind knocks them loose. The entire world shifts in the span of a second as Sam falls to his knees and clutches the front of my dress.

"*Please*," he whispers, burying his face in my chest. "I'll do anything for you, Mercy, but—" His voice cracks. "I don't—I can't—" He takes a shuddering breath. "I don't want to watch him break you. I *can't*." Lifting his eyes, they blaze with so much fury that it knocks the air from my lungs. "I'll kill him. I'll kill the fucking bastard while he's still inside you."

I run my hand through Sam's hair, trying to soothe him. "He won't hurt me." The lie feels vile, but I don't know what else to do. I need Sam there in case Kane *does* go too far... or if Zane keeps his word.

If I sleep with Kane, it might be the last thing I ever do.

"I need you there," I insist, sliding to my knees with Sam. I cup his face in my hands and fight the urge to say *nevermind*—to whisk him away from the pain I'm causing and let him keep me for himself. I know that would make him happy. But it's not what will make *me* happy. "I trust you to keep me safe, no matter what happens."

Sam clenches and unclenches his jaw, taking his time to process his response. "Only if you have sex with me first." The agony brewing in his eyes deepens. "That's my condition. I'll watch you with Reaper—" His face twists as he says Kane's nickname. "And make sure that he doesn't go overboard. But your first time—" He wraps my braid around his fist and tugs, a whine catching in his throat as our lips brush. "Your first time is *mine*."

CHAPTER 24

———

ZANE

THE PENCIL in my hand snaps in half, its splinters digging into my palm. I barely register the pain, too absorbed with the way my heart fucking shatters.

Mercy likes Kane.

She admitted it out loud. I heard her clear as day, the cameras I placed in her family's cemetery doing their job perfectly. I'd been idly watching the scene between her and Sam unfold, not entirely sure where it was going, but sure as hell not expecting *that* truth bomb.

From the way Sam's absolutely gutted, I doubt he was expecting it either.

I can't say that I blame Mercy for how she feels. If anyone gets it, it's me. The man who fell in love with a sinner. Ever since Kane admitted to sharing my feelings, we've been shacked up in our apartment, pretending that we don't have lives outside of these four walls. It's been nice for a change. Keeping track of Mercy has been easy because she hasn't left her room, and it's given me some breathing room to pity the girl instead of hating her guts for a situation that's out of her control. It's been... peaceful.

And in an instant, that peace fucking shatters.

I drag in a lungful of air. Once. Twice. Three times. But I can feel the panic rising like the tide, building and building until it carries you away, never to be seen again.

That's what I feel like—untethered. Drowning. *Hurt.*

Because when Kane finds out that Mercy not only likes him, but she wants to *sleep with* him, he's going to explode. For him, it'll be a blissful revelation that puts him on cloud nine. He's always been a sucker for watching people fall in love with him, and here we are: watching Mercy do just that.

Fall for the man who's going to kill her.

Unless.

I get to her first.

Deleting the video feed makes me nervous, but so does everything else about this situation. I can't let Kane know that she's falling for him—he'll grin like a lovesick idiot and demand to go to the party tonight. I've already refused twice on account of how many people will try to sleep with him. It doesn't matter that he insists that he's not interested, claiming that he wouldn't do that to me now that we're together, it's the principle behind the thing.

I don't want him going to frat parties like he used to.

Call me clingy or obsessed or damaged. I don't care. The only person I *might* make an exception for is Mercy, but even that feels like I'm ripping my goddamn heart out. On that, I'm sure that Sam can relate.

We don't *want* Kane and Mercy to happen, but it feels like an inevitability, and fighting fate is fucking exhausting.

I would know; I spent years trying to convince myself *not* to fall for Kane, and look how that turned out.

Miserable.

Until, suddenly, it wasn't.

Frowning at my computer monitor, I amuse myself with the idea that this, too, will end okay. Mercy and Kane can have sex, fine, but then he'll grow bored of her and move on. I'll get to kill her—or he will, doesn't matter, I guess—then we can kill Sam as a bonus, and Kane can graduate and we'll move out of the city for good.

Unless.

Fuck, that's going to be my least favorite word.

That's all peaches and rainbows and shit—*unless* Kane falls for her. Then I'm royally fucking screwed. Because getting rid of Mercy is contingent upon Kane going along with it. For now, he says that's still the plan. He's painting in his studio right now, actually, trying to picture her final moments. He's *excited* for it. But he'll be just as excited to sleep with her, and eventually, maybe, to fall in love with her, too.

Kane's always been that way. Invested. It's one of the things I love about him.

But it's also what gets us in trouble.

Tossing the pencil shards in the trash, I throw my

sketchbook onto my bed and spin around in my chair, leaping up to lock my door. I need to think. I need to plan. Let Mercy and Sam have their fun with each other —I don't give a fuck about that. It's what comes after that sets me on edge.

Because if she really does sleep with Kane, I'll have to intervene... and that might be what finally breaks Kane's heart.

CHAPTER 25

KANE

ALL OF A SUDDEN, the video on my phone disappears.

I click through the folders, thinking that my fat fingers have mis-clicked, but no. It's gone. Wiped from existence in the blink of an eye. I didn't even get to rewatch it once. It's just *gone.*

"Zane," I sigh, cracking my neck. I've been sitting in one place for hours, playing with the paints that I'll eventually use for Mercy's portrait. I normally only create a few for each target, but for Mercy, I think I'll start with half a dozen. Maybe more. I have to capture the sunlight reflecting off of her eyes just right—which is why I'm in Zane's surveillance app to begin with; I'm looking for a still image of Mercy standing beneath rays of golden sunlight when the live feed pops up, and she isn't in her room.

So I click around until I find her standing outside with Sam.

Confessing to him.

At first, I'm elated. *Finally*, they're getting some-where. Mercy has been moping in her room all week, and it's downright depressing to watch. Not that I mind the doom and gloom—it's given me an endless fountain of inspiration to pull from. When I'm not pinning Zane to the wall and kissing him senseless, I'm covered in paint as I try to embody Mercy's essence on canvas, falling just short of satisfaction.

I need to see her in person before I can finish a single painting.

And therein lies the problem; Zane's watching me like a hawk. Shacking up with him is fun—he's even more skittish now that he knows I'm liable to pounce on him at any moment—but he won't relax. Not completely. After spending years with him, I know how to read his moods. He's happier now, but he's still finding something to brood about. If I had to guess, it involves Mercy.

The minute the video suddenly disappears, I *know* it is.

What he doesn't realize is that I was watching Mercy's confession in real-time. I heard everything.

She loves Sam.

She wants to be with him.

But she *likes* me.

The cheesiest grin splits across my face, and I jump up off the floor, dropping my phone and spilling my paints. *Yes.* This is it. The wheel is in motion. By this time next year, Mercy will be madly, hopelessly in love with me. Hell, I bet I could do it in six months. Three. *One.*

Shit, could I really pull that off?

As I ponder the logistics of stealing that much of Mercy's time, I realize the huge, glaring flaw in this plan.

She already loves Sam.

But she's not *in* love with him. Wracking my brain, I think back to the night he joined our game. What was it he said? Did she have to love him or fall *in* love with him? Do the semantics even matter?

I know that Sam will argue that he's won. He'll try to end our game early. Any excuse to keep Mercy all to himself. If he can get rid of me and Zane, he'll have no competition for her heart. I was hoping that he would consider my offer of sharing her, but from how fucking pathetic he gets at the mere *mention* of my cock splitting his girl in two, I doubt he'll go through with it.

No, Samson Wright doesn't like to share.

Mercy does.

That's the linchpin. That's how we win the game. By stealing Mercy from Sam's arms. The best part is that she'll come willingly. *God*, it's going to be a bloodbath, and I am *here* for it. My cock swells at the thought of Sam and me fighting over my sweet Siren. The way those pouty lips will part as she begs us to stop, tears spilling down her face as I cut Sam down in front of her. Her heart will crack with every one of Sam's broken bones. It might not *actually* go that way—we don't usually resort to bludgeoning people to death—but a man can dream.

I drag in a breath and groan. *Fuck*, that turns me on. I grab my phone and leave the studio, flying up the stairs to tell Zane the good news. He won't be as excited as me, but I've got this infectious quality about me. By the time I'm done explaining how perfect this plan is, he'll be on board. It's even better that Mercy loves Sam, because the heartbreak is going to absolutely *kill* him.

I'm a goddamn genius.

"Zane!" I turn his bedroom doorknob to find that it's locked. "Hey, bitch, open up. I have an idea." I knock loudly. "I know how we can make things more interesting with Mercy."

"I'm busy."

"What, masturbating?" Chuckling, I lean my shoulder against his door. "C'mon, you don't have to hide it. You know I'll help." I can hear Zane shuffle around until he leans against the other side.

"What's your idea?"

"It's no fun if I can't see your face."

This isn't like him. Usually, he'll sit at his computer and let me talk about whatever's on my mind, grunting every so often so that I know he's listening. When he's worked up, I always listen. Now that it's his turn, he's hiding from me.

"Talk to me," I grumble, scratching my nails against the door like a trapped cat. For fuck's sake, we should be past this secrecy bullshit. "I'm right here. I'm not going anywhere."

After what feels like an eternity, he turns the lock and pulls open his door. I lean against the doorframe, unable to keep a smirk off my face as his eyes travel down my body, snagging on my boner. He snaps his head up and blushes.

Fucking adorable.

"I think we should bring Mercy and Sam to the cabin," he says quickly, pushing his reading glasses up his nose. He rarely wears them, but when he's been staring at a screen all day, he gets headaches. "What's your idea?"

That's not what I was going to say, but I agree with him. "Absolutely." Pushing myself off the doorframe, I slip into his personal space and grab his hips. "I never realized how slutty those glasses are." My lips curve into a wicked grin. "You should wear them more often."

A divot appears between Zane's eyebrows as he pushes against my chest. "Wait—we're not—" His blush deepens. "*How* are you still horny? We just had sex this morning!"

"Wasn't enough," I grunt, cupping the back of his head and easily licking into his hot little mouth. He moans. I love that fucking sound. "Clothes off, glasses on." I push him onto the bed and pull my shirt over my head. "Let me tell you my idea, and you can shower me in praise for how fucking smart I am." It's a brilliant plan, and I'll have fun explaining it to Zane. But what's better is the way that he can barely focus, his glasses steaming up before I've even touched him.

Yeah, I'm buying him a dozen fucking pairs of those.

"Let's invite them to the cabin." I *love* the idea of bringing her. I don't know how I hadn't thought of it already. "Then we'll tie Sam up and fuck his girl while he watches." Licking my lips, I picture it—the rage on Sam's face while I guide Mercy's pretty mouth over my cock. "He'll be so fucking broken once he realizes how much she loves it." I scrape my nails against Zane's scalp. "I know you don't really like her like that, but you could join in." Admittedly, this part is bad timing with my impromptu seduction in progress, but if we're being honest with each other, I might as well say what's on my mind. "I can't get the thought of you two out of my head."

Some of my paintings have turned into erotica of Zane and Mercy together. There isn't any definition—barely any lines or shading—but the idea is there. The *shape* is there. And it's really goddamn pretty when the two of them are together.

Zane closes his eyes and swallows, shuddering like I've just fed him the most bitter pill of his life. "I don't know." He rubs his forehead. "I don't hate her. But that doesn't mean I want to fuck her, either."

"You don't have to decide right now. I just wanted you to know." I sigh against his lips. "I think it'd be *really* hot if we tag-teamed her." I resist the urge to kiss him so that I can hear his reply.

"We've never done that before."

"Nope." I'm usually the only one who handles our targets. "But if we're exploring new things together..." I pull Zane into my lap and chuckle as he claws at my abs. "We can add this to the list."

I can't speak for Zane's list of desired life experiences, but sharing Mercy with him—and *maybe* with Sam after we rile him up first—has quickly climbed to the top of mine.

The *very* fucking top.

I've already moved on to palming Zane's ass and sucking a hickey onto his neck when he mutters a soft, "I'll think about it," driving me absolutely wild because he's open to the idea at all. The Zane I knew a few months ago would have flat-out refused.

But the Zane of today is curious.

That is my biggest win of the day, no matter how much Mercy likes me or not.

I'm in the middle of tearing Zane's pants off his legs when Mercy's voice fills the room, the tiny speaker on Zane's cell phone blaring from his jeans' pocket.

"I want you to be there."

Sam's voice is next, laced with such anguish that I almost feel bad for the man. *"Please—"*

Zane's hand slaps mine as he tries to grab his phone, but since I'm the one with his pants in my hands, I have the upper hand. I grab the device and stare at the screen, watching a recording of the video I just saw him delete from the server. I thought he hadn't even saved a backup, but here it is. Staring me in the face.

"What's this?" I ask, turning the screen towards him and waving the phone in the air. The video is time-stamped for today, barely ten minutes ago.

"I don't want to watch him break you. I can't."

I drag in a breath as a wave of excitement crashes over me. This is the part where Sam threatens—

"I'll kill him. I'll kill the fucking bastard while he's still inside of you."

Zane reaches for the phone again, but I hold it out of reach. "Give me the phone!"

Holding my ground, I listen as the rest of Mercy and Sam's conversation plays out, which means that Zane has to listen to it, too. He flinches, hiding his face, and I have to puzzle over if he's upset that Mercy made a deal with Sam to have sex with me or if he's upset that I've caught him red-handed in trying to hide it from me.

Sam's voice rumbles like thunder from an oncoming storm, heavy and powerful, as he declares in no uncertain terms that he'll be the one sticking his dick inside of Mercy first. *"Your first time is mine."* The recording loops back to the beginning of their conversation, and I cut it off.

"What is this?" I ask again.

"It's Sam and Mercy," Zane sighs, lifting his glasses to rub the backs of his eyelids. "They're going to that party tonight."

"And?" I crumble Zane's pants into a ball, wrapping his phone up with them. "Were you going to tell me?"

"I already said that I don't want you to go to the party."

"Not that part." I toss his clothes to the floor and crawl over him, grabbing his throat as soon as it's within reach. Pushing him into the mattress, I squeeze as gently as I can to get my point across. "The part where Mercy wants to fuck me and Sam agreed. Fucking *agreed.*" I bare my teeth. As long as Sam's there to watch, but that's easy to accommodate. "How long were you planning to keep it a secret? A day? A week? Forever?"

Zane's face reddens, and I have to let up before I hurt him. But the betrayal, no matter how slight, hurts. He gasps for air but doesn't try to move out from under me. "I don't know. I didn't think that far ahead."

"You know how important Mercy is to me. I've been talking about her nonstop for weeks." I interlock our fingers and hold his hands over his head, pinning him down. "The only reason I haven't gone over there and rutted her into the fucking floor by now is because of you." I've been holding myself back because I can see how much Mercy bothers Zane. But he needs to get over it. "I want her."

"I know." Zane's voice mimics Sam's from the recording, drowning in an agony I can't understand. I've been trying—I've been patient—but I still don't understand.

"Is there anything else that you're hiding from me?" Part of the reason my relationship with Zane works is because we're honest with each other. We have to be, or we'd never be as good of a team as we are. Cutting up bodies for the bratva and selling pieces on the black market is nasty business, but it gives us the freedom to live our lives how we want outside of contract hours. I thought we were on the same page about our personal endeavors. But when it comes to Mercy, I guess our normal rules don't apply.

Before Zane can answer, I let him go, throwing my legs over the side of the bed and sitting up. "Don't answer that. If you tell me any other secrets right now—" A bitter laugh cracks inside my chest. "I don't know what I'll do."

Hate fuck Zane. Skull fuck Mercy. Break into the

party and go overboard on booze and bodies. Anything goes when my mood gets bad enough, but I've been in a really good fucking mood for the past few months. Running a hand through my hair, I grab my shirt and stand up, eager to get some air. "I'm going for a walk."

"Right now?" Zane's voice pitches. He's either about to panic or beg me to stay. The problem is that neither will work. "You don't want to talk about this?"

"No." I avoid his gaze, knowing that if I look at him, I'll start to feel bad for being upset. But he's the one who lied—kept secrets—whatever! "Anything you say to defend yourself is just going to piss me off." He clearly doesn't trust me, so what's the point in talking about it? So that he can feel better?

Let him drown in guilt for a few hours, and *then* I might consider forgiving him.

I leave before he can convince me to stay, grabbing my keys, leather jacket, and boots before walking out the front door. The air is colder now that the sun has set, and I shiver as I walk up to my motorcycle. I know I told Zane that I was going for a walk, but a drive would work even better for calming me down. My heart pounds in my ears as I pull away from the curb, but the roar of the engine drowns out the sound. I lean into the icy wind, eager to let it numb the hurt inside my heart.

Because if Zane—the man who's been my rock for years—can't trust me, then what's the fucking point in trying to be any better than I am? Why fight who I am when I'm damned if I do and damned if I don't?

The miles fly past in a blur. Streetlights whiz by

alongside all of the college kids wandering the residential area in search of their next house party. Frat Row is where the Harlots reside—Greek life bastards who think they're the cream of the crop—and I'm idling in front of Sam's house before I realize which road I'm on. I don't give a fuck about the party or the dozens of rich bitches inside.

What I do care about is Mercy.

A siren lost at sea.

She doesn't belong in a place like this, surrounded by people who don't understand her. My heart twists as I throw my leg over my bike and prop it up on the sidewalk. Zane doesn't want me here because he doesn't trust me. But I'm not here for me.

I'm here for my girl.

I'm going to be the one to pull her out before she gets hurt.

Because the people who love us are inevitably the ones who fuck us over the hardest, and I don't want her to go through that. Not with me, and definitely not with Samson fucking Wright.

Not on my goddamn watch.

CHAPTER 26

SAM

I NEVER WANTED to be part of a fraternity. Befriending half the student population because of the Greek letters on my jacket never appealed to me. My father always insists that networking is key to any venture in life, and my pledging was always meant to work in his favor—after all, how better could the Wright Heir be in service to his father's fortune than by spreading his seed all over campus? But rather than sow my oats in the fertile female population, I traded in smiles and good deeds instead, eager to avoid making enemies and keep my four years of college life as simple as possible.

For the most part, my strategy has worked. I've only dated a handful of women, and I've been keeping myself open for when Mercy finally decides that she wants to be more than friends.

The fact that she's here tonight proves that the wait has been worth it. Everyone's being nice to her—all of my brothers in the frat and their girls, the pledges, even the

Runners, whose sole job is to keep the liquor flowing, are trying to keep a cold drink in her hand at all times.

I have to intervene, of course, and offer her untapped bottles and clean drinks, but I make sure to tip the Runners nicely.

All in all, it's a really good start to the night.

"Let me know when you need some air," I tell Mercy, leaning over her shoulder so that she can hear me. "We can head out back or up to my room."

She smiles at me, and I wrap my arm around her waist and press a kiss to the top of her head. Having her with me is a dream come true. If every day were like this, Greek life might not be so bad. Mercy could sit with the other girls at all of my football games, we could walk hand-in-hand at all of the seasonal bonfires and events, and she'd be my partner in the holiday toy drive.

While one of my brothers regales us with a story about a gnarly party foul from last month, I tune him out to imagine my future with Mercy. We wouldn't have to spend all of our time on campus—her family's property is just as good, if not better than, anything here. Plus, it's privately owned and secluded. We could sit under the stars at night without a single interruption, drinking hot cocoa and kissing to keep warm.

I'm so lost in the fantasy that I miss the drunken conga line circling too close, and when someone trips, warm beer sloshes all over my back, drenching my shirt in suds.

Someone cheers, and the whole room chugs their drinks.

Mercy covers her ears, laughing despite the chaos. "Are all parties this loud?"

"Usually, yeah." I tip the rest of my beer back and throw my empty cup into a trash can. "But tonight's pregame for the Championship on Saturday. Everyone's supposed to get hammered." I peel my shirt off my back and toss it onto the growing pile on the floor. House rules are that if you get sloshed, you take it off. A few of my teammates slap my back as they pass by.

"Wright!"

"Henson!"

Max Henson, our only Running Back on the team, swings by, letting his drink spill over the edge as he slams to a stop with our group. Mercy dodges just in time, but she bumps into the girl behind her and spills *their* drink. "Sorry!" she cries, stepping into my side and hooking her fingers in my empty belt loop.

"No apology necessary!" Max grins, fist bumping me. "We're all eager to take our clothes off."

Sasha, one of the neighboring sorority girls, rolls her eyes. "Speak for yourself." Her shirt is damp and her shoes are ruined, but she hasn't stripped at all. "I'm just waiting for Reaper to arrive."

That turns Mercy's head. "Reaper's coming?"

My stomach drops. I should have anticipated that someone would bring it up.

"When there's a par-tay, Reaper comes to slay puss-ay," Max cheers, laughing. "Haven't seen him yet, Sash, but don't get your hopes up. The Betas had a party last week, and he never showed. Rumor is that he's wiped."

"I'll believe it when I see it," Sasha murmurs, sipping her drink.

"What do you want with Reaper?" Mercy's eyebrows pinch together. "Unless you're, um—"

"Looking to get laid?" Sasha smiles kindly. "Yeah, babe, Reaper's the best dick there is. No offense, boys."

Max raises his beer. "None taken. He's a legend."

The huddle beside ours overhears our conversation and mixes with our group, eager to talk gossip. "But he doesn't smash twice," one of the girls says, a wistful look in her eye. "So you're out of luck, Sasha."

I try to keep my expression even throughout the conversation, but Mercy isn't as skilled at keeping a straight face. She blushes down to her roots and chugs the rest of her drink. "I think I'm ready for that air," she murmurs, tugging me by my belt loop.

"Yes, ma'am." Tossing her empty bottle into the trash, I lead her away from the crowd. Or at least, I try to. The room is packed now that the party's in full swing, and we have to shuffle alongside multiple warm bodies to get anywhere near the sliding porch door.

"Sam!"

Shit.

Ignoring Abby's voice, I pull Mercy into the dining room. Giant plastic containers filled with hunch punch cover the entire table. "Don't drink that," I warn Mercy, steering her through the room. "It'll knock you on your ass. Plus, it tastes like shit."

One of the freshmen ladling the drinks takes offense and tosses a full cup at me, unaware that I'm an upperclassman in his own frat. The alcohol arcs through the air, but the man's aim is shit. Bright red punch splashes over not one, not two, but *three* girls in the room. One of whom being my date.

"Shit! Sorry, bro!"

The two regulars smack him hard on the arm and back of his head, but Mercy stands there like a deer in headlights. Anger pulses through my veins as I walk over to him and smack the cup out of his hands. "Apologize. *Now.*" Grabbing his shirt collar, I drag him in front of my girlfriend and push him down onto his knees. "Tell her you're sorry for being an idiot." I don't even know this kid's name, but he damn near soils himself.

"I—I'm sorry. I didn't mean to hit you." He glances at the red stains on her skirt. "Or ruin your dress."

"That's coming out of your wallet," I tell the Freshman, smacking his shoulder. "Get a mop and clean up your mess."

"Yes, sir!"

While he runs away, I rub Mercy's ruffled skirt between my fingers. The punch is sticky as it dries. "I have something you can change into upstairs." Regret hits me square in the chest, and I realize how foolish I was to bring her here. "I can take you home."

Mercy hooks her arm over my shoulder and drags me down to her height. Brushing her lips over my ear, she murmurs, "The last place I want to be right now is home. I'm fine." She presses a quick kiss to my cheek. "It's just a dress."

"A beautiful dress," I counter, hauling her against me. "I hate that it's ruined. I'll buy you another one."

"It's one of a kind."

That's even worse.

She lingers near my face, blushing as she glances at my lips. "Take me upstairs?"

Gladly.

Lifting her into my arms, I grin as she squeals, clinging to my neck as I carry her across the house. We catch eyes all around the room, a few knowing frat members lifting their drinks or *whooping* as we pass, while some of the women whisper amongst themselves and glance around the room. One of them waves her hand overhead, but I don't speak girl code, so I shrug it off and keep moving.

Despite people parting the sea for us to pass, it takes a while to reach the stairs. By then, sweat trickles down my back, sticky with beer, slick with sweat, but I hardly care because of how lucky I am to have Mercy in my arms. I take the stairs two at a time, eager to lock her away in my bedroom for the night.

"Can you reach the key in my pocket?"

Mercy pats my pockets and shoves her hand inside one of them, but she comes up empty. "You don't have a key."

I definitely had one earlier.

Frowning, I set her down on the floor and gently push her aside. "Someone might be in there," I admit slowly, hating the way Mercy's face falls. "Don't worry, I'll check. Wait here."

She grabs my arm to stop me. "What if it's dangerous?"

I blink at her. "This is a frat party, baby, not a horror movie." Cupping her cheek, I press a gentle kiss to her lips, sighing at how soft and sweet they are. Damn, I'm gonna need another taste. "But I love that you care."

A chorus of shouting echoes from downstairs, with a group of men chanting *Reaper, Reaper, Reaper!*

Mercy's eyes widen, and she glances over her shoulder at the stairwell, likely thinking the same thing I am. If Reaper is here, there's only one person he's looking for, and it sure as shit ain't me.

"Hide," we both say in unison. I grab Mercy's arm and start to open my bedroom door, only to pause partway inside. A group of girls giggles as they bound up the stairs, heading for the upstairs bathroom. I don't have much of a choice; we either step inside my bedroom and face whoever is in there—not Reaper, clearly, so chances are, I can take them in a fight—or we head back downstairs and try to sneak out the back.

"I'm looking for a girl named Mercy!"

My blood runs cold as a chorus of *upstairs, man, go get her!* clashes against, *she's with someone! I'm free, Reaper! Pick me!*

Heavy footfalls sound on the stairs seconds later, and I push open my bedroom door. Hands grab me from inside, and I'm pulled *hard,* stumbling blindly into the darkness.

Mercy shrieks, clawing at my arm as we're suddenly pulled apart. "Sam!"

A girl I don't know laughs behind me in the hallway. "We'll take care of her, honey!" Shoes scuffle across the floor, and Mercy's muffled screams fill my ears.

"Yeah, we'll make sure Reaper breaks her in real good."

No!

I punch the air in front of me, colliding with someone's jaw.

"Ouch! Fucking hell, Sam!" Whoever I punched stumbles backwards and slams into my dresser. At the same time, my bedroom door slams shut and the lock slides into place. "We're doing you a favor."

I don't give a shit about any favors. I spin around and lunge for the door, but two sets of hands pull me back this time, one wrapping around my shoulders and collarbone while the other grabs my arms. "Get the fuck off of me!"

"Cool it, man. Jesus Christ."

The lights flick on, and I squint in the harsh light. The fraternity president crosses his arms over his chest and leans against the door—my only way out. "Having a good evening, Sam?"

"I *was*," I shout, "until you fucking ambushed me! What the hell, Rhodes!" His two right-hand men wrestle to keep me contained, but I'm not fucking having it. I'm not giving up this fight. "Let me go!"

"Calm down," President Rhodes grunts. "It'll be over soon."

"What the hell are you talking about?"

"Her Reaping." He cracks his knuckles. "If there's

anything left when he's done with her, you can have sloppy seconds."

"Fuck you!" Fury and fear collide inside my heart, making it beat double-time. "He doesn't rape people, so you're shit out of luck. She won't say yes."

"I have it on good authority that she's willing."

What?

He must see the confusion on my face because his shell cracks. "You said so yourself." Pulling out his cell phone from his pocket, he opens a video recording from a few hours ago. I recognize it immediately—the rows of graves, the tumbling autumn leaves, Mercy standing in her pretty dress while my hand's on her chin, holding her still as we stand in front of my truck.

Every ounce of fight in my body drains away, replaced by icy dread. "Where did you get this?" Does Reaper have cameras outside, too? Why would he send anyone this?

The video plays, beginning at the exact moment I tell Mercy to bounce on Reaper's dick. I wince, hearing the raw anger and hurt in my voice. Then I explain in detail what I expect Reaper to do to her, and Mercy replies by saying that I can't scare her. The recording ends, and Rhodes puts his phone back in his pocket.

"You looked angry, Sam. When you showed up with her tonight, we figured you were too hung up on her to break things off."

"We're doing you a favor," one of the VPs says, repeating himself from earlier. "She's trash, Sam. She's been leading you on for years."

"You've been wound up tight. You need to let her go."

"Once she fucks Reaper," Rhodes joins in, "she won't want you anymore."

"Do you hear how crazy you all sound?" I grit my teeth and fight against the VPs, but they lift just as many weights as I do. It's a struggle to move six inches, let alone six feet. "I'm not letting him touch her. Get the fuck off of me!" They don't know anything about our situation. Mercy needs me to be there. She *asked* me to be there. As much as it kills me, I have to stand next to her and watch her get railed.

I need to make sure that she makes it out alive.

"Why don't you date Abby instead?" Rhodes genuinely looks concerned, but for all the wrong reasons. "She's cute. Perky tits. Won't shut up about you."

"I don't want Abby!"

The only person I want is being held against her will at a party that I dragged her to, completely unaware that I'm trapped and can't get to her. She's going to think that I abandoned her. That I let this happen.

That it's all my fault.

CHAPTER 27

MERCY

THE NEXT FEW minutes are a blur of girls laughing and cheering as they tear my dress off in the hallway bathroom. While one girl unzips the back, another unbuttons the front. Then someone gets impatient and grabs the top collar and *riiiips* it off my arm while a fourth girl breaks the buckles on the straps over my ankles.

I try to fight them off, but they come at me from all sides, ruining my dress in the span of thirty seconds and leaving me in my underwear.

"Have fun!" One of them cheers, genuinely looking pleased with herself. They open the bathroom door and shove me back into the hallway, where I collide with a wall of warm muscle. I scream, but all he does is pick me up and toss me over his shoulder, grabbing my ass as soon as the opportunity presents itself. We bounce down the staircase to a chorus of insults.

Dirty slut!
You're about to get that cherry popped!
What a whore!

Meanwhile, the monster carrying me down the stairs is greeted with enthusiasm.

Fuck her up, Reaper!
Tear that virgin pussy!
Get her nice and wet for the rest of us, killer!

Tears streak down my face, blurring the crowd. I ball my hands into fists and beat the ever-loving hell out of Kane's backside, but he barely flinches no matter how many times I strike. "Stop it! I don't want this!"

I've known of Reaper's reputation for years, but I've never witnessed the main event. Parties, sports matches, club activities after dark, wherever the Reaper appears, someone gets fucked. I used to think that it was a metaphor—maybe he's a boxer—but then I heard rumors about his massive cock and realized that no, people *literally* get fucked.

But Kane wouldn't do that to me. Not in public. Not *here.*

Not with Sam standing directly over our heads.

"Kane!" I twist my body and grab his hair, pulling as hard as I can.

He yelps. "Fucking bitch! You asked for this!"

What?

Someone throws a drink in my face, and I'm blinded, the alcohol burning my eyes. I can't stop the sob that escapes my lips, and my next plea isn't for Kane. It's for my best friend. "Sam!" I scream, kicking and clawing. "*Help!*"

But Sam doesn't appear on the stairs. He doesn't jump through one of the open windows or fall from a hole in the ceiling. My protector is nowhere to be found, and I can't help but feel like it's my fault.

I told him that I loved him, but he wasn't enough for me.

I also wanted Kane.

Maybe this is the price for being greedy. Normal girls don't keep two men—they sleep with one and marry the other. Isn't that how the game goes? *Fuck, Marry, Kill?*

If I'm fucking Reaper, I'll still get to marry Sam because he'll let me break his heart, and when Zane comes after me for losing the game, he'll kill me before I could ever kill him.

Except, that's a game of pretend. Only one of those is coming true. Sam isn't here to save me, and Zane is nowhere to be found. It's just me and Reaper, in the end. Exactly how it was the night we first met in the mausoleum.

As I desperately wipe the alcohol from my stinging eyes, we move to the center of the living room, the floor now clear to make way for our arrival. Reaper spins around to show off his prize, giving me enough leverage to find an escape route. But as soon as my gaze lands on a flimsy pop up table in the center of the room, suddenly cleared of beer pong, my heart sinks. Streaks of warm beer and spilled punch glaze its surface, bouncing all around me as I'm thrown onto my back on the table. I kick as hard as I can, slamming my heel into Reaper's jaw.

A flash of anger in his dark eyes makes me heart race. He's going to be rough on purpose.

I scan his body for weak points, scrambling to think of any self-defense I've learned over the years, but all I notice is the shitty paint job. Concrete gray body paint covers his torso and arms. It's devoid of any markings—not even the usual skeleton—and slapped on haphazardly, like he was in a hurry and didn't care about the finished product. His cruel eyes rake down my body, and his brunette hair falls over his forehead.

An artist would never slap paint on like this.

"You're not Kane," I realize, feeling so incredibly stupid. This isn't *the* Reaper. It's a cheap imitation.

A girl straddling a shirtless man's shoulders pumps her fist in the air. She's familiar somehow, but that doesn't matter when she's yelling for Reaper to "Fuck The Dead Girl!" The chant picks up speed until that's all I can hear. My own heartbeat goes deaf in my ears.

Maybe I really am dead.

A silent tear tracks down my cheek as "Reaper" pulls his pants down to reveal a lackluster cock. He strokes it, trying to make it bigger, and I can't stop the laugh that bursts from my chest. You have *got* to be kidding me. They should have vetted the substitute before letting him ruin Reaper's reputation.

"*That's* your mighty weapon?" I push up onto my elbows and grin maliciously. I could cry and scream and play the victim—*or*, I could fight back the only way I know how. "I've seen the real Reaper's dick, and it's twice as big." Staring at his penis, I lift an eyebrow. "Is it gonna grow any more, or is that it?"

Someone pulls my hair, yanking me flat against the table. My scalp screams. My shoulders ache. Everything *hurts*.

"Make her choke on it, Reaper!"

I laugh again. *Louder.* Maybe it's the trauma. Maybe I'm crazy. But now that I've started, I can't stop. Tears fall freely, and I can hardly catch my breath.

I should have stayed home, surrounded by dead things. At least there, I fit in. I'll never belong in a place like this.

Someone slaps their dick on my face, and a chorus of laughter erupts around the room. Maybe I'm laughing, too. I don't know. I don't feel like I'm laughing anymore.

"Open up, Dead Girl," Fake Reaper orders, hanging the back of my head over the edge of the table. I don't know when he moved. I guess it doesn't matter. He's here. I'm here. Just a warm, wet hole for someone to fill.

I wish Sam was here instead.

I wish Kane were here, too.

I want it so badly that I imagine hearing his voice. "Get the *fuck* off my Siren!" A growl. The heavy *thud* of a punch. Shouting.

Commotion stirs across the room, but I'm too busy fighting off oral invasion to pay attention. Thankfully, the girls who aren't fleeing the room are stepping up and voicing their doubts. One even tries to pull "Reaper" off of me, but she's quickly thrown to the shirtless hyenas circling their prey and lost among them. Someone shouts. Something crashes and shatters on the floor. The dick hanging over my face disappears, and all I can do is laugh and cry and try not to throw up.

Someone crashes into my table and I fall, slamming into the hardwood and knocking the air from my lungs. My ears ring as I crawl on my hands and knees, desperate to move. Desperate to flee. I don't know where I'm going, but it has to be better than here.

A heavy hand wraps around my ankle and *yanks*, dragging me across the floor. I scream and kick as I'm flipped over, coming face to face with Fake Reaper, his nose bloodied, teeth stained red, a malicious gleam in his eyes. He pulls his fist back, and I scream.

Blood splatters across my body, and something wet falls on my chest as a gunshot pierces the air. We both stare at the hole in his fist as blood pours from the wound, covering what little remains of his hand and dripping down his wrist. I glance down at my chest and find the bloodied stump that used to be his thumb. With a shriek, I fling it off of me.

Kane kicks the bastard over, toppling him to the floor. As Fake Reaper tries to scramble away, Kane stomps on his spine, snarling. "I *said*, get the fuck off of her." He cocks the gun, loading a bullet into the chamber. "She's *mine*."

A second gunshot pierces the air, then a third, and a fourth. Kane empties the magazine and stomps on the corpse's head repeatedly. "You dumb fucker," he growls, "piece of shit copycat!"

Anyone hiding on the second floor quickly descends the stairs and flees, a few girls crying as they cover their tits with their hands. Shouting echoes from above, and one of the football players tumbles down the stairs, going limp as soon as he hits the bottom landing. Kane spins around, quickly loading a second magazine and holding up his gun. Glancing at me, some of the anger drains from his face. "Stay there, beautiful; give me a minute to clean up." Blood clings to his face and neck, staining his clothes. He storms over to the stairs and yells. "Get the fuck down here!" Planting his foot on the unconscious man's chest, he aims at his face. "Before I shoot this fucker, too!"

"Wait!" Two men appear from the upper floor, holding their hands up as they take slow, careful steps down the stairs. One's got a busted lip and the other's looking over his shoulder, clearly pissed off. "Get the fuck down here, Sam! This is your fault!"

The one with the split lip stares at his buddy on the floor. "Shit, man, you killed Thomas!"

"He's still breathing." Kane's smile curves like the sharp tip of a knife. "For now." He waves the gun impatiently. "C'mon, c'mon, we don't have all day."

Sam appears at the top of the stairs last, following the other two down. His eyes search the room until he finds me, and the color drains from his face. Most of it, anyway —he's got a black eye and a bloody nose, torn shirt, ripped jeans. "Mercy, baby, I'm so sorry."

The gun swings in Sam's direction. "Don't you fucking talk to her."

"I wasn't in on this, I swear!"

Kane growls. "I will *kill* you, Samson fucking Wright!"

"Go ahead!" Sam throws his arms out and keens like a wounded animal. "It's what I fucking deserve!"

The men in front of Sam flinch, stopping on the stairs. "No you fucking don't," one of them yells. "Jesus, Sam, get a grip. She's just a girl!"

"Don't throw your goddamn life away!"

"Enough!" Kane shoves off of the stairwell and sighs, walking over to me in record time. Keeping the gun aimed behind him, he searches my face. "What do you want me to do, Siren?"

I feel numb inside, barely able to lift my head off the floor. I don't know when I laid down. "Why are you asking me?" My heart stirs, but all I feel is the aching echo of its beat.

Kane's voice softens. "Because he's your boyfriend." He runs a gentle hand over my hair. "And you're the victim here. You should decide his fate."

I don't want to decide anyone's fate. I want to go home.

A few seconds pass in silence before Kane sighs. "Alright, Siren. We'll hold onto him for you until you're ready." When he turns back around, only Sam remains. The other men fled when the opportunity presented itself.

But not Sam.

He stands six feet away, completely ignoring Kane to stare at me. "Mercy—"

"Don't," Kane snaps, holding the gun to Sam's forehead. He snarls, using the barrel to shove Sam. A streak of red cuts across Sam's forehead, the tip of the gun slicing through his skin. "*God*, I wish I could shoot you. Do you know how many times I've pictured it?"

Sam speaks, but his heart isn't in it. "I've thought about killing you a hundred times."

"Bet you're glad you didn't, huh, Pretty Boy? Because who was here to save your girl? Sure as shit wasn't you."

Wincing, Sam lowers his head, blood dripping down his face. It slides between his eyes and past his nose. "You're right." Our gazes lock, and he drops to his knees. "I'm at your mercy, baby, but please—"

Agony reflects in his eyes.

"Don't go easy on me."

The Price of Mercy is waiting for you.

Thank you so much for reading *Begging for Mercy!* Please consider leaving a rating or review if you enjoyed spending time with these angsty babes. ♥ The best way to promote an indie author is to spread the word about our books. We couldn't do this without you!

Join my Discord for sneak peeks & book discussions: Discord Link

Join my email newsletter for free books: Email Newsletter Link

About the Author

Just a smut-lover listening to angsty love songs on repeat.

Misti Wilds is a lover of all things romance, especially when the spice is habanero hot and the men are morally gray and dangerous. She devours angst like her favorite M&M cookies--all at once with no regrets. When she isn't writing romance, she can be found floating in the lake with her favorite sun hat or playing video games while surrounded by Squishmallows. She lives in Southern USA with her number one fans (an adoring husband and two precious pups).

ALSO BY MISTI WILDS

Baranova Bratva:

Rule of Three

Reign of Four

Brutal Beauty:

Brutal Beauty (prequel)

Claimed by Rage

Tempted to Rebel

Bound by Ruin

Born to Riot

Dying for Love:

Begging for Mercy

The Price of Mercy

9 798990 269569